RIVER *of* GLASS

JADEN TERRELL

RIVER *of* GLASS

THE PERMANENT PRESS
Sag Harbor, NY 11963

For information, address:
   The Permanent Press
   4170 Noyac Road
   Sag Harbor, NY 11963
   www.thepermanentpress.com

Library of Congress Cataloging-in-Publication Data

Terrell, Jaden—
   River of Glass / Jaden Terrell.
        pages cm. — (A Jared McKean mystery)
   ISBN 978-1-57962-360-9
        1. Private investigators—Tennessee—Nashville—Fiction.
   2. Mystery fiction. I. Title.

PS3620.E753R58 2014
813'.6—dc23   2014023887

Printed in the United States of America

For Mike Hicks, whose unfaltering support blesses my life, heals my heart, and makes me believe everything is possible.

Acknowledgments

To name everyone who has offered me support, encouragement, and assistance with this book would take volumes, so let me apologize in advance for the incompleteness of this list.

My thanks go first and foremost to my husband, Mike Hicks, my mother, Ruthanne Terrell, and my brother, David Terrell, for their ceaseless love and support.

Thanks to my agent, Jill Marr of the Sandra Dijkstra agency; my publishers, Martin and Judith Shepard of The Permanent Press; cover artist Lon Kirschner; copy editor Barbara Anderson; and fellow Permanent Press authors Chris Knopf, Len Rosen, David Freed, and Baron Birtcher.

Thanks to Clay Stafford and the whole Killer Nashville Crew for taking up the slack while I finished this book.

Thanks to those who shared their knowledge and expertise with me on everything from law enforcement to HIV. Among them are Dan Royse, Mike Breedlove, and Patrick Looney of the TBI; Sgt. Derek Pacifico of the Writer's Homicide School; Gene Kleiser for information about Vietnam; Susan Harris for her expertise in all things equine; and Greg Herren for providing information about HIV and AIDS; and Sheila L. Stephens for her insights into private investigation techniques.

I would be remiss if I didn't also express my gratitude to the Mystery Writers of America, Sisters in Crime, Private Eye Writers of America, the Hardboiled Collective, and the Quill and Dagger Writers' Group. An extra thank-you to authors Timothy Hallinan, Eyre Price, Rob Pobi, and Stacy Allen.

Thanks to my friends and teachers at World Champion Productions. And as always, thanks to my friends at Measurement Incorporated, with special shout-outs to Christina Wilburn, Jeff Kirchner, Mary Beth Ross, and Steve Jones.

There are so many of you to whom I owe a debt of gratitude. You know who you are. Much love to all of you.

Tuyet

*T*he girl called Worm hugged her knees to her chest and shivered, listening to the storm. Wind shuddered the walls of the shed and whistled through the cracks. Rain hammered on the roof and trickled in through the seams where the steel walls met the concrete floor.

In another life, she had been Tuyet, and she clung to the name now, lips moving in a silent recitation: *My name is Tuyet. No matter what they call me, I will always be Tuyet.*

She blew on her hands to warm them, then rubbed her upper arms. Her nylon slip shifted, clammy against her skin.

From a window in the ceiling, too high for her or the other women to reach, a wash of sooty light spread downward and was swallowed by shadows. The glass was gray with night and rain, but if she squinted, she could make out the other fourteen women in the dim light. She would have known them even without the light—by their shapes and by their voices, even by their smells. Fear and self-preservation might turn them against each other in time, but for now, this dank shed that smelled of sweat and shit and sex had made them sisters.

The youngest and newest, a Japanese girl known only as Grub pressed her forehead against the shoulder of a young Chinese woman called Maggot. Maggot, who had suffered a beating for sharing that her true name was Hong, wrapped an arm around the younger girl and rocked her as if she were a small child. The gesture made Tuyet think of her mother, and that made her chest tighten and her eyes burn.

She closed her eyes and let herself feel the touch of her mother's hand on her cheek, let herself remember the smell of her grandmother's coffee shop and the taste of pho soup—the savory broth, the tang of fish paste. She gave herself a few minutes to remember that other life. Then she pushed the thoughts away. A little memory could give you courage. Too much could make you weak.

A Thai girl with a barbed-wire tattoo around her neck ran her fingers around the rim of her plastic dinner bowl as if an extra grain of rice or a sliver of fish might have appeared there. She was called Weasel, and while she too must have had another name, Tuyet had never heard it.

A crash of thunder rattled the walls. Weasel moaned and pounded her thin mattress. Grub pressed her face to Hong's shoulder and whimpered like a child. Someone groped in the shadows for the chamber pot, and a few moments later, the air grew sharp with the smell of urine.

Weasel coughed. Hong began to hum. There was a lightness in the room that came, not from the rain, but because of it.

The men would not come out in this weather.

Hands outstretched, Tuyet made her way to the back corner of the shed. The rain had seeped in, and a puddle of rainwater chilled her bare feet. Where the two walls met the floor, there was a small gap. She knelt on the damp concrete, forehead almost touching the floor, and sucked in the smells of earth and rain, then laid her palm flat against the metal and pressed hard. With a tiny shriek, the gap widened. Moonlight and rainwater poured in.

"You make trouble," a reedy voice said in fractured English. Tuyet looked up to see a flat-faced Thai girl called Beetle behind her, arms crossed, jaw set. Like Hong and Weasel, Beetle knew even less Vietnamese than she did English, so by default, English was the language they used among each other. "Boss man catch you, he make everybody unhappy."

A few feet away, a Vietnamese girl called Dung huddled on her filthy mattress, scrawny arms curled around her stomach.

Her magenta hair, now black at the roots, hid most of her bruised and swollen face. She was the smallest of them, but she had fought the hardest and the longest. Just this morning, she had raked her nails across the boss man's neck and, without even flinching, he had caught her hand and snapped two of her fingers. The broken fingers and the bruises were partly punishment and partly an example for the rest of them: See what happens when you disobey?

Tuyet thought they would kill the girl soon. Or maybe she would kill herself. Surely no one could take so much abuse for so long. The girl's eyes, fixed on the gap in the wall, shone in the dim light.

Tuyet said, "He make everybody unhappy anyway." She pushed again, and more water washed through. Did they have monsoon season here in America? If it rained like this for weeks, would the men stay away? How long before, half starved, she and the other women fell on each other? As much as she hated the men, she hated her dependence on them more. "Anyway, I only looking. See what see."

"See nothing," Beetle said. "Nobody get through there. Even if can, too sharp glass, too high wall. Too many ghost."

Tuyet shivered. She had never seen the shallow graves behind the shed, but she knew from the fear in the long-timers' eyes that they were there. "I know. But maybe . . ."

"You think maybe hope? Is no hope. You go sleep now, forget this foolish." Beetle stomped back to her own mattress, her lips a thin line in her flat face.

Another flash of lightning lit the room. Then a loud crack, followed by the sounds of breaking wood and the crunch of glass. Tuyet lay down on her stomach, heedless of the water soaking through her slip, chilling her breasts. She pressed the wall outward with her palm and peered out through the gap.

Forget this foolish.

Rain pelted her face and chilled her skin, but she didn't care. She would never get her fill of that smell.

Across the grass, rain sparkled on a river of shattered glass. Beyond that stood a high stone wall, also topped with glass, if the long-timers told the truth. But who would know? Who could cross the river of shards to find out?

Tuyet blinked. Wiped rainwater from her eyes and looked again. A tree, split by lightning, lay across the wall, its trunk and branches stretched like a bridge across the glass. Only four or five feet separated the trunk from the grassy turf. Four or five feet across the shards. It would hurt, it would hurt a lot, but it could be done.

She looked over at Dung. The smallest of them.

Tuyet climbed to her feet and brushed water and grime from the front of her slip. Then she pressed her shoulder against the wall and pushed as hard as she could. The metal squealed. The gap widened.

Beetle looked up and wailed.

Shoulder still pressed to the wall, Tuyet gestured for the other women to help. There was a way out, she said, and told them about the fallen tree.

Beetle moaned. "Boss man come, put you in pit for sure. Maybe me, us, too."

Dung, who had once spent three days in the pit, whimpered.

"No one come tonight," Tuyet said. "Too much storm. We hurry, have plenty time."

Hong looked pointedly away, then buried her face between Grub's shoulder blades. Beetle covered her face with her arms and keened, while Weasel turned her back and lay down on her mattress. The others were as still as stone.

"I do it myself," Tuyet said. She pushed, pushed harder. The gap widened to the size of a pumpkin, then held. Was it enough? She had lost weight since she'd been here. If the gap would stay open . . .

She shifted her weight backward, and the metal popped back into place, only that small gap at the bottom.

She pushed again. Pushed until her muscles trembled and sweat popped out on her upper lip. She pushed until her shoulders ached and her eyes stung and her breath came in ragged gasps and whimpers. She pounded a fist against the ungiving metal, then flung herself against it.

Again. And again. Until she had no more strength. Panting, she laid her cheek against the cool metal.

"Please," she whispered. She turned her face toward her sisters and made her voice louder. "Please."

No one moved. Fear held them in place, and how could she blame them? There had been so many tricks, so many false hopes offered and then snatched away. But not even the boss man could call lightning from the sky.

No, God or her ancestors, or whatever benevolent spirits there were, had given her this one small chance. She would not let her sisters' fear steal it from her.

She looked at Dung.

Dung blinked.

"You can do it," Tuyet whispered. "Only you."

"They kill you," Beetle said, from across the shed. "They kill you both. Then kill rest of us."

Tuyet said, "They kill us anyway." She looked back at Dung. "But I think they kill you first."

Dung looked at the gap in the corner. Such a small gap. Tuyet knew what Dung was thinking—what she herself would be thinking, in Dung's place. What if Tuyet had exhausted herself and the gap closed before Dung was through? The metal was heavy, the edge sharp. Would it slice through a leg? A spine? Would the next grave behind the shed be hers? Tuyet imagined a long line of dead women, a field of ghosts between the shed and the river of glass. She wrapped her arms around herself to keep herself from shivering.

Dung's lips moved, but no sound came out. She licked her lips and tried again. "I hear the dead."

"Only the wind."

"No."

Tuyet waited. What could she say? The dead were there beneath the grass. Maybe they walked, and maybe the wind carried their voices. Maybe one day soon Dung would be one of them. Maybe they all would.

After a moment, Dung pushed herself up and scooted to the edge of her mattress. She moved like she had something broken inside.

"Wait." Tuyet lifted her mattress and slipped a creased photograph from a slit in the bottom. She pressed the photograph into Dung's hand and said in Vietnamese, "Go to this address. Tell the man you find there about us. Bring help."

She made the girl repeat the address three times. Then Tuyet pressed her shoulder to the wall again and said, "Go."

"I bring help," Dung said in English. "Thank you."

Dung pressed herself flat against the concrete and inched into the gap headfirst. She was small, and starvation had made her smaller still. Even so, she cried out as the metal scraped her shoulder blades, then her buttocks, and finally the backs of her thighs.

Tuyet held the gap open until she thought her back might break. She watched Dung disappear inch by inch. Knees. Calves. Ankles. By the time Dung's feet passed through the gap, Tuyet was trembling with exertion.

She stumbled backward, and the metal sprang back into place, leaving only a small gap at the bottom where the metal had bent.

She sank to her knees, then lay down on her stomach and pressed the metal outward with her palm so she could watch Dung push herself to her feet and stumble toward the fallen tree. Rain lashed Dung's face, and the wind caught her small cries as the glass bit into her feet.

"Run," Tuyet whispered. Tears stung her eyes and ran down her cheeks, mingling with the rain. "Run far from this place."

She tried not to think of what the men would do when they realized what she had done. If there was anything she had learned since the day a man she'd trusted had brought her here, it was that there were so very many ways to be hurt.

1

The storm blew itself out around midnight and by dawn, a new bank of clouds had rolled in. They filled the sky from horizon to horizon, gray and roiling, swollen with rain. A few scattered drops fell throughout the day, as if God were spitting on us.

That afternoon, I put on my father's leather bomber jacket, locked my elderly quarter horse in the paddock, saddled my Tennessee Walker, and rode out into the woods behind the house. The air was cool and damp, thick with the smells of mud and moss, the mulchy scent of deadwood, and the occasional far-off whiff of skunk. The trail twisted like a copperhead, littered with broken branches and mottled with gray light.

The wind rose and rattled the leaves. Crockett tossed his head and picked up his pace, hoof beats muted by the rain-softened earth. When I gave him his head, he slipped into a running walk, hips lifting and falling as his hind legs stretched beneath him in a smooth, ground-covering gait.

He faltered at a side trail, turned his head toward it. The underbrush made the trail seem darker there, the air somehow less clean. Crockett drifted toward it, but I'd had my fill of darkness. I nudged him forward and past, into a band of sunlight.

The saddle creaked as I shifted my weight and squeezed with my lower leg. I closed my eyes, felt the wind brush my cheeks, and the black gelding broke into the rocking-horse canter typical of his breed. His shoulder dropped, and my eyes snapped open as the trail bent sharply to the right. Just beyond, a downed maple crossed the trail. No time to pull up. I lifted my weight from the saddle, wrapped both fists in Crockett's mane to keep from pulling on the reins, and squeezed his sides again. Another burst of speed, then his muscles bunched, and we were in the air, a moment of suspension that felt as close to flight as I would ever come.

One rear hoof skimmed the trunk as we sailed over. His hooves struck the ground, and we skidded sideways, hurtling toward a wall of green. He scrabbled for a moment, got his legs beneath him, and veered back onto the trail.

Grinning, heart pounding, I sank into the saddle and lifted the reins. Crockett slowed, then drifted to a stop and lowered his head to pluck a few blades of grass from the side of the trail. I leaned back, let him graze. Tilted my head back into a shaft of muted light and listened to the quiet sounds of afternoon—the riffle of wind through branches, the trill of a bird and the answering call of its mate, the sound of grass between my horse's teeth.

Somewhere to my right, the wheeze of Frank Campanella's Crown Vic broke the stillness like a chain saw in the wilderness. I knew it was Frank, even without benefit of sight. He'd had the Vic long before he and I had worked homicides for Metro Nashville's now-defunct Murder Squad, probably before I'd graduated from the academy at nineteen, possibly since before I was born.

A thousand scenarios flashed through my mind—car crashes and drownings and God-knew-what-else involving my son, my ex-wife, my nieces, my brother and his estranged wife . . . Frank was my friend, but there was no good reason for him to show up at my home unannounced.

Dread closing my throat, I got off and walked my horse around the fallen tree, then climbed back on and urged him toward the house.

When I rode out of the woods, Frank was on the porch, a glass of lemonade in his hand, my friend and housemate, Jay Renfield, hovering anxiously beside him. I'd known Jay since kindergarten, and our friendship had survived both his revelation that he was gay and his ongoing struggle with AIDS.

Frank looked up as I bent to open the pasture gate. He said something to Jay, set his glass down on the porch railing, and started down the steps. By the time I led Crockett across the pasture and into the barn, Frank was waiting for me.

He was a cinder block of a man, shoulders straining against his regulation suit. Square jaw, bristling eyebrows, silvering hair. He ran a hand through it, leaving a ruffled patch above one ear. Then he gave me an awkward man hug and said, "How you doing, Cowboy?"

I gave his back a thump and turned back to loosen the latigo of Crockett's saddle. "You didn't come here to ask me how I'm doing."

"No, but now that I'm here, the question has crossed my mind."

"I'm fine," I said. "Or was, until you stopped by."

"I'll try not to take that personally."

"It's not personal. You know what they say about shooting the messenger. You have your bad news face on."

"I have a bad news face?"

"It's like your regular face, but squintier."

He let that pass. "Did you go to the office today?"

"What are you, the office police?" I tugged the cinch loose and lifted the saddle and pad from Crockett's back. There was a saddle-shaped patch of sweat beneath. I ran my hand over it, checking for tenderness, and found none. "I did a skip trace and a couple of background checks. Nothing I couldn't do from here."

He cocked his head. Gave me a narrow look. "Skip traces. Background checks."

"It's honest work. Pays well. Plus, I can do it from my couch."

"You're wasted on it." He jammed his hands into his pockets, pretended to study Crockett's saddle. "Jared, what happened to Josh wasn't your fault."

A vision of my nephew lying limp in a tub of bloody water shot a sharp pain through my temples. If I'd done things differently . . .

"I know that," I said. "But you didn't come here to tell me that, either."

He looked pained, but let it pass. "A situation's come up. Malone asked me to come by and ask you to take a look at a crime scene. A courtesy."

"From me to her, or from her to me?"

"From the department to you," he said. "And vice versa."

"Paul has a Cub Scout meeting tonight." I slung the saddle over the saddle rack and looked pointedly at my watch. "I'm just about to go pick him up."

Frank shook his head, his lips pressed tight.

"Aw, shit," I said.

He held out a clear plastic evidence bag, and in it was a sepia-toned Vietnam-era photo of a young guy in fatigues, a small Asian girl on his shoulders and an infant in his arms. The photo was creased, as if it had been crumpled in a fist, and there was a rust-colored stain on one corner. He flipped it over, and I saw another stain, like a bloody thumbprint, across the back. Scrawled in pencil beneath the thumbprint was a phone number and address. My office number and address.

"What's this?" I said.

"You know who this is?"

"Of course I know who it is." The crooked grin, the shock of buckskin-colored hair, the slant of the jaw . . . I saw them every day in the photo on my bedside table, saw similar features in the mirror every morning. *So like him*, my mother used to say, and trace my cheekbones with her thumbs.

I reached for the bag, as if a closer look might prove me wrong, and after a moment he handed it over.

"You know the routine," he said. "Don't open it."

I knew the routine. I looked at the picture, smoothing the plastic over the photo with my thumb to reduce the glare. "Where'd you get it?"

"We got a call, one of those Strip-o-Gram girls works downstairs in your building."

I worked out of an office on the top floor of a former boarding house. One of the downstairs offices belonged to a grandmotherly type who ran a call-out strip business. Bachelor parties. Birthday parties. Boys' nights at the office.

"They prefer to be called women now," I said, because I couldn't think of anything else to say. "Or so I'm told."

"This one looked like a girl," Frank said. "Eighteen, nineteen, maybe. But then, they all look young to me these days. She went out to toss a trash bag in the dumpster—guy who works on the second floor carried it out for her—and when they opened it, there was a dead woman inside. Asian." He nodded toward the photo in the evidence bag. "That was in her hand."

"That's not possible."

"And yet, there it is. So what we need to know—what I came here to ask you—is why this dead girl in your dumpster had a picture of your father in her hand?"

I studied the photograph. It was my dad, all right. Late teens, early twenties. Tall and rangy, like my brother and me. A few years younger than in the photo I had on my dresser. In that one, he was standing on our front porch, staring out toward a coming storm. In this one, he stood in front of a reed shack with a sloped roof and stilts that raised it a few feet off the ground. An attractive Asian woman in a white blouse and a long dark skirt leaned against him, one hand on his forearm, the forefinger of the other hand clutched in the baby's fist.

"Maybe it's an orphanage," I said, a queasy feeling settling in my stomach. "Didn't a lot of soldiers volunteer in orphanages?"

"Uh huh."

"I've never seen this picture, and I don't know your dead girl."

"How do you know?"

Crockett nuzzled my shirt pocket, and I reached inside it for a peppermint. "I don't know any Asian women. Not to speak of."

"Could be she's one of the kids in the photo. One of those . . . orphans."

"I wouldn't know. So why are you here?" I asked. "Why you?"

"Dispatch gets a call. Dead body in a dumpster. A couple of uniforms go in, check it out. One of 'em sees the photo and dials the number on the back. Gets your office. Calls Malone, who sends Harry to the crime scene and calls me in to—"

"You and Harry are back on homicide?"

A new commissioner had broken up the Homicide and Murder Squads, leaving only a small core of cold-case investigators in the downtown detectives' offices. The rest, he'd spread out among the precincts with the idea that generalization was preferable to specialization. It might have sounded good on paper but had sent the homicide solve rate plummeting. Homicide investigation requires some special skills, not the least of which are the abilities to compartmentalize and detach.

Frank said, "The Squad's still defunct, but most of the precinct commanders are starting to wise up and let us do what we do best. Unofficially, at least. Anyway, we get there and I take a look at the photo and whattaya know, it's a picture of your dad."

He'd have recognized it. For the seven years we were partners, I'd kept a picture of my father on my desk to remind me of the kind of cop I'd hoped to be.

"So Malone sends you to sweet talk me into coming in. I told you, I have a Scout meeting. Paul's getting a progress bead tonight. One more, and he gets his Wolf patch."

"Jared," Frank said. "The scene's being processed even as we speak. You know how important those first forty-eight hours are. We need you to come down there and take a look at this girl."

"I've been down this road before, Frank. Am I a suspect?"

"Not in my book."

"In anybody's book?"

He shrugged. "Dead girl found in a dumpster behind your office with a picture of your father and your phone number in her hand. Somebody's gonna think you're a suspect."

I cued Crockett to step back, and when he did, I fed him the mint from the flat of my palm. I wanted to feel angry or indignant, but all I could manage was tired. After a minute, I sighed

~ 20 ~

and said, "Guess I'd better call Maria and tell her I'll be late to the meeting."

Frank said, "There'll be other meetings."

"That's not the point."

He didn't answer, just nodded and put his hands back in his pockets, waiting. I sighed again and said, "Am I riding with you, or can I take the truck?"

"Whatever you want."

He wasn't treating me like a suspect, which made me feel marginally better. I put Crockett into the paddock with Tex, stepped inside to tell Jay I was going out, then climbed into my black and silver Silverado. Frank slid into the Crown Vic.

As I followed him down the driveway and past the mailbox, I heard the distant rumble of thunder.

2

Traffic was light on I-40, so I dialed my ex-wife, Maria, on the way.

"Hey, Cowboy," she said before I had a chance to speak. Once, I might have called it ESP, but now it seemed more likely to be caller ID. The warmth in her voice made me smile and ache at the same time. "How's everything?"

"There's a situation."

I told her about the dead woman in the dumpster, and when she said, "Who is she?" her voice had lost some of its warmth.

"I don't know. That's what they're hoping to find out."

"Paulie's been looking forward to this all week. He's been wearing his uniform since he got home from school."

"I'm sorry. Can D.W. take him?"

"Of course."

There was no anger in her voice, only resignation. Maria understood about the job. She hadn't been able to live with it, but she understood. I didn't like the way she said it, though, the unspoken message behind the words: *D.W. would never miss his son's Scout meeting because of a dead woman in a dumpster.*

Of course he wouldn't. D.W. was safe. Dependable. Duller than dishwater. That was why she'd married him.

A baby's cry broke the silence on the other end. With a heavy sigh, Maria said, "I've got to get Sofia. Come when you can. I'll explain to Paul."

I hung up and eased into the middle lane behind the Vic. By the time the Nashville skyline with its two-pronged AT&T

"Batman Building" came into view, the back of my neck had begun to throb. I tailed Frank to the Broadway off-ramp and swung left toward West End and Vanderbilt University. A few blocks later, we turned onto a narrow street jammed with unmarked police cars and blue-and-whites with their lights flashing. At the center of the chaos was the three-story, pseudo-Victorian building I worked out of. A Channel Three news van parked at the edge of the hubbub signaled the presence of news anchor Ashleigh Arneau.

The throbbing in my neck spread to my shoulder blades.

In high school, she'd been Ashley Arnold—head cheerleader, drama diva, star reporter for the *Golden Bear Claw* student newspaper, and a force of burgeoning sexuality that drew in guys like me and turned them to ash. We hadn't dated then, but a few months after my divorce, Ashleigh and I had a brief but tempestuous relationship. Heated arguments and hotter sex that ended when I was fired for an inexplicable leak of confidential information to the press. I gave Ashleigh the bad news from my cell phone and came home to find her removing the bug she'd planted in the receiver of my home phone. Suddenly things got a lot more explicable.

Scowling, I parked across the street from the van, then joined Frank on the sidewalk, where a knot of spectators jostled against the crime scene tape. A harried-looking uniform waved them back from the line. He looked fresh out of the academy.

Ashleigh stood at the front of the crowd, craning her neck to see past the emergency vehicles and personnel. She wore black slacks and a raspberry blazer that reminded me of an ice cream sundae. In the afternoon light, her skin looked like ivory.

Just behind her stood a skinny cameraman and a pretty young woman in a short skirt. Platinum hair swept to one side. Red lips parted in an eager smile. Blue eyes riveted on Ashleigh like a barn cat eyeing a mouse.

Interesting.

Ashleigh tucked a stray lock of chestnut hair behind her ear and shoved her microphone into the young officer's face. Asked him a question I couldn't hear. He frowned, and she shook her hair back and flashed him a smile. A goofy grin spread across his face.

Poor guy. He didn't stand a chance.

Ashleigh's cameraman pressed a button on the side of an oversized camera that looked too heavy for his shoulders.

I nodded toward the uniform and said to Frank, "You better go rescue that guy. Unless you want to see all the gory details on the five o'clock news."

Frank groaned and changed trajectory. He plucked the microphone out of Ashleigh's hand and glared at the kid in uniform.

"No comment," Frank said into the mic, and handed it back to her.

Ashleigh started to protest. Then she spotted me behind Frank, and her eyes brightened.

"Detective Campanella. Is Mr. McKean a suspect?"

Frank ground his teeth together and said, "Mr. McKean is a consultant."

"Consultant? Hasn't he been—"

"No comment means no comment."

The smile slipped off Ashleigh's face. She glanced over her shoulder at the blonde woman, whose eager grin had turned smug.

Frank lifted the tape, and I ducked under it. Ashleigh's voice rose above the hubbub. "We've just seen private investigator Jared McKean, whose office seems to be at the epicenter of the activity."

Epicenter. For Christ's sake.

Frank said, "That woman ought to come with a warning label," and pointed me toward the office.

A forensic tech squatted on the entrance walk and snapped a photo of something on the concrete while two more techs stretched a plastic tarp above her head and affixed it to metal poles, creating a makeshift tent. A drop of rain splatted against the plastic, and the woman swore softly and snapped another picture.

We skirted the photographer, and I knew why Frank had asked me if I'd been to the office. If I'd come in, I'd have seen the drunken line of small bloody footprints that led toward the front steps and ended abruptly in a cluster of smears and droplets. I'd have known they meant bad news.

On the front porch, an earnest-looking detective interviewed a young blonde woman in jeans and a clingy white tank top. One of the Strip-o-Gram girls. Bridget something-or-other. Probably the one who'd found the body. She fidgeted with her necklace. Shifted her weight. Dropped her hands and toyed with the string of plastic shamrocks someone had wrapped around the porch railings. Yesterday, they'd looked kitschy and hip. Today, they just looked cheap.

"Around back," Frank said, and I followed him along the side of the building and into the alley behind, where more tarps flapped in the breeze and a team of forensic detectives worked the scene with a sense of urgency heightened by the threat of rain.

Frank nodded toward one of the techs, who handed me a paper jumpsuit, cap, and booties sealed in a clear plastic bag. We suited up and went to join Harry beside the dumpster.

The dumpster had a sliding door on each side, and Harry Kominsky stood at the near opening, pointing a Nikon digital camera inside. On the other side, a forensic technician in a paper suit bagged a soiled disposable diaper and labeled it with a Sharpie, while another photographed a tattered leather shoe with a ruler beside it for comparison.

Measure, photograph, bag, label . . . Processing a crime scene is tedious work. It's done in layers, each item and its relative position documented in such a way that, years from now, an investigator could take the stand and tell how many quarters had been in the victim's purse. If the girl had been alive, it would have been different. Saving her would have trumped preserving evidence. But she wasn't alive, and they could take their time with the scene.

The technicians looked grim, and I couldn't blame them. I was none too happy myself, and I wasn't the one who was going to have to tag and bag a half ton of garbage.

Harry glanced up as Frank and I rounded the corner. "You gonna ID our victim for us?"

"Probably not," I said. "But move over and I'll take a look."

Harry edged to his left, and I stepped into the space he'd left behind. The stench of sour milk, soiled diapers, and rotting vegetation rolled over me. No smell of decomposing flesh. It was too soon and the weather too cool for that.

I realized I was already detaching, preparing myself for what was in the dumpster.

"He killed her quick at the end," Harry said. "But before he did . . ." He shook his head.

I put my hands in my pockets and leaned forward to look inside, feeling Frank's solid presence at my back.

"Jesus," I said.

She was a small woman. Thin legs. Small breasts. Her collarbone stood out against her skin as if she'd been starved. She lay curled on her side in a pile of bulging garbage bags, the dark plastic a stark contrast to her magenta hair and the stained white slip that had ridden up her thighs. Bruises in various stages of healing patterned her body in purple, yellow, and a sickly green.

Looking closely, I could distinguish flat facial features and epicanthal folds over the eyes, but the face was too swollen to tell how old she was or how pretty she might have been. Young, I thought, from the smoothness of her skin. Something past puberty, not more than twenty. Too young to be either of the children in the photo Frank had shown me.

"Poor kid," I said.

Frank nodded. "He wanted to hurt her. But he didn't want her permanently disfigured. Looks like he's been at her for at least a month or so."

Her eyes were open and had begun to flatten as the fluids in them dried out. Fresh bruises at her throat and small broken capillaries in her eyes said she'd been strangled, though it was too early to say if that was what had killed her. Her head lolled at an impossible angle, a tell-tale bulge at the throat where her killer had broken her hyoid bone.

One hand lay open, fingers curled toward a bloody palm. Probably the hand that had held the photograph. The other arm was twisted behind her, where it must have fallen when her killer pushed her in.

Horrible way to die. But then, the list of good ways to die was a short one.

Harry said, "Look at her feet."

They were bare, crusted with dirt and blood, bits of glass and gravel embedded in the flesh. "She walked a long way," I said. "But from where? And why come here?"

"You don't know her?" Frank said.

"I don't know her. When did she die?"

"Sometime between one and five this morning. Much earlier, and the rain would've washed away the footprints. Any later, and someone would've seen him dump her." He nodded to a small clapboard house across the alley. "The woman who lives there came out at five to eat breakfast on the back patio. Not much chance to dump the body after that."

I nodded. The neighborhood wasn't exactly a bustling metropolis, but with Vanderbilt's campus and West End Avenue just a few blocks away, we got our share of joggers and other foot traffic.

I pointed to a scar in the cleft where the girl's neck met the collarbone. "What's that?"

Harry pulled out a penlight and shone it on the mark, a raised white scar, pink around the edges and shaped like something you might see on a Chinese menu.

"Looks like a brand," Frank said.

"You think he's a collector? Marking his property?"

"Maybe. Or could be traffickers."

"I read about that big ring you guys busted up. Bunch of Somalis?"

"It's not just the Somalis." He rubbed his palms over his face. "Turns out those three interstates that make us all so happy during rush hour also make us a trafficking hub."

"That'll look good in the tourist brochures."

I looked at the woman again, the wasted body and misshapen face. The thin, bloodstained fingers that had plucked glass from her wounded feet and then fingered my father's photograph. A rush of anger slipped beneath the curtain of detachment I'd pulled up over my mind. Someone had brutalized this girl, systematically and over time. Whoever he was, I wanted to snap his neck.

Frank said, "Could have been her pimp. There's one over on the east side brands his girls. But he uses a double helix. Like DNA."

I found my voice, pushed the anger down. "Interesting choice."

"His name's D'Angelo Norton Albert. Initials DNA. Guess he thought it was clever."

"Clever pimps. What's the world coming to?"

"Sign of the apocalypse for sure." Frank cracked a grin. "You're sure you don't know this girl? Never met her, never dated her best friend's sister's cousin?"

"I don't know her."

"'Cause we really need to catch this guy."

"I can't help you, Frank. I don't know who she is."

"She's connected to you," he said, an edge to his voice. "Your dad's picture, your address and phone number. This isn't random."

"I get that."

"Maybe somebody's sending you a message."

"Somebody who'd have a decades-old picture of my dad? Why wait this long to pull it out of the hat?"

We looked at the body in glum silence. When I thought I'd paid due respect, I said, "Can I go now? I can still make Paul's meeting."

He glanced at Harry, who signaled his acquiescence with a twitch of the shoulders.

"Fine," Frank said. "As soon as you give me your statement."

It wasn't much of a statement. No, I'd never seen the girl before. No, I had no idea who she might be.

I finished my statement and peeled off the paper jumpsuit, cap, and booties. Frank flipped his report book closed. He looked tired, and I suddenly remembered something he'd said back at the house.

"Hey," I said. "It's Thursday."

"So?"

"So, you haven't missed a shift since bread was invented. Why'd they have to call you to come in?"

His grin came a beat too late. "I'm not sure you're in a position to throw stones."

"Not throwing stones. Just—"

"Mac," he said. "Go to Paulie's meeting. Everything's fine."

"If you need—"

He held up his phone. Waggled it. "I've got you on speed dial."

Since pushing Frank was about as effective as trying to levitate a tank with the power of your mind, I let it go. He'd tell me when he was ready. He led me back around to the front and lifted the crime scene tape. As I ducked under, Ashleigh called my name and started in my direction. I trotted across the street to the Silverado and pretended not to hear.

3

I slipped into the meeting room of the Mount Juliet community center just as the last boy was receiving his progress bead from the Cubmaster, a scrawny guy named Leon Musgrave, who wore Coke-bottle glasses and had an Adam's apple the size of a nectarine. In the front row, beside D.W., Paulie slumped in a metal folding chair, his cap pulled down too far in front, his new bead clenched in one stubby hand.

When we'd first learned our son had Down syndrome, we'd wondered if he'd ever ride a bike, play baseball, even dress himself. Now I felt a swell of pride at the sight of him in his blue uniform, his yellow scarf knotted at the base of his throat.

Musgrave gave an affectionate pat to the last Scout's cap. With a broad grin, the boy clomped down the stage steps, and as if on cue, a horde of chattering youngsters surged out of their seats and swarmed toward the refreshment table, where a guy in a well-floured apron was setting out cookies. D.W. said something to Paul, who shook his head and slumped lower in his chair. His lips looked a little blue, and for a moment, my throat closed. Kids with Down syndrome are prone to heart defects, and Paul had had a murmur since he was a baby. Then I saw the cup of purple Kool-Aid on the seat beside him and let out a relieved breath.

I commandeered another cup of Kool-Aid, wrapped a couple of chocolate chip cookies in a napkin, and took them over to him. He looked up and scooted closer to D.W. He might as well have carved my heart out with a screwdriver.

"Hey, Sport," I said, and held the cup and cookies out to him. He ignored them.

"Cub Scout is honest," he said, reproach in his gravelly voice. "You said pick me up."

"I'm sorry, Sport. Something came up. Police stuff."

D.W. stood and stretched. "I'm gonna go get a cup of that Kool-Aid myself," he said, and wandered off.

Paul said, "I hate police stuff."

"I hate it too sometimes." I slid into the seat D.W. had vacated. Held up the Kool-Aid. "You sure you don't want this?"

After a moment, he reached for it. Took a long sip. I handed him a cookie, and while he nibbled at it, I ate the other one. By the time he'd finished the cookie and the juice, there was a purple ring around his upper lip, and he was sitting up a little straighter.

"Look," he said, and opened the hand with the head.

My chest loosened. "It's terrific. I'm proud of you, Sport."

He climbed onto my lap and chattered about the upcoming Blue and Gold banquet, where he would become a full-fledged Wolf. Then I set him on the floor and held out my empty hand. He took it, palm damp and a little sticky, and I led him over to D.W., who was watching with a bland, enigmatic look on his face that made me want to punch him.

"Glad you could make it," he said. I listened for a judgmental undercurrent, but he seemed sincere. "Maria said you got tangled up with another homicide. Good Lord. You just attract this stuff, don't you?"

There was no good answer to that. It was my dumpster, even though I shared it with four other offices. It was my father in the photo and my phone number on the back. If I wasn't attracting it, something was.

D.W. shrugged into his jacket, and I helped Paul into his. I walked them to the parking lot and watched as D.W. pulled away, Paul waving furiously from the back window.

*

THE DEAD girl had nothing to do with me, and everything to do with me. The photo was a seeping wound. I worried at it on the drive home, past the blazing lights of a shopping complex with the optimistic name of Providence. The space between street-lights grew longer. Then the road narrowed, lit only by head-lights. I passed a state park the size of a postcard and home to an endangered wildflower, and three minutes later, no closer to an answer, pulled into our gravel driveway and parked the Silverado next to Jay's new Lexus. No sign of the red BMW 3 Series that belonged to his lover, a sculptor and graphic artist named Eric Gunnerson.

Eric had paid his way through art school drawing avatars for role players, and while our friendship had gotten off to a tenuous start, his ability to draw a portrait from a verbal description had made him useful to me on more than one occasion.

Another raindrop fell, then two more. My foot hit the porch steps just as the rain began in earnest, and I pushed inside, where the air was thick and sweet with the smell of carmeliz-ing peppers. The skitter of nails sounded on the hardwood, and Luca, the Papillon pup we'd inherited from Jay's former lover, skidded around the corner. I scooped him up and cradled him like a football, and he licked my fingers while I sifted through the mail on the foyer table.

Cable bill, a request for a donation to the firemen's fund, and a check from my brother in Alaska. No message. No return address. I put down the dog and stuffed the check into my wallet.

Jay came out of the kitchen wearing khakis and a pale blue shirt, buttoned to the collar. His new regimen of meds seemed to be working, and he looked good, if a little pale.

"What did Frank want?" he said.

"He asked me to identify a body. A courtesy, he said."

"And could you? Identify it?"

"No."

"What made him think you could?"

I filled him in. The picture, the address and phone number on the back. He tipped his head to one side, blew out a long breath.

I said, "Whatever it is, it isn't going to follow me here."

"I wasn't thinking that."

"Maybe you should be." I looked away. "Maybe I should leave. At least until this is over, whatever *this* is."

"Don't be ridiculous." Absently, he toyed with the top button of his collar. "If someone comes here looking for you, do you think he'll shake my hand and thank me when I say you're gone?"

"Not when you put it that way. So maybe you should leave for a while instead."

"Does Frank think the killer is on his way here?"

"Not that he mentioned."

"Then let's wait and see what's what before we do anything dramatic." He disappeared into the kitchen and called, "Stuffed peppers for dinner."

I hadn't thought I was hungry, but the peppers were good, and by the time Jay started to clear the table, my plate was empty. He washed, I dried. Then he picked up the dog and said, "Let's see if your dead girl's on the news."

"She's not my dead girl."

I brought him a beer, kept one for myself, and settled onto the couch while he flipped on the TV. He clicked past Channel Three, a quick flash of Ashleigh's bleached smile, and landed on Channel Five, where an anchor we didn't know and had no reason to dislike reeled off the news with a solemn, trust-me expression.

The top spot went to the murdered girl. The anchor reported the story with appropriate gravitas, but said nothing I hadn't already heard from Frank. The weathergirl came on, pointed to a swirl of green on the map, and assured us that, while scattered showers seemed probable for the foreseeable future, major flooding was unlikely.

Jay tipped the neck of his bottle toward the television. "Probable. Unlikely. Could she *be* more definitive?"

An interview with a farmer whose prizewinning cow had birthed a healthy two-headed calf was followed by coverage of an explosion at a meth house. Not unusual in itself—meth labs were always exploding—but this time someone had left a typewritten note in the mailbox: *For Justice. This is only the beginning.*

If he hadn't left the note, he could have cleaned out a dozen labs before anybody bothered to run the odds. But the kind of guy who leaves a note isn't looking to clean things up. He's looking to get noticed.

The news went off, and Jay switched the channel to an old BBC comedy. I went upstairs and roamed from room to room, opening drawers and banging them closed, putting stray paperbacks back on the shelf, plucking out a couple of half-hearted songs on my guitar. Thinking about the dead girl. Trying not to think about the photograph.

I put away the guitar and took a velvet-lined box from my closet. Fingered my father's medals and his Metro police badge, then pulled out my mother's photo albums and stared at Dad's pictures as if I might see the shadows of Vietnamese orphans in his eyes.

He looked impossibly young. At thirty-six, I was older than he'd ever be.

Downstairs, the television went off. Jay's footsteps padded toward his bedroom. His door snicked shut.

I pushed the album away and opened my laptop. Tapped in a search for killers who branded their victims. Three million hits, most for commercial marketing/branding sites and a metal band called Serial Killers. After twenty pages of dreck, I typed *human trafficking* into the search engine.

Sixty-three million hits. Good God.

I added *Nashville* to the search terms. Ten pages of local news stories and a special report from the Tennessee Bureau of Investigation. Better.

I scrolled through the articles. Most centered on the Somali case and on a young Hispanic woman who'd been kept chained in an apartment for six months. Several dozen mentioned rescue organizations, and of those, more than half referenced a group called Hands of Mercy. Founder, artist/art therapist Claire Bellamy. Executive Director, investor/philanthropist Andrew Talbot.

Both were cited as consultants and said to work closely with the law enforcement triumvirate—FBI, TBI, and local police.

The Hands of Mercy website looked slick and professional, with tabs leading to articles on trafficking, testimonials from rescued women, and opportunities for sponsorship. A photo on the home page showed Bellamy and Talbot on the courthouse steps, Bellamy blonde and earnest-looking in a pencil skirt and peasant blouse, Talbot suave and polished in a tailored suit. The caption said: POLICE WORK WITH RESCUE EXPERTS TO NAIL HUMAN TRAFFICKERS.

The pimp Frank had mentioned, D'Angelo Albert, aka Helix, also had a website. It looked slick and professional too, with a photo of a handsome black man in a tailored suit at the top and a disclaimer at the bottom that said the information provided was for entertainment and educational purposes only. His book, *How to be a Mack Pimp*, was available for immediate download, and for the paltry sum of $14.99, I too could learn how to target and manipulate vulnerable young women.

Instead, I ran his name through SearchSystems and a few other databases, then cross-checked with Metro Nashville's public arrest records. He had a few arrests, no convictions. No surprise there. Pimps are notoriously hard to convict. The surprise was his degree in business. A real degree, from an accredited four-year university.

Somehow that made it worse. A college diploma, and his idea of being an entrepreneur was branding women and selling their services to strangers.

Disgusted, I shut down the laptop. Nothing more I could do until Frank and Harry identified the murdered girl. I dashed out through the rain to feed the horses, came back thirty minutes later soaked and shivering. As I peeled off my wet shirt and jeans, I glanced at the bedside table, where my phone blinked up at me—*Missed message*. I flipped it open, found a text message and a voice mail. The text was from a woman I'd been dating on and off since Christmas. She was on sabbatical, starting a school for rural kids in South America. Just as well, maybe. She had baggage, I had baggage. A little time apart might do us both good.

The text said: *Bought supplies. Heading up to the village tomorrow. No signal for a few weeks. How was your day? I miss you.*

My thumb hovered over the keypad as I imagined my day encapsulated in a text box. *Missed Paul's Scout meeting, dead girl in dumpster.*

Right.

Learned dad had secret life in Vietnam, dead girl in dumpster.

No good.

Finally, I tapped in: *Miss you too.*

The voice mail message was from Ashleigh: "Hey, Cowboy. Buy you a drink if you'll give me the scoop on what happened today."

I sent her a text message too: *No comment.*

4

Morning came, wet and hazy. I cashed my brother's check and drove the money over to his wife's house. When no one answered my knock, I slipped the envelope through the mail slot and went around back to offer a mint to the rescued Arabian I'd given my nieces. They'd been good for him; his coat was glossy, and he didn't flinch when I rubbed my hand over his blind eye.

I did another background check from the cab of my truck, took a few pictures of a cheating husband and a few more of a cheating wife, then referred a man with a missing son to another agency. I had neither the time nor the heart for another lost boy.

The storms lingered through the weekend. Between squalls, I took a chain saw to the fallen tree and cleared the debris from the trails, trying to ignore the dead girl prodding at the edges of my mind. On Monday morning, with Frank's shrewd gaze still fresh in my mind, I pulled up to the curb in front of my office a little before nine. The crime scene tape had been removed, and the rain-washed street looked much as it had before the murder. No cops. No reporters. Not even a rust-colored stain on the concrete walk to say a woman had died here.

At the top of the porch steps, I fumbled with my keys. The locks were new, like the new buzzer system the tenants had pitched in for. Now clients who wanted in had to push the buzzer with my name on it and identify themselves via intercom so I could buzz them in. Or not. It might have made a lesser man giddy with power.

Finally, my key turned and the door swung open. Inside, an Asian woman sat on the steps, a small leather purse slung across her shoulder, a misshapen duffel made of olive green canvas at her feet. She looked up as I came in.

One of the Strip-o-Gram girls, I thought at first. Then I saw the scars. Angry, puckered scars that flowed down her right cheek and disappeared into the neckline of her blouse. It looked like one side of her face had been melted.

The scars ran out the right sleeve of her shirt and past the elbow, where they converged in a patch of shiny, puckered flesh at the end of a stump.

She was too old for a Strip-o-Gram girl too. Late thirties, early forties, maybe older. The scars made it hard to tell. The fingers of her left hand toyed with the necklace at her throat—a jade monkey on a silver chain. The buzzer system, it seemed, wasn't foolproof.

When she saw me, she came to her feet, smoothed her slacks with her good hand, her only hand, and peered closely at me. "You know Jay Pee Mac Kean?" she said. "You look like. A little."

Her accent was thick. Vietnamese, I guessed, considering the circumstances.

I said, "J.P. was my father."

"My father too."

"Bullshit."

"Not believe not make not true."

While I untangled that, she said, "You see my daughter? Tuyet?" Her voice was calm, but the tension in her jaw betrayed her.

I said, "Why would your daughter have come to see me?"

"We need talk. Go you office?"

She was about five-four and slim. No sign of a weapon, nothing feral in the way she moved.

"Upstairs," I said. "Third floor, on the right."

She hoisted the duffel and ducked her head under the strap. I gestured for her to go up ahead of me.

At the top floor, I unlocked my office door and stepped aside so she could go in. She'd seemed confident downstairs, but now she looked around like a lost child—at the wildlife prints Maria had given me while we were married, at the horse magazines on the coffee table, at the second-hand sofa and the massive oak desk. My Wyatt Earp desk with its bullet scars and the scorch marks on one side.

"You need new desk," she said.

"I love this desk," I said. "It survived the Civil War and the Wild West, and now it gets to have a nice life here where I only occasionally bleed on it. What can I do for you, Ms. . . . ?"

"My name Khanh," she said. "Jay Pee Mac Kean my father."

"You said that already. I don't believe it any more than I did downstairs."

"I show." She reached into her purse, and even though she probably wasn't reaching for a weapon, I slid my hand beneath the desk, where a Glock .40-caliber was tucked into a holster fastened to the wood. Good gun. Reliable. You could drop it into a rock quarry from a helicopter, and it would still fire. I had another in a shoulder rig under my jacket and another one, custom-made with an external safety, at home in my living room.

She pulled out a photo, and I let my hand fall away from the Glock.

"This picture. My mother, Phen, my father Jay Pee. This picture, I two year old, my sister Trinh just baby."

She handed over the photo. It must have been taken around the same time as the one Frank had shown me the day before, but in this one, my father and the Asian woman were sitting side by side, laughing, heads close together, each holding one of the girls. Behind them, a troop of monkeys groomed each other in the shadow of the hut.

"My grandmother take this picture," Khanh said. "Right after Mother and Jay Pee marry."

"He was already married."

She wagged her head no. "Traditional Vietnamese wedding. My grandparent not so happy."

I stared at the photo. Tried out the orphanage theory again. It didn't hold water. He looked too happy. No. He looked too in love. They both did.

I closed my eyes and tried to remember the photos I'd seen of him with my mother. They'd seemed happy together too. If he'd seemed wistful or a little melancholy even, that was the specter of the war and the treatment he and the other soldiers had gotten when they'd returned.

He'd done multiple tours in Nam. That had always seemed heroic to me. Now it seemed like maybe something else.

She said, "Mother say he try get us out, but too hard, nobody get out then. Jay Pee send money. Many letter. Come back soon, he say. But never come." She lowered her eyes an instant too late to hide the flash of hurt and anger. "Then soldier come, take us education camp. Too much move then, too many camp, too many village. Mother say he never find us."

I thought of my father, sending letters out into the vast unknown, hoping for an answer that would never arrive. I wondered if my mother had known.

"That was a long time ago," I said. "Why are you here? Why now?"

She clasped her hands in her lap and said, "Mother very sick. Medicine very expensive. We have no money, but if no medicine, Mother die. Tuyet say she come here, come America, find my father. Her grandfather. Make him pay. She very young. Very stupid."

"He couldn't have helped her if he'd wanted to," I said. "He died thirty-two years ago."

She bit her lip and then said softly, "What happen him?"

"He went out to buy cigarettes. It was just down the street, and he didn't take his service gun. He should have. You're supposed to have it with you all the time. But that time, he didn't. And there was a robbery at the convenience store."

She cocked her head, eyes questioning. "Not know con-ven-yunce store."

"It's a little box store where you can get snacks and soft drinks. Aspirin. Beer. That sort of thing. There was an old guy behind the counter, and this young punk was robbing the store. Kid pulled a gun on the clerk and my dad stepped in. The kid shot him."

"And old man?"

"Dad was bleeding out, but he managed to get hold of the kid's gun. He shot the bad guy, and the clerk went home to his family."

She bowed her head.

I said, "But none of that explains why you're here."

"No money for medicine. No money for Tuyet and me come America. You ever hear of *cái gió?*"

I shook my head.

"Mean wind tree. Deep in jungle, very dangerous go there." She opened her hand, showed me the cracked, raw skin of her palm. "Very difficult. But very precious. Much money. Blood of wind tree . . ." She stopped. "What is word for blood of tree?"

"Sap?"

She nodded. "Sap. Use make incense for religious ceremony. Also make medicine. I know someone, he take me there. But take long time." She closed her hand. Looked down at her lap. "Too long."

I pictured it as she pieced it together, the cramped, sweltering bus ride, the long trek into the steaming jungle carrying a knapsack almost as heavy as she was. Skin glistening with sweat as she slashed a narrow corridor through dense foliage, machete in one hand, the stump of the other raised to protect her face from the brush.

"You left your daughter behind. To keep her safe."

"My daughter, she almost twenty. Old enough, I think, stay with my mother. Take care her. Take care each other. But I gone too long." Her voice broke, and she pressed her hand to her mouth, eyes squeezed tight, holding in tears.

When it looked like she had a handle on it, I said, "And while you were gone . . . what happened?"

"Tuyet tell all friend, everyone she know, she want come America. Finally, someone know someone who know a man. He say he buy ticket, she pay when she get money from my father. Everyone warn her, this not wise action, but Tuyet . . ." She made a helpless gesture. "She like my sister. Never listen nobody. She call Mother one time from airport in Nashville. Then . . . no more call. First, Mother think, so far away, maybe bad phone, but is too long time. Something happen her. I come home, have money from *cái gió*. But Tuyet gone."

Her eyes welled, and she covered them with her hand, like she was shielding them from the sun.

I said, "So you came here to find her. How long has she been gone?"

"Almost four week."

Four weeks. Anything could happen in four weeks. In law enforcement, as Frank had said, the magic window was forty-eight hours. If you didn't find a missing person by then, chances were you never would. I kept my expression neutral, but she saw it anyway.

"Too long. I know. But not easy come America. Find someone take care mother, pay bribe for visa. Take time. But I come here, look for our father in you big yellow book. No Jay Pee Mac Kean, only you name. I think maybe . . ." She stopped.

"Jared. J.P. You thought maybe I was him."

"I see you, I know. You too young, but same eye, same hair. Same, same."

Until a few days ago, I would have been proud of that. Now I wasn't sure.

She said, "You not Jay Pee. But you find people. You help find my daughter?"

"I don't know how to tell you this," I said.

She searched my face, saw something in it that made her sink down onto the leather visitor's chair across from my desk. "Something happen Tuyet?"

"There was an Asian woman . . . She was holding a picture a lot like this one." I gestured with the photo. "It had my phone number on the back. What did—what does she look like?"

Her face softened, and for the first time, I saw the hint of a smile. "Very beautiful. Black hair like me, but long." She gestured to the small of her back.

"That doesn't tell us much. Hair can be cut."

"She proud her hair. Never cut."

There were people who would cut it just to break her. I didn't tell Khanh that. I suspected she knew.

"You know something." She closed her eyes. Took a deep breath, bracing herself. "She . . . die?"

"Someone died. I know it's hard, but maybe you could come down to the—come down and see if you can identify her."

"I have picture," she said, reaching for her purse.

I thought of the swollen face. "That might not help."

Her face was expressionless, but her fist clenched against her stomach. "Yes. I come."

5

Frank picked up on the fourth ring.

"There's an Asian woman in my office," I said.

There was a silence on the other end. Then, "Alive or dead?"

"Alive. She might be related to the—" I glanced toward Khanh, who sat stiffly on the sofa, left fist clenched against her knee, stump pressed tight against her stomach. "The victim from the other day."

"And she showed up at your office, why?"

I hesitated a moment before I told him. "She's one of the girls in the photo you showed me." I left out the part about the traditional Vietnamese wedding.

"So she's your sister."

"Half sister."

"And our vic is the other one?"

"I don't think so. Maybe a daughter. I thought we might come by or meet you at the . . . facility . . . unless you already have an ID."

"We got nothin'," he said. "Her prints aren't in AFIS, INS hasn't got her in the system. That leaves us with nada. Thing is, I'm not at the office."

"You're always at the office."

"Which is why I need a day off."

"Frank, what's going on?"

He blew past that as if I hadn't said it. "Malone has copies of the crime scene photos. They're pretty thorough, so you won't have to put your girl through a trip to the morgue."

"She's not my girl," I said. "Are you—"

"I gotta go." He cleared his throat. "We'll touch base later. Call Malone."

I didn't want to talk to Malone twice, so I called the front desk instead. She was in, but I left a message with the desk sergeant anyway, imagining the little furrow between Malone's eyebrows, the quirk of her mouth when he told her I was on my way over. The image wasn't entirely without its charms.

Since Khanh had come by taxi, I shepherded her downstairs to the Silverado and opened the door for her. She shoved her duffel into the front seat and eyed the distance between the pavement and the floorboards. She was a small woman, and it was a big truck. After a moment, she gave her head a little shake, and I boosted her into the cab.

We didn't make small talk. Khanh opened her mouth when we passed the full scale Parthenon replica in Centennial Park, then closed it again without speaking. I thought about telling her how it was built for the Centennial celebration back in 1897 and how, except for the gilded statue of Athena, the friezes and sculptures had been molded from the originals. It would have filled the time.

But she wasn't a tourist, and I wasn't a tour guide, so I let the moment pass. A few minutes later, I turned into the West Precinct parking lot. Malone was standing just outside the automatic doors, sucking on a cigarette and tapping her feet. The damp air had frizzed her hair. "You."

I forced a grin. "I admire your ability to sublimate your natural enthusiasm for my presence."

"Smart ass. You here to add something to your statement?"

"This is Khanh. She might be able to ID the woman in my dumpster."

"I wouldn't be so quick to claim that dumpster," Malone said. "Seeing as how there was a body in it." She brushed a stray tendril of red hair out of her eyes and looked past me at Khanh. "So she knows the victim. What are you here for?"

"Moral support."

"Ha," she said. "Don't make me laugh."

The animosity was more habit than real. A few months earlier, she'd just as soon have shot me as look at me, but she'd mellowed since then. Or maybe my charm and boyish good looks had finally won her over.

She said to Khanh, "I'm sorry. He has that effect on me."

I cocked an eyebrow. "I have an effect on you?"

Khanh stopped us with a glance. "My daughter?"

Malone blew out a spume of smoke, tamped out the cigarette on the bottom of her shoe, and flicked it into the white sand in the ash receptacle. "In here."

I checked my Glock at the security desk, along with the Beretta in my ankle holster, and Malone swiped her security card. When the lock clicked, she twisted the handle and pulled open the heavy metal doors that led us into a warren of offices and cubicles.

I filled Malone in on the way, focusing on Tuyet's disappearance and skimming the parts about my father and his other family. The hall was quiet, except for the sounds of our footsteps— the click of my boot heels, the muffled tap of Malone's flats, the soft shuffle of Khanh's embroidered slippers.

Malone pushed open a door that had a brass plate with her name on it. "I have to warn you. These photos, they won't be easy to look at."

Khanh gave her a long, flat look. "Easy, not easy, I look."

Malone gestured toward two chairs across from her desk, then went around and dropped into the ergonomically designed computer chair on the other side. Her desk was polished, neat. Pens and pencils in a ceramic pen holder, spiral-bound calendar open to the current month. I thought of my scarred desk with the bullet holes. I liked it better.

She opened a drawer and pulled out a thin file. Pushed it across the table toward Khanh.

Khanh closed her eyes. After a moment, she took a deep breath and opened the file. Picked up the photo on top. I looked over her shoulder. The dead girl, curled like a sleeping infant in the mound of garbage bags. Khanh took a quivering breath and moved the picture to the back of the pile.

She took her time, studying each one carefully and lingering over the close-ups of identifying marks. A mole on the side of the neck. A dragonfly tattoo on one shoulder. The scar that looked like a Chinese ideogram.

In the photos, the scars and bruises were more noticeable. A small sound, almost a chirp, escaped Khanh. Then she let out a whoosh of breath and said, "Not her. Not Tuyet."

"You're sure?" Malone said. "There's a lot of damage. The face is kind of . . . misshapen."

Khanh closed the file and handed it across the desk. Her voice was calm, but her jaw pulsed. "Tuyet not so small. Bigger breast. Longer leg. No . . ." She fumbled for the word. "On shoulder. No tattoo." After a moment, she frowned and said, "She must know Tuyet. Maybe steal picture."

Malone said, "Or maybe Tuyet gave it to her. Or maybe she got it from someone else who knew your daughter."

I looked at Khanh. "Who was the man who bought Tuyet's ticket?"

"She call him Mat Troi," Khanh said. "He Amerasian, like us."

"Probably why she trusted him," Malone said. "Assuming he's involved in this. But you don't know that he is—or that she isn't. If this girl was a rival—"

Khanh's hand curled into a fist. "Tuyet never do this!" Her stump waved toward the file.

"Relax," Malone said. "I didn't say she would. I said she might. We don't know what happened. We don't even know she's missing."

"She missing. Too long, no call."

"Maybe," Malone said. "They don't, always."

She asked Khanh all the right questions—the flight number, time and date of the flight, everything she knew about the man who had bought the ticket. Khanh knew the time and date of the flight, not much else.

"You have a picture?" Malone asked.

Khanh reached into her purse and pulled out a candid photo of a laughing young woman on a motorbike. Tight jeans. No helmet. One hand brushed a windblown strand of long black hair from her face. She had Khanh's eyes and mouth, my father's nose and cheekbones. She was beautiful.

I thought of the girl in the dumpster, her battered face, her shredded feet. Her killer had kept her a month, maybe two, Frank had said. Tuyet had already been missing a month. If she was still alive, she might not have much time.

Malone scanned the photo into her computer and handed the original back to Khanh. I picked up the file before Malone could protest and flipped to the picture I wanted. "Khanh. You see this mark?" I pointed to the scar, the one that looked like a Chinese symbol.

"Yes. Mean eye of dragon."

"Frank—Frank Campanella, he's working the case—says it might be a brand."

"I not know brand."

"It's a mark, like a scar. It shows possession. Like, cattlemen used to brand their livestock so other ranchers would know those particular animals were theirs. So if a rustler stole somebody else's cow or horse, other people could recognize it and know who the real owner was."

She looked aghast. "You do this people?"

"No, psychopaths do this to people." At her blank look, I added, "Bad men who like to hurt things."

She took in a hitching breath. "You think Tuyet with . . . sigh-ko-pat?"

Malone shot me a glare. "It's too soon to speculate. She could be shacking up with the guy she came here with, she could be—"

"She could be anywhere," I said. "She obviously got as far as looking up my office number, just like you did, but you showed up on my doorstep, and she never did. Whatever that means, it can't be good."

Khanh was quiet for a moment. Then, "You help me find her."

"That's what we do," Malone said. "But it will take time. It's a big world out there, and we don't have much to go on."

"Big world," Khanh repeated. She hugged herself with her good arm and whispered, "Too big, sometime."

6

"What now?" Khanh asked. She hauled the duffel bag across the passenger seat and into her lap. It was too big, but she propped it on her thighs and wrapped her arms around it as if it were a child. Her left hand cupped her other elbow, just above the stump.

I said, "You heard her. They're looking for your daughter. They have more resources than we have."

She glared at me through narrowed eyes. "You give up."

"Nobody's giving up. I'm just saying, this is a homicide investigation. Leave it to the professionals."

"These professional," she said, "how hard you think they look?"

As hard as they can, I wanted to say, but she was right. Nashville detectives were good, but what did they have? A dead girl they couldn't identify and a missing foreigner they couldn't prove was missing. My father's photograph linked them, but how many links might be in that chain was impossible to tell.

"This sigh-ko-pat," Khanh said. "Maybe hurting her right now." She gave me a pleading look. Big brown eyes like Maria's, with epicanthal folds like Paul's. This was not my problem, but I felt my resolve faltering. Something skittered at the edges of my mind. I pushed it down, thought of my father and the Vietnamese family in front of that shack in the rice fields. *No. I don't owe her anything. I don't owe either of them anything.*

I wasn't sure if I meant Khanh and her daughter, or if I meant Khanh and my father. The thought made me feel petty, but there it was.

"Please," she said, maybe seeing something in my face, some sudden coldness. "I know we nothing you, but for you father . . . for you ancestor . . ."

"I'm not feeling very chummy with my ancestors right now. You were doing better when you said she might be being tortured somewhere."

"That still true. Please. I read you sign. You find lost people. My daughter lost."

Another lost teenager. The weight of it was a pressure in my gut, a clamp around my chest. Frank had it right. All those months when I'd been dodging cases more complex than faithless spouses and skip tracing for bill collectors, I'd been running from a deeper question:

What if I wasn't good enough?

For a moment, I couldn't breathe. I gripped the steering wheel, found my voice, and said, "I find people who have credit cards, driver's licenses. People who leave trails, even if they don't mean to."

"You hear police lady," she said. "Tuyet grown woman. Maybe go away. Maybe meet man, fall in love."

"Maybe she did." At her baleful expression, I held up a hand and said, "I'm not saying that's what happened. I'm saying, isn't it possible?"

"No. Not possible."

I drummed my fingers on the steering wheel. With the Murder Squad defunct and the department understaffed, the Cold Case division was Khanh's best hope of solving the unidentified Asian woman's murder and finding Tuyet. They were among the best in the country. But it would be a year before the case would be officially cold, and by then it would be too late for Tuyet.

If it wasn't already.

I weighed the options, came up empty. Khanh and her daughter needed help. Good enough or not, I was what they had.

"I'll look for her," I said, finally. "But just until we figure something else out."

"We look for her."

"I work alone."

She stared straight ahead, not frowning, not smiling. "Okay. You work alone. I come with you."

I started to tell her it was too dangerous. Whoever had killed the girl in the dumpster wouldn't hesitate to kill again. And Occam's Razor said that whoever had killed the girl either had Tuyet or knew the men who did. Then I thought about the wind tree and the long trek into the jungle. I thought about vipers. Bandits. Tigers.

"Fine," I said. "But if you get in my way . . ."

"Not get in way," she said. A smile flitted across her lips. "Where we start?"

"We canvass the neighborhood. My building first."

This was ground Frank and Harry had already covered, but I wanted to ask my own questions, hear the timbre of voices, watch for physical reactions. Witnesses were sometimes more relaxed and therefore more forthcoming with civilians than with police. And sometimes less, but there wasn't much I could do about that. The hunger to gossip might make up for my lack of a badge.

Since it was too early for the Strip-o-Gram ladies, I knocked on the door across the hall. *Shawna Reese,* said the placard on the door. *Counselor for Abused Women.* She answered the door, scowled when she saw me, and talked to us in the hall, arms crossed tightly across her chest, one knee jiggling as she talked. She kept regular office hours and hadn't been there at the time of the murder, she said, then went on at length about the Asian woman's tragic death and the perfidy of men. She punctuated her speech with hard looks in my direction.

Pretending not to notice, I thanked her for her time and turned toward the stairs.

"Wait," she said, touching Khanh's elbow with her fingertips. "I hope you find your daughter. If you find her, she'll need to talk to someone. You know where to find me." She shot me a final glare, stepped inside, and closed the door.

"No help," Khanh said.

"Onward and upward." I led her up one level and tapped on the psychedelic poster on the door of the Society for the Legalization of Controlled Substances. No answer. The door was locked, and a faint odor of marijuana hovered in the hall. I knocked again, and finally the chain rattled and a barefoot, bleary-eyed guy in faded jeans and a tie-dyed T-shirt opened the door. A haze of cannabis smoke boiled from the room. I coughed and waved the smoke away.

"Dude," he said.

"I'm following up on that murder from last week."

His eyes cleared a little. "I thought you weren't a cop no more."

"Private."

"Can't help you, man. We was crashed out in the back when it went down."

"How do you know when it went down?"

"Cops asked where we was between midnight and five A.M., wasn't too hard to figure. We worked late stuffin' flyers into envelopes, had some pizza around nine, crashed around eleven. Didn't hear nothin' until we woke up around noon the next day. Well, except for the big crash."

"Big crash?"

"Sometime between two and three. Sounded like it came from next door."

"Warfield's office?"

"Naw, more like outside. But then it got real quiet again and we went back to sleep."

"You tell the police about this big crash?"

"Hell, no, and I ain't gonna, neither. Too bad about that chick, though."

I glanced at Khanh as the door closed. "Yeah, too bad."

The last occupied office belonged to Casey Warfield, a nondescript man who shuffled nondescript packages to and from Tokyo, Bangkok and Shanghai. I'd never noticed any postmarks from Vietnam, but then, I hadn't had reason to look for any. Suddenly he seemed a lot more interesting.

His door opened as I lifted my hand to knock. His eyes widened, and he stumbled backward a few steps, shielding his body with his briefcase and an oversized presentation folder. Recognition seeped into his eyes, and he lowered the briefcase a few inches.

"Dear God, you scared the life out of me." His gaze moved past me to Khanh, lingering on her scars a little longer than was polite. He was a few inches shorter than me, with prematurely thinning hair and a pasty complexion. He tucked the folder under one arm and used his free hand to straighten his tie. "I don't have time to talk. I've already missed one meeting because of you."

"Me?"

"Don't tell me that dead girl in the dumpster didn't have anything to do with you."

"A little respect." I nodded toward Khanh.

"Next of kin?"

"No, but her daughter's missing. There's a good chance it's connected."

He rolled his eyes. "Of course it is. Why wouldn't it be?" The folder slipped, and he propped the briefcase against his calf while he adjusted the folder. "But I can't help you. I already told the police everything."

"You do a lot of work in Asia, right?"

"With, not in. I've actually never been out of the country." He stopped suddenly, eyebrows lifting. "You're not thinking I had anything to do with—"

"I'm not thinking anything. Yet."

"Look. Finding that . . . seeing her . . . that was the worst thing that ever happened to me. I hurled my lunch all over the alley. It's burned on my retinas, man."

"You're the one who found the body?"

"I was just about to leave. To another meeting. And somebody knocked on the door. It was that hot-looking blonde stripper, and she had a trash bag in her hand, you know? And she said she was going out back to put it in the dumpster and would

~ 54 ~

I mind going with her, since she didn't like going in the alley all by herself. I was running late, but I said okay, because . . . well . . ." He gave an embarrassed laugh.

"Because she was hot."

"Hot *and* a stripper, you know?"

"She ever ask you do to anything like that before?"

"Hell, no. Thought it was my lucky day."

"And in the alley, you didn't see anything else out of place?"

"You mean, besides the body? Man, I couldn't see anything but that. I couldn't get that picture out of my head. While I was puking, the stripper called 911, and then we went inside to wait for the cops and I canceled my meeting. It was an important one too, but what can you do, right?"

"What about earlier that morning? Or the night before? See anything unusual then?"

"I come in at nine, leave at five. And no, I didn't see anything. Do you mind?" He held up his watch. "My client was gracious enough to reschedule, and I can't afford to be late."

I stepped aside, and Khanh moved with me, her presence an angry heat behind me, her breath between my shoulder blades quick and shallow. I said to Casey, "What is it you do, exactly?"

He locked the door behind him and held up the presentation folder. "Comics. Anime. That sort of thing. I'm a procurer."

I wondered if he procured other things, but that was a question for another time. Beside me, Khanh cocked her head and listened to his footsteps clatter down the stairs. "He very big creep," she said. "Woman die, Tuyet missing, he only care about stupid meeting."

"He cared about the stripper," I said. "For what it's worth."

"Not worth much," she said. "Not even know her name."

We stepped out into the cool, gray morning and made our way up my street and down the next, alternating sides, covering the apartment complex on the corner and the row houses that backed the alley. All dead ends. Not even old Mrs. Corcoran, who lived three doors down and spent her nights watching classic films and peering out the curtains at her neighbors, had seen anything out of the ordinary.

A little after one, Pat Freeman's Chrysler pulled into the driveway next door. The driver's door popped open, and Pat leaned his seat back so he could pass his wheelchair, sans wheels, across his body and onto the driveway. Standing, Pat would have been around six-four, with broad shoulders and a heavily muscled torso, but a bad tackle in his senior year had left him paralyzed from the waist down. Now he made his living freelancing for sports magazines and spent his off-hours kayaking and training for the Paralympics. Like Mrs. Corcoran, he was a night owl.

By the time Khanh and I got there, he had pulled both wheels out of the back seat. He looked up at us and grinned. "Hey, Cowboy," he said. "Who's your friend?"

I didn't ask if he needed a hand. I knew he didn't. Instead, while he reattached the wheels, I said, "Her daughter, Tuyet, is missing. Nineteen years old. Maybe related to the murder last week."

He regarded her for a moment, then stuck out his left hand. She clasped it awkwardly with her good hand and gave him a self-conscious smile.

With the chair assembled and the right brake on, he lifted each leg out from under the steering wheel, then swung himself into the chair. "So you're tracking down the missing daughter?"

"Something like that. Any chance you saw anything that night?"

"Only thing I saw was that little Strip-o-Gram girl. I don't know when she came in, but she left around two thirty. I know because I heard a crash outside my garage, and when I looked out the window, I saw her hightailing it across the yard. She'd knocked over my garbage can."

I turned it over in my head. "She didn't find the body until that afternoon. So what scared her at two thirty that morning?"

He paused, hand stretched toward the chair arms in the passenger seat. "She didn't find the body."

"What do you mean?"

~ 56 ~

"I saw the news. It was a blonde girl found the body."

"Bridget. Right. That's not who you saw running across your yard?"

"No. It was the little Mexican. Lupita. You've seen her. Petite. Hair like a black silk curtain, ass that won't quit." He glanced at Khanh and slid the chair arms into place. "Beg pardon, Ma'am. Talked to her a couple of times, but her English isn't too good."

"You describe her to the police?"

"I haven't talked to the police. I was away all weekend, covering a wheelchair basketball tournament. I'm just now getting back."

He couldn't add anything more, so we shot the bull for a few minutes, and then he said, "You guys want to come in for lunch? I make a mean PB and J."

"Next time, maybe. I need to confer with my client. And you might want to let the police know about Lupita."

He gave me a mock salute. "Will do, Captain."

As I walked Khanh back to my building, she poked me in the arm and said, "Client?"

"You wanted me to tell him you're my maybe-half-sister from when my dad screwed around on my mom during the war?"

She shrugged. "Why not? Thing happen sometime. Nobody fault sometime. Get over it."

7

I didn't answer. My head knew she was right. My father had been a young man in wartime, a long way from home. Lonely, scared, not knowing if the next day would be his last. Who knew what I might have done, in his shoes? But knowing and believing were two different things. I'd spent my life trying to live up to him. Now it seemed like there were some things not worth living up to.

It didn't matter, in the long run. Khanh existed. She and Tuyet needed me, or someone like me, and whether or not any of us liked it, I was what they had.

I nudged Khanh up the porch steps.

Ina Taylor, owner of Strip-o-Grams, opened the door on my second knock. A cap of white curls framed a sweetly wrinkled face, and a pink sweater draped her bony shoulders, sleeves knotted at the chest. She looked like a kindly piano teacher—until you looked behind her wire-rimmed glasses into eyes as clear and cold as an Arctic winter.

She gave Khanh a quick, appraising glance, then dismissed her and turned her attention to me.

"Come in, Mr. McKean. Forgive the simple decor."

Simple was an understatement. Hardwood floors. Beige couch and a couple of chairs on one end of the room, an open space with a ballet barre and a stripper's pole at the other. A crocheted afghan thrown over the back of the couch for a splash of color.

I got down to business. "Ms. Ina, the girl who reported the body . . ."

"Bridget."

"Tall, blonde, wearing jeans and a tank top when she talked to the police."

"All right, Mr. McKean, we've established you know who she is. What's your point?"

"She told police she found the body."

"She did find the body."

"She found it in the afternoon. But what about earlier? Say, around two thirty A.M.?"

She tilted her head and scanned my face with narrowed eyes. "She was coming back from an appointment, wanted to shower before she went home. She heard something in the alley, like a scuffle. It scared her."

"Then later that day, she got Mr. Warfield to go with her to take out the trash, and that's when she found the body."

"So?"

"How many times you think she's taken out the garbage around here?"

She pursed her lips. "A few."

"She never asked Warfield for help before."

"I told you, she'd heard something out there that scared her."

"Or maybe she already had an idea what was in that dumpster because Lupita told her."

She sucked in a little gasp of surprise, then caught herself and raised a calculated eyebrow. "Lupita?"

"She knocked over Pat Freeman's garbage can. Pat recognized her. And then you staged it so Bridget would have a witness when she found the body later in the afternoon. Why wait so long?"

She picked at the knotted sleeves of her sweater. I could see her weighing it—how much we knew versus how much we were guessing. Whether it would be more trouble to tell the truth or lie. Finally, she straightened her shoulders and went for truth. "We hoped someone else would find it and save us the aggravation."

"But no one did. Look, my—" I stopped, *my client* hanging on my tongue. "We don't care about her immigration status. We're just trying to find a missing girl. If Lupita saw something, she could maybe help us keep the same thing from happening to Khanh's daughter."

Khanh leaned forward, left hand wrapped around the monkey pendant between her breasts. "Please."

The doorknob rattled, and Bridget strode in, her blonde hair pulled into two ponytails. She flashed us a smile, then tossed her gym bag into a corner, peeled off her sweatshirt and sweatpants, and began a series of dance stretches, clad only in a sports bra and a g-string.

For a moment, I lost the power of speech.

"Perk of sharing office space," Ms. Ina said. "You've been a good neighbor, but that doesn't mean I'll sell out my girls for you."

I tore my gaze away from the floor show. "Just ask Lupita. I promise I'll keep her name out of it."

"You can do that?"

"You have my word. I keep her out of it unless she gives me permission not to. We just want to find Tuyet."

She gave her curls an absent pat. "Suppose I agree. What's in it for us?"

"I'll pay. Your regular rate. Just to talk to her."

"I don't think so. It could be dangerous. For the girl, and possibly for me. Inconvenient, at the least."

"Double the rate, then."

"Double. And a favor."

"What favor?"

"I don't know just yet, but one day, I'll ask you for one, and you'll say yes."

"I'm not killing anybody."

She smiled. "Good. I can't think of anybody I want killed."

I glanced at Khanh, saw the tension around her eyes.

"Okay," I said. "Within reason."

Ms. Ina hunched a bony shoulder. "I suppose that will do. But if she says no . . ."

"We're no worse off than we are now."

"Except for the favor. You owe that, either way." She gave a curt nod and pulled her cell phone from her purse. "I'll be right back."

While she was in the next room, I watched Bridget dance. Every few moves, she'd catch my eye and give me a practiced, enigmatic smile. Her real smile was better. She was just finishing her routine when Ms. Ina came back, cell phone in hand.

"She'll meet with you," she said. "An hour from now at the Dairy Diner near Briley and McGavock Pike. You know where it is?"

I nodded.

"If you screw us over . . ."

"I won't."

Bridget put her right foot in her right hand and lifted it over her head. Laughed as I sputtered a good-bye. As the door closed behind us, Khanh nudged me in the ribs. "She like you."

"She's too young for me. Besides, she wasn't looking at me. She was looking at my wallet."

"You handsome man," she said, exaggerating her accent. "For round-eye American."

I didn't know what to say to that, so I didn't say anything. She ducked her head, but not before I saw her faint smirk.

"Come on," I said. "We're burning daylight."

"My mother say all time," Khanh said, her voice tinged with wonder. "Burn daylight. Not Vietnam words. You father say?"

"My brother always said it. It's a pretty common phrase around here, but I guess he could have gotten it from Dad."

"Early bed, early rise," she said. "Not count chicken still in egg."

"Don't count your chickens before they hatch," I said.

Half a world away, my mother had said those same words to my brother and me. A big world, Malone had said. And yet, sometimes, so very small.

8

I pulled out my cell phone and called Eric, Jay's lover and my sometime sketch artist. After I'd filled him in, he agreed to meet us at the Dairy Diner. Thirty minutes later, we settled into the parking lot, Khanh and me in the Silverado, Eric idling in his Beamer, head tipped back against the headrest, fingers tapping on the steering wheel in time to some lively music we couldn't hear. The lot was about half full, not bad for the middle of the afternoon.

Khanh and I sat in uncomfortable silence. I fidgeted with the radio. Poked my bobble-head Batman. Drummed on the steering wheel with considerably more vigor than Eric. Khanh sat perfectly still, eyes forward, jaw clenched. A muscle pulsed in her cheek, but her breathing was even. In for a count of four, out for a count of four. Calming breaths.

At three fifteen, a rusty pickup splashed through a puddle and pulled into the lot. In the bed of the truck were six swarthy, wiry men in painter's pants and wife-beater T-shirts spackled with paint. The passenger door of the truck swung open, and Lupita climbed out wearing an orange and yellow Dairy Diner uniform. She looked younger in the uniform, no makeup, with her hair pulled back in a ponytail. A paper hat with interlocking Ds on it was clipped to her hair.

"Wait here," I said to Khanh and got out of the truck. I glanced toward the BMW and caught Eric's eye. He'd wait for a sign from me before he did anything.

The driver said something that made Lupita grimace and wave him on. Behind me, the door of the Silverado slammed. Obviously, someone needed to teach my half-sister the meaning of *wait here*.

Lupita pushed back her bangs and watched me approach, weight shifted onto the balls of her feet as if in preparation for flight. "I have only a few minutes," she said in heavily accented English. "I have to make biscuits and red-eye gravy."

I gestured toward Khanh, who had padded over and stood just behind my left shoulder. "This is Khanh. Her daughter might have been taken by the man you saw kill the girl at our office."

The girl hugged herself. "I . . . hear about . . . what he did. He is a very bad man."

"You knocked over the neighbor's garbage can around the time of the murder. We need to know what you saw."

"No, I . . ." She tilted her head, tugged at her ponytail. "Señor Freeman make a mistake."

"I didn't say it was Mr. Freeman." At her uneasy glance toward the diner, I added, "We're not here to make trouble for you. We just need to know what you saw. Did you see his face?"

"This is a mistake. I tell Señora Ina I don't want to talk to you. I should not have agreed."

She started toward the building and I stepped in front of her, barring the way. "Look, I get it. You're illegal, and you're scared."

Her cheeks flushed. "I'm Mexican, so I must be illegal?"

"Why else wouldn't you go to the police?"

She lowered her head. "You saw what he did."

"Yeah, I did. Did you? Because I'd think you'd want to get this son of a bitch off the streets. Especially if he knows you saw him. Does he?"

She tugged at her ponytail again, the blood leeching from her face, and choked, "I don't know. I don't think so."

"If you could talk to the police—"

"No! No *policía!*" She sidled away, and I held up a hand to stop her.

Khanh came around me and touched Lupita's shoulder. "No police," Khanh said. "Only you, me, us. You help me find daughter. Please."

Lupita bit her lower lip. She looked young and frightened, and I knew she was thinking about green cards, deportation, and a limp, bruised body in a dumpster.

I pointed toward the BMW. "You see the man in the red car? He's an artist. You tell him what you saw, he'll draw it. We take it to the police. We keep you out of it."

"My family," she said. "I don't want trouble."

"No trouble. You just tell him what you saw."

"You *policía?*"

"No *policía.* That missing girl I told you about? She might be my niece."

"Might be?"

"Long story. Or maybe just an old one." I pulled a note pad and a pen from my jacket pocket. "Could we start at the beginning? What were you doing at the office at that hour?"

"I have a . . . date. He needs to get home, so I have him drop me off on West End and think, I'm so close, I walk to the studio and practice my dance routine before I go to work at the diner. I do that sometimes."

"You have a key?"

"How can I practice if I have no key?"

"So you got there, and it was dark."

"Pretty dark. Not much moon. But there is light from the front porch."

"Did you go in?"

"No. I'm almost there, and I see a car. There is a man driving, but I can't see him so good. It pulls up to the curb, and a woman gets out. She is wearing a . . ." She frowned, searching for the word. "Like a dress, but underwear."

"A slip."

"*Sí.*"

"Did you recognize her?"

"I never see her before. She looks Chinese." She glanced at Khanh. "Like you."

I said, "Asian, anyway. Go on."

"She walks like her feet hurt, no shoes. I think maybe somebody beat her."

"The man in the car?"

"Maybe. He lets her out, and she goes to the front door, but she can't get in. The door is locked."

I thought of the new security system, suddenly sick. If she'd gotten in, could she have barricaded herself? Kept her killer out?

I swallowed bile and said, "And then?"

"The car drives away."

"Did you see the license number?"

"A little." She rattled off a string of letters and numbers, which I jotted on the note pad.

"And the car?"

"Silver, I think. In the dark, is very hard to tell the color."

"Two-door or four-door?"

"Two, I think."

"Anything else you can remember about the car?"

"A sticker on the back. 'Be nice to nerds. Some day you will be working for one.' Or something like that. Big letters, shiny in the light. And that's all."

"Then he pulled away?"

"Sí. And I'm about to go over to the Chinese lady, see what she wants, maybe let her in. Only a man comes out of the shadow, from behind the building."

Khanh sucked in a sharp breath, pressed her hand to her mouth.

I asked Lupita, "Did you see his face?"

She wiped away tears with the heels of her hands. "Sí. He came into the light."

"Did he see you?"

"I was in the shadow. Behind Señor Freeman's garage."

"What happened then?"

"She sees him and tries to run, but her feet are too hurt. He catches her so easy, and he puts his arm around her. Here." She touched her throat with her fingertips. "I want to say something, but my voice is frozen. She makes a sound like she can't breathe and he lifts her off the ground. Her feet are kicking and kicking, and he says something. I can't hear it all. Something about taking his time, making an example for women who run." She shook her head, all the color drained from her face. "I make a sound, and he looks up. Right at me. I don't think he can see my face because of the shadows and the darkness, but he knows I'm there. His face is so cold. He gives her neck a hard squeeze, and I hear a snap and she goes limp. I know I should help her, but I am so afraid. I just run." She covered her face with her hands. "If I had not run . . ."

"You might be dead too. No use second-guessing yourself. Do you remember what he looked like?"

She nodded.

"Could you describe him to my friend? It won't bring the dead girl back, but it might help us save Tuyet."

"No *policía*?" she asked again.

"No *policía*."

"Okay. I will talk to your friend."

With Khanh at our heels, I led Lupita around to Eric's BMW and opened the passenger door for her.

She hesitated.

I said, "You've known me, what? A couple months, right? Seen me in the hall? I'm one of the good guys."

She squeezed her lower lip between a thumb and forefinger. After a moment, she let out a sigh and sank into Eric's passenger seat. I closed the door behind her, and Khanh and I climbed into the back.

Eric sat in the driver's seat, sketchbook propped against the wheel. He gave the girl a reassuring smile, pencil poised above the paper, and said, "*Yo sé que estás asustado. Pero mi amigo se encargará de ustedes.*"

I said, "Since when do you speak Spanish?"

"I learned it in college. Spent two summers with a beautiful boy I met backpacking in Paraguay, hardly spoke a word of English. Not that he needed to." He turned back to the girl. *"Qué usted ve la noche que murió la niña?"*

He drew her out with questions and reassurances delivered in a sonorous tone. I didn't understand most of the words, but I knew he was leading her through it, focusing her memories on the killer's features. I'd seen him do it before, coaxing out information in a way that was almost like hypnotism. Her answers were hesitant at first. Then, as she watched the features come to life on the page, she grew more animated, pointing to a curve of the chin or the slope of an eyelid.

"Sí!" She tapped a finger on the finished picture. "This is the man I saw."

The man in the picture had dark hair and heavy eyebrows that met in a "v" at the bridge of a bulbous nose. Unkempt mustache. Broad jaw. Thick neck dark with stubble. Heavy eyelids over hooded eyes. Eric shaded in the irises lightly. It had been too dark for her to see the color.

A tattooed manticore framed the right side of the man's face, one claw arcing across his eyebrows, its scorpion tail curling along the edge of his jaw.

He'd come out of the shadows, Lupita had said. On foot. He must have parked some distance away and chosen the dumpster on impulse, because if he'd had a car behind the building, it would have been easier to stash the girl in the trunk and dispose of her more efficiently later.

He'd mentioned taking his time, which meant the crash of Pat Freeman's garbage can had sealed the girl's fate. The crash meant a witness, which meant no time for fun. But the scars and bruises said he'd already had plenty of fun before she ran.

"You catch this man?" she asked, a quiver in her voice.

"We'll catch him." Or the police would, once I gave them Eric's drawing, but given her obvious fear of the police, I kept that part to myself. "Could I get a phone number? In case I need to talk to you again?"

"You don't need to talk to me again."

"Probably not. But if I do . . ."

She grimaced. "You know where I work. Here and Señora Ina's. Where else am I going to go?"

She climbed out of the BMW. Khanh followed, and together they walked to the door of the diner, speaking quietly, heads close together.

Eric watched them leave, then flipped the sketchbook closed and handed it to me. "You think she'll be okay? Lupita, I mean."

"Are you talking about trauma, or about the guy maybe seeing her?"

"The guy."

"Hard to say. Unless he got a good look at her and can figure out who she is, she's probably fine."

"What are the odds of that?"

"Fifty-fifty. Either way, I think it would be riskier to come after her than to let it lie. But that only matters if he isn't crazy."

"He murdered a woman and threw her in a dumpster. Of course he's crazy."

"If he's crazy, he'll screw up. The police will catch him pretty quick, with or without this picture. But this guy . . . He may be twisted, but I don't think he's crazy."

"I'm not seeing the difference."

"Crazy, he's out of his head. Maybe hallucinating, maybe hearing voices. He might've thought she was possessed or trying to kill him with her mind, or like that guy in California back in the seventies who thought his blood was turning into powder and the only way to save himself was to drink other people's blood. Killed a bunch of people, and they caught him wandering around drenched in gore. Horrific stuff, but in his mind, it was self-preservation."

"My God."

"It's the guys who aren't crazy that get away with it for a long time. BTK. Bundy. Those guys who do it for fun—or the ones who do it because it's just a job. Twisted, maybe. Evil for sure. But they know what they're doing."

"Then he'll do it again?"

"If he's a serial killer, yeah. If he's something else . . . probably. Guys like this . . . they always do it again."

"Tuyet?"

"Sooner or later, if he hasn't already. If he's the guy, he's had her a long time."

"Does Khanh know?"

"Here," I said, touching my finger to my temple. Then, palm over my heart. "Not here."

9

The kid at the front desk of the West Precinct was a guy I'd seen before. Red hair, bored expression, dog-eared paperback propped in his left hand, frosted Pop-Tart in his right. Crumbs dotted the front of his shirt.

"Malone," I said. "Tell her it's Jared McKean."

He picked up the phone and punched in a number. Told the person on the other end we were there, then grunted and punched the button that unlocked the door to the detectives' offices. I waved a thanks and headed that way, Khanh following in my wake.

Malone was behind her desk, pecking at her computer keyboard and scowling at the screen. She didn't look up when Khanh and I came in, but gave a quick nod toward the chair across from her. I gestured to Khanh, and after a brief hesitation, she reluctantly sat.

I said to Malone, "I found something."

A few more taps, and she punched *Enter* with a flourish. Looked up with a smile that couldn't hide her impatience. "That was quick."

I handed her a copy of Eric's composite.

"Who's this?"

"The guy who strangled your Jane Doe."

She stared at the picture. "Where did you get this?"

"There was a witness. Don't ask me who she is. I can't tell you."

The skin around her eyes tightened, and she swung around, tipped back in her chair. "Can't?"

"She only talked to me because I promised her no cops."

"*You* promised." She looked from me to Khanh, then back again. "You don't get to decide that."

"Talk to Pat Freeman, the next-door neighbor. I didn't promise *him* anything."

"I'm not Frank, McKean. You can't pull that cowboy shit on me."

"What cowboy shit? You knew I was going to investigate this. I'm bringing you what I found."

"I need the witness."

"I'm not giving you the witness. I'm giving you this." I gestured toward the drawing.

She blew out an exasperated breath. Looked at the picture again. "Tough guy. Pretty distinctive tat."

"There's something else too. Partial plate." I gave her the numbers and a description of the car.

"Your phantom witness saw all this but didn't come forward?"

I shrugged.

"I appreciate your help, McKean. I really do." Her tone suggested that, whatever she was feeling, it wasn't appreciation. "But I want everything you have, everything you find, and that includes witnesses. If you can't handle that, then now that you've done your part as a good citizen, butt out of my investigation. Note I said citizen. You haven't been a cop in a long time."

"Not that long. But that's beside the point. Do you know who she was? The dead girl?"

The furrow between her eyebrows deepened.

I said, "That's what I thought. This picture, that partial plate. That's all you have."

She glanced at Khanh again, cheeks reddening. "Freeman's on our call-back list. We'd have gotten this in a day or two. You want to investigate this, I can't stop you. But if you mess up so much as a fingerprint, I'll have you in jail so fast your head will spin."

"I gave you everything I have."

"Everything except the witness. If you'd given her to me first, I'd have her in protective custody by now, and when we find this guy, we could use her for the lineup. As it is . . ." She held up her hands, palms up. "Fifty-fifty, we can make it stick. Face it, McKean. You fucked it up."

I glanced at Khanh, who sat perched on the edge of the chair. Spine rigid, lips pressed tight, nostrils flaring.

"You gonna run that or not?" I said.

"I'm gonna run it." She turned back to her computer screen, dismissing us. "And if anything turns up, you better hope we find a lot of evidence, since you may have lost our fucking witness."

10

Back in the Silverado, Khanh rubbed at her stump with the fingers of her other hand and said, "You fuck up?"

"No."

"Malone think yes."

I looked out the window, saw a sky filled with clouds the color of bruised plums. "Malone is a jerk. If I'd gone to her with this first, Ms. Ina would have warned Lupita, and she'd be on her way back to Mexico before morning."

Khanh gave a slow nod. "Maybe yes. But . . ."

"Malone is pissed because she's embarrassed. It's not her fault or Frank's that Pat was out of town all weekend, but she doesn't like it that I got there first."

Khanh lowered her eyes, picked at the zipper of her duffel bag.

I said, "Right, wrong, it's done. Nothing to do now but roll with it."

We spent the afternoon canvassing the rest of the neighborhood, though for all the good it did, we might as well have spent the afternoon working jigsaw puzzles on the kitchen table. Nobody else knew anything.

I said, "Maybe we should start fresh in the morning. Where are you staying?"

She pulled her duffel a little closer to her chest. After a pause, she said, "I come plane, go straight you office."

"Do you have a reservation anywhere?"

"I think I stay you office, maybe."

"It's not set up for guests. I could take you to a hotel."

"You no trust?"

"It's not about trust."

I remembered how she'd gotten here, how her mother's medicine had taken most of what she'd earned from selling the sap of the wind tree. The plane ticket had probably taken the rest. I said, "Exactly how much money do you have?"

Mr. Tactful.

She flicked her tongue across her lower lip and said, "One hundred American dollar."

"You'll run through that like it's water."

"I have what I have."

My hands tightened on the steering wheel. "I guess you're staying at my place."

She looked away, and I guessed she was no happier to accept my charity than I was to give it. "Vietnam, family take care family," she said, finally, "but I pay you back. Send money I get home."

"Let's worry about that when the time comes. For now, let's just find Tuyet."

Khanh stared out the passenger window, watched the landscape flash past until we pulled into the open area at the top of the driveway.

"This is it," I said.

She scanned the two-story farmhouse, the barn with its stalls open to the pasture, the horses stretching their heads over the fence to scarf up the grass on the other side. She said, "You have lovely home."

"It belongs to a friend. I just rent the upstairs." I pulled in between Jay's Lexus and the pasture fence. Eric's red Beamer sat to the right.

She glanced again at the horses, and I said, "You ride?"

"No horse my village, only ox."

The Papillon pup met us at the door. I tucked him into the crook of my arm and glanced at the foyer table. Nothing but an L.L.Bean Catalog and a couple of ads for magazine subscriptions. From the living room, Jay was laughing at a *Big Bang*

Theory DVD while the smells of fresh-baked bread and apple crumble emanated from the kitchen. I stuck my head into the living room, where Jay and Eric sat on the couch, Eric's arm around Jay's shoulders. Jay looked up, pointed the remote at the TV, and clicked *Pause*.

He grinned. "It's the one with the robot contest. Classic. Dinner'll be ready in about twenty minutes. And this . . . ?"

"Is Khanh. She'll be staying in the spare room for a while."

Jay slid out from under Eric's arm and stood, extending his right hand. Noticed Khan's stump and switched hands as smoothly as if that had been his intent all along. His gaze flicked briefly across her scars.

"I hope you like squash casserole," he said to Khanh.

She forced a smile. "Never have squash casserole."

"You'll love it," Jay said. "I'll show you your room. Jared, seriously, you let her carry her own bag?"

"I carry." Khanh swung the duffel up.

"She's the independent type," I said. "Plus, she thinks I'm going to steal her bag."

She grimaced at me.

Jay flashed her a smile. "You don't need to worry about him. He hasn't been arrested in days."

He came back down a few minutes later, and not long after, Khanh followed, dressed in black yoga pants and a clean white blouse. Her hair was damp, and as she passed, I caught the scent of sandalwood. My shampoo.

The casserole was hot and cheesy, the bread warm and crusty, the apple crumble sweet with a touch of cinnamon. Khanh picked at her food while the rest of us made stilted conversation. Thoughts of death hovered like another presence at the table. We might as well have set out another coffee cup.

It was a relief when we finally pushed our plates away and retired to the living room to watch the news.

Khanh said, "If Tuyet you daughter . . . you sit home, watch TV?"

I picked up the Papillon and set him on my lap. "I want to see if there's anything about your daughter or the dead girl on the news."

"Oh." She tilted back in the lounger and curled her knees toward her chest, arms wrapped around her shins. The fingers of her good hand clasped her stump. "You do big favor, I too big hurry. I know."

Jay pointed toward the screen. "Look."

Ashleigh Arneau sat behind the anchors' desk, a strained smile on her face. Beside her, looking young and fresh and chipper was the blonde woman I'd seen at the crime scene.

"What does that look like to you?" I asked.

Jay chuckled. "Poetic justice."

Neither Ashleigh nor her apparent understudy mentioned the murder. Old news now, especially with no breaks in the case. The new, hot news was another explosion, this one in East Nashville. Five dead, two injured. The photos of the victims showed glazed eyes and prison tats. This time, the message read: *For Justice. No mercy.*

"My God," Eric said. "He's going to be a fucking folk hero."

"For a while." I pushed out of the lounger and handed Jay the remote. "Until he kills someone who matters."

Khanh scowled at the screen. "Many police there."

I knew what she was thinking, because I was thinking it too. All the man-hours that would be going into finding the bomber.

Hours that would not be spent finding Tuyet.

Tuyet

*I*n the corner of the shed, Tuyet scratched a line into the metal. There were five lines now, one for each day Dung had been gone. They looked like white hairs against the paint. Tuyet imagined her grandfather's face when Dung handed him the photo, pink skin turning ashen, gray eyes widening in surprise. *What is this?* he would ask, and somehow Dung would make him understand.

The doorknob rattled, and Tuyet dropped her hands to her sides and sidled back to her mattress. The other women in the room looked at each other, their faces sallow in the sooty light.

The door opened, and the boss man strode in, Mat Troi and the tattooed man a step behind. The boss man's jaw was taut, his lips thin and white. Tuyet's throat tightened until her breath was a thread.

Mat glanced in her direction, and she forced a smile, as if she still thought there was something special between them, as if she still found him beautiful. He didn't smile back, but there was hunger in his eyes.

The boss man said, "Dung is dead." He reached into the jacket of his expensive suit and pulled out a photograph. A shiver started in Tuyet's stomach, spread to her arms and legs. She wrapped her arms around herself to keep the men from noticing. "She betrayed us, and you helped her. One of you, some of you . . . maybe all of you. And by helping her, you made this happen."

He thrust the photo toward Hong's face, then Weasel's, then Beetle's. Hong sucked in a sharp breath and curled her hands into fists. Weasel flicked a nervous tongue across her lips. Beetle stared at the picture with dull, flat eyes. He passed down the aisle between the mattresses, flashing the photo at each of the women, and stopped in front of Tuyet. Held the picture up to show the broken doll that had once been Dung, curled into a nest of plastic garbage bags. In bright red letters, someone had stamped: Police file—confidential.

Tuyet's eyes stung. She had not even known Dung's name.

"Look at the date," the boss man said. "Five days ago. She didn't have time to talk to anyone. She didn't ask for help. So if you were thinking some white knight would come bursting in here to save your pretty little yellow asses, you're wrong. No one is coming."

Tuyet willed the tears from her eyes. She would not give him the gift of her tears.

He tucked the photo back into his jacket pocket. "Do you know why I waited this long to tell you?" He cupped her chin and tilted her head up, his thumb and fingers digging painfully into the sides of her jaw. "Answer me."

"Hope," whispered Tuyet. "You want us hope."

"That's right. Five long, glorious days of hope. And now you see there is no hope, and never will be."

He gestured toward the man with the tattoo. "You all know this man. You know what he can do. Now you have a choice. Tell me who helped Dung escape, and only the guilty party— or parties—will be punished. Protect the guilty, and . . ." He paused, smiled. "Let's just say the manticore will have a very busy night."

No one spoke. Tuyet's heart pounded, the pulse of blood in her ears like the sound of the ocean in a seashell.

Then, as pointedly as if they had shoved her into a spotlight, the other eight women looked in her direction and slowly turned their heads away.

For an interminable moment, the boss man studied her face. Then his fingers closed around her arm, dug painfully into her flesh.

"Wait." Mat wrapped his hand around Tuyet's other wrist. "This one is mine."

11

After the news, while Jay took his meds and Eric made a missing-person flyer, I called a woman I knew at the DMV. It was after nine, but she'd be up for hours yet, working Sudoku puzzles and watching nature documentaries on TV.

Beatrice Sandowski had started with the Department of Motor Vehicles the year I was born. She had five daughters, one a lesbian, two divorced, one a career bachelorette, and one married to a guy who'd been unemployed for the past three years and spent his days smoking pot and playing online war games. Beatrice had a soft spot for me, which probably had something to do with her none-too-secret hope that I might one day make a more suitable son-in-law.

Her voice warmed when I said hello.

"Hello, handsome. You still single?"

"Seeing someone."

"Dang."

"Got a favor to ask. A partial plate."

"It'll cost you."

"Cost me what?"

"Meatloaf on Sunday. You can even bring your girlfriend, if you want to break my heart."

"She's out of town." I glanced at Khanh. "But I might bring someone anyway."

She tsk-tsked. "When the cat's away?"

"Nothing like that. It's . . . she . . . might be my sister. Half-sister."

"Might be?"

I looked at Khanh again. She sat stiffly in the recliner, pointedly not watching me. "It's still up in the air. This partial plate I need you to run. It's connected to a missing girl, this woman's daughter."

Her voice softened. "Oh, honey. Look, you give me the numbers and I'll see what I can do. I'll take a rain check on the meatloaf."

I thanked her and flipped the phone closed. Slipped it into my jacket pocket.

"Might be?" Khanh said. "Still in air?"

"Don't push it," I said. "It's not like there's a paternity test."

"We find Tuyet," she said. "Then we go away, you close eyes, no more sister."

"Promises, promises." I told her where the extra blankets were and went outside to feed and water the horses. The night air chilled as I picked out their hooves, combed their manes and tails, and brushed them until they gleamed. Through the stable doors, I could see the flicker of the television behind the blinds. Then the lights went out and there was nothing but the moon. It was past time for bed, but I lingered in the comforting presence of the horses.

I was feeding Tex molasses treats from my palm when the front door opened and Khanh came out. She wore one of Jay's sweaters, and my mother's afghan hung loosely around her shoulders. I tried not to let that bother me.

"Couldn't sleep?" I said.

She pulled the afghan tight around herself. In the moonlight, the scars on her face seemed softer, like the shimmer of heat.

After a moment, she said, "You think Tuyet okay?"

"I don't know." I moved to the next stall, and Crockett nudged my hand. I asked him to target my other palm, and when he did, I gave him a treat. "We have to work it as if she is. And we have to assume she hasn't been shipped off somewhere. We have to assume she's someplace we can find her."

She rubbed at her upper arms. "My country, many ghost. People die from war, die from mine. No body, no ritual. No one pray over." Crockett put his head over the stall door, and she gave his nose a tentative stroke. "No rest. Become *con ma*— hungry ghost, cause *bi ben tah*—mean ghost sickness. If Tuyet die, we need find, make good ritual. Make sure she no hungry ghost."

"I don't believe in ghosts."

"Believe, not believe. Not believe not make not true." She pulled Jay's sweater tighter, drifted to the open door of the barn, and stared out at the house. It stood in shadow, an isolated square of light in the upstairs window.

I rubbed the flat space between Tex's eyes and said, "There are no ghosts here."

"You wrong," she said, clasping the edges of the afghan just beneath her chin. "This place, many ghost."

12

If there were ghosts, they kept to themselves. I slept unmolested and woke to the smell of buckwheat pancakes. Outside, leaves rattled in the wind, and the trees waved their branches against an angry sky. While Jay and Eric armed themselves with umbrellas and left to plaster have-you-seen-this-woman flyers in coffee shops and grocery stores across the city, I loaded Tuyet's photo and Eric's drawing of the suspect onto my phone and laptop.

Khanh, fumbling with the buttons of a sweater Jay had given her, looked over my shoulder as I printed out hard copies and Googled the address for Hands of Mercy, the rescue organization that had featured so prominently in the news articles I'd read.

"Why we go there?" she asked, as I tapped the address into my phone. "You think they rescue Tuyet?"

"No. If she'd been rescued, she would have called. But if someone's buying and selling Asian women, these folks might have them on the radar." I handed her the folder with the copies in it. "Hang on to these for me, would you?"

We stepped out into a brisk wind, too cold for the season. I flipped the collar of my jacket up. Khanh held the folder against her chest and pulled Jay's sweater tight around her.

I waited until we were on the interstate to dial Frank's number. Got his voice mail and hung up without leaving a message, punched in Malone's instead. She answered on the fourth ring.

"What now, McKean?"

I grinned. Her phone knew who I was. "What do you know about Hands of Mercy?"

After a beat, she said, "They do good work. Rescue and rehabilitation. Why?"

"We're heading over there now. I just wanted to know if they were legit."

"Something wrong with your computer?"

"I know what the public records show. I want to know what you think."

There was another silence while, presumably, she weighed the consequences of talking to me. "They've helped us build a few trafficking cases, consulted on a lot of others. Claire does the hands-on work with the women. She's a painter and photographer, had a few gallery showings—very successful, as far as I can tell. Then she gave it up and got degrees in psych and art therapy. Started Hands of Mercy right after graduation."

"Takes a lot of money to run a show like that."

"She comes from money. Plus grants. Plus she exhibits her artwork and donates the proceeds."

"Altruistic."

"Seems that way. Plus, Andrew does a ton of PR and fundraising."

"Busy folks."

"It's a big job. Claire does the therapy, Andrew directs the rescue operations."

Claire and Andrew. She felt comfortable enough to call them by their first names. I said, "I thought you guys handled the rescue operations."

"The big-time traffickers are smart, McKean. They cover their tracks. What groups like HOM do is gather enough evidence to get us involved. And Andrew's thorough. All the dots and crosses in place by the time it comes to us."

"Have you asked him about Tuyet?"

"I have. He doesn't know of any local groups trafficking Asians. I told him you'd probably be in touch anyway. Don't make me regret it. As soon as you have anything . . ."

"You'll have it too." I started to tap the *End Call* button, then said, "Malone? One more thing. What's going on with Frank?"

There was silence on the other end. Then she said gently, as if to ease the sting of her words, "That's not mine to tell, McKean. If he'd wanted you to know, I'm pretty sure he would have told you."

~~~

HANDS OF Mercy was housed in a renovated factory building in walking distance of Belmont University. Its aged glass-and-brick veneer was a sharp contrast to the university's classic southern architecture. I pushed open the glass double doors, stepped aside to let Khanh enter, then followed her into an open lobby with exposed brick walls, a few mismatched vinyl chairs, and a metal magazine rack filled with booklets and brochures on trafficking.

Artwork lined the walls—acrylic paintings, raw and primitive, in cheap frames. A few were unsigned. The rest had first names scrawled in the lower right corner. Anya. Tamika. Emily. Ruth.

Between the lobby and the hall beyond, a pretty blonde woman in jeans and a navy blazer sat behind a cluttered desk. Pink silk blouse beneath the blazer, collar open to reveal a moonstone necklace on a silver chain. She looked younger than she had in the photos I'd seen online. A pair of beaded paperweights bracketed the brass nameplate in front of her, which said, *Claire Bellamy*. She was bent over a leather-bound book, brow furrowed, mouth open in a little "o" of concentration. The pencil in her hand turned and turned again, and a few moments later, a woman's face emerged beneath the beveled point.

Khanh tucked the file folder under her arm and stretched a hand toward the magazine rack, ran a finger along the edge of a booklet called *Trafficking in America*, then dropped her hand to her side.

I said, "Ms. Bellamy?"

The woman looked up from her sketchbook with a sheepish smile. "Sorry, I get lost in it sometimes. Please, call me Claire."

I introduced myself and Khanh, then pulled out my phone and showed her Eric's drawing and the photo of Tuyet. "We're looking for these two people. The girl is Khanh's daughter. We think she was trafficked from Vietnam."

"By this man?"

"An Amerasian she called Mat Troi, but this guy is probably involved."

She traced the manticore tattoo with her index finger. "This is remarkable work. I'd remember it if I'd seen it."

"The guy who drew this guessed at the details, but this is the gist of it."

She picked up Tuyet's picture. "Beautiful girl. You were able to track her this far?"

"She told everybody she knew that she wanted to come here. We figure eventually it got to somebody who knew the guy who snatched her. You could say she fell into his lap."

She shook her head. "Youth. It's a wonder any of us survive it. Andrew does more of the outreach work than I do. He may recognize one of these people, or know someone who might."

We trailed her down a narrow hall to what looked to be a boardroom. A man about my age, midthirties, bent over a projector in the center of the conference table. From his tailored suit and expensive haircut, I guessed he spent a lot of time glad-handing potential donors.

He tapped a button on the attached laptop, and a PowerPoint title page popped onto the wall behind him—*Slavery in Modern-Day America: How to Spot It, How to Stop It.*

Claire slid her hand along his shoulder and rested it on the back of his neck. More than colleagues, then. "Andrew, these people are looking for a missing Vietnamese girl."

Andrew Talbot looked up from his laptop and gave her a distracted smile. To us, he said, "You must be the detective Lieutenant Malone told me about."

I introduced myself and Khanh, showed him my license. He gave it a quick glance and said, "Lots of things can make a girl go missing. What led you to trafficking?"

"We're not sure it is, but it fits what we know." I told him all of it, beginning with the mysterious Mat Troi and the ticket to Nashville and ending with the dead girl in the dumpster. "We figure it was too good for him to pass up, a pretty girl asking around for a ticket to his base of operations."

"You have some reason to think he's based here?"

"The wounds on the dead girl were in various stages of healing. He—or someone—had been going at her for quite a while. Months, maybe."

"That doesn't necessarily mean it happened here. She could have been brought from anywhere."

"She had a photo that belonged to Tuyet—my client's daughter. They definitely crossed paths. Hard for it to have been anywhere but here." I took my folder from Khanh and handed over two copies of each picture. "You can keep these. Maybe post them somewhere so your people will know to keep a lookout?"

"Of course. Whatever we can do. Claire can put these on the community board and post them on our website."

"The mark this guy uses . . ." I showed him the drawing of the dead girl's brand. "Have you ever seen this? Know anyone who uses it?"

He took the drawing and studied it. "It's not uncommon for slavers to mark their victims. We once rescued six women who all had portraits of their pimp tattooed on their buttocks. It was the first thing he did when he turned out a new girl. Another guy carved an asterisk on each woman's left breast. He called himself Snowman, and the asterisk was supposed to represent a snowflake. But this one's new to me."

"Ever hear of a pimp called Helix?"

Claire said, "We rescued a young woman from his stable a few weeks ago."

"Could we talk to her?"

Talbot moved the mouse and clicked the PowerPoint file closed. "If she's willing. But I doubt he has the resources for the kind of operation you're talking about. He's probably never even been out of East Nashville. This way."

As he led us back into the hall, I said, "Malone spoke well of you both. How'd you get into this?"

"I knew someone who'd been trafficked. My stepmother. She had a big influence on my brother and me. I guess you could say that pushed us toward activism."

The news stories hadn't referenced a brother. "He works with you?"

"No, no, not really. Just donations, some repair work, the occasional minor errand. He's never much cared for the spotlight."

Claire grinned, winked. "Unlike the rest of us."

"Don't listen to her," Talbot said, starting up a narrow flight of stairs. "She was a rising star. Her last painting sold for half a million dollars, and she walked away from it to start all this. Ask her why."

She looked over her shoulder, cheeks pinked. "Nothing dramatic. A friend gave me a book on trafficking. *A Crime so Monstrous*, by a guy named Ben Skinner. I couldn't believe it."

"I know what you mean," I said. "The vastness of it. It's not like the random crazy who keeps a woman in his basement. That, you expect."

"Well, I didn't expect even that. I was very naive. So for me, it was like being smacked in the face with a wet rag. I read some more, watched some documentaries, talked to police. And I thought my God, how lucky I was, how blessed, and these women, even when they get free, they're so damaged, they have so far to go. And I thought art is such a great healer. I can't explain it. I just knew this was something I was supposed to do."

Talbot said, "She gets frustrated with rich, well-meaning people."

Claire gave a self-conscious laugh and said, "People like me."

The stairwell opened up into a fifteen-bed dormitory, each bed paired with a four-compartment wooden cubby for clothing and other essentials. A few young women sat or lay on the beds, reading fashion magazines or painting their fingernails. The smell of acetone hung in the air. Over his shoulder, Talbot said, "Her name's Marlee. Has a lot of promise. If she doesn't go back to her pimp, the way so many do. It's one of our biggest challenges."

I'd seen that on the job, too. Abused women who couldn't wait to run back to the men who'd broken their noses and blackened their eyes.

Claire said, "These men have a whole playbook on how to target and manipulate vulnerable women. It's a lot like brainwashing."

"It's exactly like brainwashing," Talbot said. He stopped a few feet from a pretty young woman with olive skin and green eyes. "Marlee, could we speak with you a moment?"

Marlee looked to be in her late teens, a slim girl in jeans and a sleeveless white blouse knotted below her breasts. A lotus tattoo circled her navel, and just below her collarbone was a pale, puckered scar in the shape of a double helix.

Talbot said, "These people are looking for a missing girl. They'd like to ask you some questions."

I showed her Tuyet's picture, then Eric's drawing of the killer. She gave each a cursory glance and said, "Never seen 'em."

"Does Helix run any Asian women?"

"Black, white, yellow. Long as she got a pussy, he don't care."

"Does he always use the spiral mark? Or could he use different marks for different kinds of women?"

"I never seen any other marks."

Claire said, "Could it be something new?"

The girl scratched at a chipped tooth with a Manchurian nail. "I guess. He started a new string of bitches about a year ago. Elite, he called 'em. Guess he might mark 'em different."

I said, "These elite girls. How many of them does he have?"

"Don't know. He don't answer to me."

"Did he keep you locked up someplace? Keep you from calling anybody?"

Her laugh was harsh. "Who'd I call? Santa Claus?"

"Marlee." Talbot gave his head a small shake. "They're trying to help someone. A young woman in trouble, like you were."

She looked away. "He didn't lock me up. He loved me nice. Made like he was the only person in the world who cared about me. He gave me coke. No meth, he don't hold with that on account of it makes you ugly."

I said, "Did he ever beat you?"

"Sure he beat me. He got a pimp stick and knows how to use it." She pushed down the waistband of her jeans and brushed her fingers across a web of pale scars. "But that's on me. I got it coming, you know?"

Claire said, "You didn't have it coming."

As if she hadn't heard, Marlee touched the spiral on her collarbone. "I thanked him for this. Pretty fucked up, huh? He said it told the whole world I's his. It made me proud."

I said, "How does it make you feel now?"

"Lots of things. I still got to sort it all out."

Talbot looked at Khanh and asked, "How long has your daughter been missing?"

I answered for her. "Four weeks, give or take."

He shook his head. "If she was trafficked even four days ago, there's a good chance she's gone. She could be anywhere."

"We think he's holding her here. He kept the other girl a long time."

"It's possible, yes. But not likely. I'm not saying don't look," he added quickly. "I'm just saying don't get your hopes up."

13

That moment when hope dies is like the last breath of a nestling after a hard fall onto concrete. You want to cup it in your hands, to save it somehow, but it's too fragile and too late. Khanh's hope hadn't died yet, but watching the play of emotions on her face as I shepherded her out of the Hands of Mercy building and back to the Silverado, I didn't need to be psychic to know what was going through her mind.

There was a limit to how long you could pursue a cold trail. Even if, God forbid, it were Paulie who'd been taken, there'd come a time when life would intervene. Grass had to be mowed. Rent had to be paid. You didn't give up, but you moved on. You fit your search—your hope—into the empty spaces around work and bills and washing the car. I could afford to give Tuyet my undiluted attention for a while, but not forever. How long, Khanh must be wondering, before the clock stopped ticking?

"Khanh," I said. "He didn't mean we shouldn't try."

"Please," she said, her voice small. "Not talk now."

I drove a silent grid through downtown, then midtown, around the bypass and onto I-65. Traffic pressed in around us, slowed us to a creep. The silence was a palpable pressure, as if the cab of the truck were a submerging submarine. After a while, I parked in front of an upscale nouveau southern restaurant called Urban Grub. Fish pit, oyster bar, outdoor patio with brick fireplaces. The bar tops were glossy and textured, made from oyster shells and recycled beer and wine bottles. The ambience said rustic funk.

Too upbeat for our moods, but maybe that was the point.

"Lunch," I said. "And don't say you're not hungry. *I'm* hungry."

Khanh frowned. "Look expensive."

"My treat."

"You think poor sister from Vietnam must need charity?"

"I think poor sister from Vietnam should save her money for medicine."

She bit her lower lip, looked down at her lap. "Expensive place, take long time. Cheap food, finish quick."

I knew what she was thinking. What if we took an hour for lunch, and then when we found Tuyet, we found we were an hour too late? The if-onlys would kill you.

I said, "This isn't gonna be a sprint. Whether we eat here or hit the drive-through at McDonald's, finding Tuyet is going to take time. Besides, I've got a lot of questions. This is as good a place as any for you to answer them."

Our server, an aspiring actress with café au lait skin and a smile that could have dazzled a sea urchin, brought two waters and handed us each a menu, casting discreet glances at Khanh's scars. Taking my cue from Khanh, I pretended not to notice. I ordered the wood-oven trout and the berry and butternut salad. Khanh hesitated a moment, then followed suit.

When the server had gone, I said, "Tell me everything you know about this guy who bought your daughter's plane ticket."

"I never see."

"You know he was Amerasian."

"Mother tell."

"What else did your mother tell you?"

"Tuyet say he very handsome. He rich American."

"She called him Mat Troi. Last name first, right? That would make him Mr. Mat?"

She thought about it. "Maybe."

"Maybe?"

"Vietnam name very complicated. Last name first, but last name family name. Nobody use. Mat maybe middle name, Troi first name. Or maybe some other middle name, Mat Troi both first name. Be Mr. Troi or Mr. Mat Troi. Maybe."

"Mister and the first name? Is that how it would be on his passport?"

"Maybe. But Tuyet say American. Maybe have American last name. No way to know."

"So all we have is Mat. Tell me that's not a common name."

"Plenty name Mat," she said.

"Here too." I shook my head. "An Amerasian with a common name. And it could have been Matt, short for Matthew. Matt Troy. Did she say where she met him?"

"Friend of friend, she say." She blinked hard. Looked skyward. "Probably bar."

If she'd known the name of the bar, and if the bar had been in town, I'd have gone there and shown Tuyet's picture around. But she didn't, and it wasn't. I said, "I guess we're stuck with the Mexican stripper."

"You not very respect."

"She doesn't want to be called a stripper, maybe she shouldn't be one."

"You stupid man," she said. "Think everything simple."

I bit back a retort as the server brought our food and refills on our water and Khanh's coffee. When she'd gone, Khanh took a deep breath and said, "Not mean that. Just feel . . ." She made a helpless gesture. "Want hit everything."

"I wouldn't mind punching a wall myself," I said. "But let's both restrain ourselves."

She jabbed at a dried cranberry. "I try."

I tested the trout with the edge of my fork. Flaky inside, crisp and golden outside. "So, this Mr. Mat Troi bought Tuyet a ticket to the United States. Round trip?"

It was how I'd do it, if I were Mat. A round trip ticket would have reassured her.

"One way," Khanh said. "She get money for ticket back from you father."

"Assuming she found him."

"She not so good at think ahead."

"Tell me about her," I said. "Everything you can think of."

She stared into her coffee cup. "This help find her?"

"I don't know what will help find her."

"She beautiful. Smart. Stubborn. She like pretty thing. Always want more." She touched the jade monkey at her throat. "She buy necklace, one me, one my mother. Save money long time."

While I ate, Khanh told me how Tuyet had draped silk scarves over lamps to brighten their one-room home and how she'd sold her grandmother's favorite earrings for money to buy a new dress, then saved her money for the next six weeks to buy them back.

Khanh said, "She bar girl. I tell her no need dance in bar. Mother and I own coffee shop, make enough for food, clothes. And Mother . . . she call spirit sometime. People pay, talk to ancestor. Or husband maybe. Get advice. Plenty money get by, before Mother sick."

I tried to imagine the woman in the photo Frank had shown me sitting across a table, telling fortunes—reading palms, or maybe tea leaves. "Your mother is a psychic?"

"She spirit caller."

"Spirit caller. Right. Why didn't Tuyet listen when you tried to talk her out of working at the bar?"

"She think rich American man come take her away. Always she pray for rich American boyfriend."

"Prayers the Devil answers," I said.

She cocked her head, quirked an eyebrow.

"It's an Appalachian saying. Like a monkey's paw. You get what you asked for, but in a bad way. Like you pray for a thousand dollars, but then your husband dies in an accident and the insurance payout is a thousand dollars." I pushed my plate away. Nothing left but a couple of lettuce leaves and a few flakes of fish. "Okay, let's go talk to some more folks. If you're finished."

Khanh laid her silverware neatly across her still-full plate. "I finish."

Tuyet

*H*e made love as if they were in a hotel bed in Ho Chi Minh City and not in a walled compound where she'd been beaten, raped, and starved for days on end. Lying on his side, gazing at her across the pillows, he ran the tips of his fingers across her cheek, swept a few strands of hair away from her face.

She smiled to hide the churning in her stomach and forced the tension from her body, deep breaths in and out, forced her limbs into a post-coital lassitude she didn't feel. Might not ever feel again.

"So beautiful," he said in Vietnamese. "Remember that day in the park?"

A tiny nod. They had strolled through the gardens hand in hand, then made love behind a topiary tiger. "You bought me quail eggs in rice paper. Then we walked on the Thu Thiem Bridge. We dropped petals into the water."

He had been another man then. A better man. She could still feel the warmth of his lips against hers, the way his gaze softened when he looked into her face. Surely, it had not all been a lie.

Not all.

She said, "I thought we were happy. I thought I made you happy."

"You did." He ran a thumb across her lips. "You used to shine."

"I shine for you. Only for you."

She drew in a long breath and summoned images of her mother, her grandmother, the sweet drink her mother made

~ 95 ~

from heart leaves and sugar, even the little monkey she had doted on as a child. Everyone and everything she'd ever loved. She opened her heart to them and poured that love out through her eyes. As if it were for him, for him alone.

It was beyond belief that she should feel these things for him, after all he'd done, after all he'd allowed to be done to her. Beyond belief that she would want to be his woman. But she did want it, more than anything, because to be his was not to be theirs. To be his was to be safe from the man with the manticore tattoo.

"You think you're special?" He propped himself up on one elbow, studying her face. "Is that it?"

"I want to be your woman," she said softly. "That's all. You said I made you happy. Why should you share with strangers? With _him_?"

He rolled onto his back, covered his eyes with his forearm. "You have to be punished. You know that. Karlo is waiting."

Her breath caught, but her voice, when she spoke, was strong. "I know. But after."

She laid a gentle hand on his chest. No lower. If she reached beneath the sheets, he would know she was trying to control him.

"If you live," he said at last. There was something in his voice, a sadness that chilled her bones and froze the smile on her face. "If you live, then maybe."

14

There was a missed call from Beatrice on my cell phone. I called her back from the Silverado, and she answered in a voice as warm and sweet as fresh-baked blackberry cobbler. "Got something for you, darlin'. How do you want it?"

"Can you fax it to my office?"

"It'll be there in five. Just don't forget about the meatloaf."

We stopped at the office to pick up the fax. Seven pages, small print. It would take days to get through it. I faxed a copy to Jay's home computer so he and Eric could narrow the field and pass the likely prospects on to me.

The new-message light on the answering machine was flashing. While Khanh stood in the doorway shifting from foot to foot, I punched the *Play* button. A man's thin voice stammered a story about a cheating spouse. I could have used the money, but the resignation on Khanh's face made me hesitate.

My father had failed her. Hell, life had failed her. Not wanting to be one more letdown on a long list of letdowns, I suppressed a sigh and called back to refer him to another agency.

Khanh gave me a tentative smile. "You good man. What now? Make more plan?"

"I don't know enough to make a plan," I said. "All I know to do is cast a wide net and hope we catch something."

I stopped at the ATM and took out three hundred dollars in twenties. Then, with Khanh at my heels, I spent the afternoon questioning hookers, pimps, and self-styled businessmen on the wrong side of the law. Some I'd met when I was in vice, and some I'd cultivated after I went private.

The message I left was always the same: *An Amerasian guy and the man in this picture kidnapped the girl in this other picture. Help us find her, and we'll make it worth your while.*

It was another cool, wet week, and we spent the better part of it dripping our way from one informant to the next. I bought Khanh an umbrella, and when the rain slanted in from the sides, found her a plastic poncho. Titans blue, with the team logo on the front. I exchanged my father's leather jacket for an Australian stockman's duster and a waterproof Outback hat with a broad brim. We made two more visits to the ATM, spreading around a chunk of my diminishing savings, twenty dollars at a time.

No one knew the man with the manticore tattoo. Their denials were sincere. No shifting gazes, no nervous tics. He might have been a manticore himself, more myth than man.

I asked about Helix too, with better luck. He had a reputation as a player, strictly minor league until about six months ago, when he'd stashed two high-end call girls in an uptown penthouse. He still kept his third-string girls in a cheap rent-by-the-month hotel, but he'd refurbished an old boarding house in East Nashville for his second string, each room decorated to facilitate a different fantasy. He was making a play for the high rollers, and if they wanted an Asian woman, he would either have one in his stable or find a way to come up with one.

It sounded promising, but if he had a partner, Amerasian or otherwise, either no one knew, or no one was willing to talk about it.

On Tuesday afternoon, the rain subsided into a fine mist that silvered Khanh's hair in the light. As we climbed into the truck to warm up and dry out, she wiped the rain out of her eyes and said, "Why not go Helix house, see if Tuyet there?"

"It's on the list." I punched the heater on. "But right now nothing points to him. Nothing concrete."

"Wish we check anyway. Make sure."

"After we find the guy with the tattoo. The manticore. I want some leverage before I talk to Helix."

"Bird in hand," she said, tilting the vent up to warm her face. "Father say that too."

I nodded, though I wasn't sure which was the bird—the one we knew was involved but couldn't find, or the one we could find but had no evidence against.

There were two more bombings that week, both meth houses, and by Thursday, *For Justice* T-shirts and bumper stickers had begun to crop up around town. A letter to the editor in the *Tennessean* called the bomber an American hero, filling a void left by an impotent law enforcement system. A guy selling shirts on lower broad waved one at us as we passed. It said: *Justice: It's a Blast!*

Another showed a bald man in white holding a burning stick of dynamite: *Mr. Clean—Keeping Nashville free from scum.*

While Khanh and I worked our way through the city's seediest pawn shops and strip clubs, Jay and Eric pinned posters on community bulletin boards across the city. Then they made their way down Beatrice's DMV list, searching without luck for our Good Samaritan.

By Friday, Khanh and I had run out of things to say to each other. My feet hurt, and I wanted a hot shower and dry clothes. I wanted to find the tattooed man, too, but wanting something didn't mean you got it. As my mother used to say, *People in Hell want ice water*.

"One more place," I said, pulling into the parking lot of a dingy pink shoebox bar with peeling paint and a neon sign gone dim on one side. Khanh followed me to the front door, and when I opened it, a cloud of cigarette smoke rolled out into the wet night like a spume of volcanic ash. "I know a hooker used to work out of here, street name Amber. She used to get around, keep her ears open. If she's not here, we'll call it a day."

But she was, sitting alone at a table near the front door, where customers would see her when they came in and again when they left. She looked older than I remembered. Bottle-blonde hair, still damp from the rain. Heavy makeup that didn't quite hide the sores on her hollow cheeks. Thick eyeliner, false lashes, flame red lipstick over blistered lips. She wore a red suede mini-skirt and a black lace blouse with a red bra underneath. Black heels and white lace stockings held up by garters. One leg swung up and down beneath the table, dissipating nervous energy.

She looked up at me and blinked. Then recognition dawned in her eyes, and her mouth stretched to reveal a jumble of stained and rotting teeth. Meth mouth.

"Hey, baby." Her voice was husky, an emphysema hack. "Ain't seen you around in a while. Heard you was off the job."

"Gone private." I pulled a chair out from the table for Khanh and slid into the one beside Amber. A bored-looking waitress took our orders and came back with a pair of Budweisers for me and a Kirin for Khanh. I pushed one of the Buds toward Amber and kept the other.

Her chipped nails picked at the skin of her forearms, where a patch of scaly green skin said she'd been mainlining krocodil. Known as a poor man's heroine, the Russian drug was made from codeine, gasoline, paint thinner, and other toxins, and was known for rotting the user's body from the inside.

Amber was walking dead. She just didn't know it yet.

Or maybe she did.

She squinted at me through the cigarette haze. Didn't flinch when I touched the skin beneath her eye, where there was a bruise too dark for the makeup to hide.

I said, "Jerome do this to you?"

She waved my hand away. "Could be. Or maybe some john. All the same, you know? What brings you here, baby? Slumming?"

I showed her both pictures and ran down the story, and when I'd finished, she sat back in her chair, scratching at her cheeks like she had bugs under the skin. "I seen that guy around."

"He a john?"

"Maybe, but I never did him. Not his type, I guess. And I'm not sorry, either. Dude got crazy eyes. Mean, you know?"

"Where can I find him?"

She shifted in her seat, breasts pushed out, legs spread. "Little somethin' to make it worth my while?"

I gave her a twenty from my new wallet.

"Big spender," she said, and stuffed it into a pocket sewn inside the waistband of her skirt.

"It's pretty generous, considering you haven't actually told me anything. If what you've got pans out, I'll bring you another one."

"I seen him at Ray Salazar's place. You know, down off Broad. Adult videos, sex toys, peep booths in the back. I was givin' a little show, and this guy comes in. I remember on account of the tattoo."

"He watched your show?"

"For a while. He jerked off, and then he laughed this real mean laugh and called me some names in another language and got up and left."

"What other language?"

She shrugged. "It wasn't Spanish or French. Or Chink or German. He sounded kind of like Dracula."

"Then how did you know he was calling you names?"

"The look on his face, he sure as hell wasn't calling me sweetheart." She scratched at her arm, then held up a bloody fingernail and grimaced. "This guy targets working girls? Should I be worried?"

"We don't know enough to tell, but I'd say it's just as well for you you're not his type."

The waitress drifted by, and I paid for the drinks. Then Amber walked out with us so anyone watching would think I'd paid for services rather than information. We stood under a leaky awning and waited fruitlessly for the drizzle to dissipate. "Need a ride?" I said, finally. "Drive you to rehab."

She barked a laugh. "Been there, done that. Didn't take. Besides, I still gotta bring in another couple hundred or Jerome'll—" She stopped, looked into my face. "I forgot what a Boy Scout you are. You get any redder, you're gonna bust a vessel."

I drew in a calming breath, blew it out. The Zen detective. "He'll kill you one of these days. If the kroc doesn't get you first."

"No great loss. Might be a relief, I guess. But just as likely he'll get himself offed."

"And then?"

"There's always another Jerome. A girl's got to have somebody watchin' out for her."

"He's watching out for you, all right. He'll watch you right into the boneyard."

For a moment, anger cleared the glaze from her eyes. "Two years, I don't see you. Now you wanna come here and get all up in my business? Fuck that. Fuck rehab. And fuck you."

Khanh watched her go, then looked at me and said, "She like you wallet. But not so crazy about you."

15

Ray Salazar's Adult Emporium was wedged between a comic book store and a barbershop. There was a narrow alley beside it and a poor excuse for a parking lot behind. The asphalt had buckled, and weeds grew up through the cracks. The security light came on when I pulled in and parked between Salazar's junker and a burgundy Impala. Ours were the only vehicles in the lot.

Salazar carried erotic novels, movies, and sex toys, but video was his stock-in-trade. He sold commercial titles and a low-budget porn series he filmed in his basement. He'd done time a few years back for trading in snuff films, but now he swore he was out of the death business.

I turned toward Khanh. "You sure you don't want to wait in the truck? Could be embarrassing."

"Not care embarrassing."

"Suit yourself."

We went through the alley and around to the front door. I pushed it open, and when the bell rang, Salazar, who was ringing up a stack of DVDs for a blushing middle-aged couple, looked up.

At first I thought he was wearing a dirty turban. Then I got closer and realized what I'd thought was a turban was a tattoo. A realistic depiction of a rattlesnake.

"What have you done to your head?" I asked.

He stroked his bald head. "You like it?"

"What's not to like?"

The couple stared fixedly at the counter. The woman tugged at the man's sleeve. Salazar tucked the DVDs and receipt into a plain plastic bag and handed it to the man, who clutched it to his chest with one hand and pushed the woman out the door with the other.

Salazar shook his head and grinned in my direction. "First-timers," he said, and gave his head an affectionate pat. "I can see you're wondering about the tat. This here's a symbol of danger, mystery, and virility. Which is me, to a T."

"Funny, I never thought of rattlers as particularly virile."

"The serpent, man. You don't really think God got all bent out of shape over an apple? Hell, no. That was all about sex." He winked at Khanh. "What can I do for you two? I know you ain't with the police no more, so I'm guessin' this visit is personal?"

"Not exactly. I'm on the private payroll these days. Khanh is my . . . client. Her daughter's missing."

His eyes went wary. "I wouldn't know anything about that."

"Not you. But maybe someone you know. Someone who's into Asian women, likes to play rough. He's killed at least one girl we know of."

"I don't deal in snuff films no more, man. And even when I was, it was strictly trade. I was never on the production side."

"But somebody might ask to buy one. Or sell one. And if they do, maybe you could give me a call."

He rubbed his head absently, thinking it over. "What're you offering? Now that you're on the private payroll?"

"Depends on what you deliver."

"Ballpark."

I looked at Khanh. Imagined my savings as a dwindling pile of dollar bills in a Scrooge McDuck bank vault. A tiny pile, getting smaller by the minute. "Two hundred if you give us something that pans out."

"Shit. I seen rewards for dogs higher than that. Last week, I seen a thousand dollars for a lost Chihuahua."

"I give you a thousand dollars, I'll have to go live in a refrigerator box."

"Five hundred, then."

"Three hundred."

"Four."

"Three fifty, but only if we find her."

"Done."

I doled out another card and gave him a twenty for his time, which he tucked into his shirt pocket. Then I showed him Tuyet's picture and the drawing of the man with the tattoo. "Ever seen either of these people?"

He squinted at both pictures. "The girl, no. The guy . . ."

"He's been in here?"

"Yeah, I remember him. Who could forget that ink?" He jerked a thumb toward the back. "We got to talkin', and turns out we use the same artist." He gave his head a fond pat. "Soon's I saw it, I figured as much. My guy got a distinctive style, you know? Anyways, this guy Ka . . . uh, Karl, he special-ordered a video, so there's a good chance I have his name and address on file."

"You remember the video?"

"Something about prisoners of war, I think. Blondes with big bazongas and bad accents wallowing in the mud with rifles." He came around the counter and pointed to a stained coffeemaker against one wall. "Be right back. Help yourself to coffee—if you like it strong and black."

I took a pass on the coffee but glanced around at the wares. Videos to the left, books along the back wall, fetish gear to the right, and blowup dolls and sex toys in the center aisles. While Khanh glared at the floor, I picked up a pink rubber vibrator that looked like a squid. Put it down again.

Khanh rubbed at a stain on the floorboards with a toe. Her back was rigid, her mouth thin with disapproval.

I said, "What's eating you?"

"What? I very quiet. Say nothing, even when you make deal with asshole for daughter life."

Heat rushed to my face. "You think these people are going to talk to us out of the goodness of their hearts?"

"I—" She stopped. Lowered her eyes. "No. Not think that."

"I'm going to do everything I can to find Tuyet. But I can't promise what I don't have."

"You rich American. Big house. Nice truck. Two horse."

"Jay owns the house, and Wells Fargo owns the truck. I plead guilty to the horses, but I'm a long way from rich."

"You go bank, take out three hundred American dollar easy," she said softly. "Seem rich to me."

The door to the back swung open, and Salazar came out carrying a sheet of paper that looked like it had been ripped from a memo pad. He held it up, just out of reach. "Here you go. Karl Sanders. Got the address right here."

I gave him another twenty, and he handed me the paper. I slipped it into my wallet.

With business out of the way, Salazar seemed more chipper. "That tattoo," he said. "It's called a manticore. Karl, oh uh, old Karl, he told me it was the perfect metaphor for a real man."

"The perfect metaphor."

"Body of a lion for physical strength, wings to rise above the shit life throws at you, tail of a scorpion, because a scorpion kills without mercy, and mercy is for the weak. And finally, the face of a man, for man's superior intellect, the most dangerous weapon of all." He chuckled, stroked his rattlesnake tattoo. "He's a thinker, old Karl. Me, I'm more the primal type."

He told me a story about a woman who had a fanged vagina tattooed onto each thigh and another about a woman who wanted a picture of her dead infant tattooed onto her stomach. Then he said, "I hit the jackpot in the movie biz, though. Zombie porn. It's huge, man. I mean, huge. A few years ago, it was vampires and werewolves, and you sometimes still get some goobers askin' for those, but zombies are the new vampires. Only, you got to be careful about the makeup, you know, cause you want the girls to be hot, and it's hard to be hot when your skin is rotting off, you know what I mean?"

I told him I did.

When we left, he was stroking his head and reading a book called *How to Eat Another Man's Wife*.

That Salazar. All class.

16

It was after nine when we left, circling around through the alley and to the parking lot. There had been a security light on when we came in, and when we came out, it had gone out. The mist had stopped, and the full moon glowed through a veil of gray clouds. To either side of it, dark striations raked the sky like claw marks.

The hairs on the back of my neck prickled. Nothing psychic about it, just something registering underneath the surface, like a shadow within a shadow, or a faint disturbance in the air, perhaps caused by a stranger's breath.

I looked around. Saw nothing.

Khanh rubbed her upper arms and shivered.

I pulled my keys out of my pocket and flipped to the truck key. Punched the unlock button. The headlights flashed, but there was no obliging click of the locks. I punched it again. Still nothing. I pushed the key into the lock, met resistance.

"Wrong key," Khanh said.

"It's not the wrong key." I bent to get a closer look at the lock.

A shadow flashed past the corner of my eye. I started to turn, saw a figure in black coming up on my left, moving fast. Big. Bulky. His face was smooth and black, completely featureless. For a moment, I thought of Salazar's zombies, then realized no, the man was wearing a mask. His arm came up, and the dirty light of the alley glinted on the metal pipe in his hand.

I threw up my left arm as the pipe came down, the thwack of pipe against bone like a rifle shot in the dark. A burst of pain shot from my elbow to my wrist. The arm went dead, and for a moment, my mind went blank. All I wanted to do was cradle the arm and vomit.

I choked back bile and shot a kick at his knee, but he was already moving. I caught his calf with the edge of my heel as he went by.

Khanh shouted something in Vietnamese and leapt onto his back, stump clamped around his neck, fingers of her left hand clawing at his mask. He grunted and bucked her off. She stumbled backward, hit hard on her tailbone. The pipe came down, and Khanh crabbed away as it swished past her ear.

I tugged the Glock out of my shoulder holster, tried to rack it, but my left hand was still numb. It didn't want to cooperate. The masked man's foot slammed into Khanh's gut, and the breath went out of her in a whoosh. Her back slammed hard against the wall of Salazar's shop, and she slumped against it, small and boneless in her poncho.

I hooked the rear site of the Glock on my belt loop and chambered the round. Pointed it at the guy in the mask. "Hey!"

He swung his head toward me, and his gaze froze on the gun. He hadn't made a sound yet, but now he chuckled. "I do not think you will," he rasped, a touch of Eastern Europe in his voice.

My finger twitched toward the trigger. If I killed him, we'd lose our only connection to Tuyet. While I wavered, he stepped into the shadows between the barbershop and the comic book store. The pipe clanged to the pavement, and he bolted for the alley.

I bolted after him, ignoring the throbbing in my arm. We plunged into the alley and down it, across a vacant lot. Brambles caught at my jeans. Bits of broken glass crunched beneath my feet. I splashed through a puddle, stumbled on uneven ground, twisted an ankle, bit back a curse.

Halfway across the lot, he turned and tugged something out of his waistband. His arm came up, and this time there was a pistol in it, something heavy and military-looking. It was too dark to see the make.

I threw myself to the left and rolled. Another burst of pain as my arm hit the ground. Then I was up and scrambling for cover, gritting my teeth against the fire in my arm and ankle. The gun popped twice, the *paf paf* of suppressed rounds, and a chunk of grass and earth flew up a few inches from my boot. I raised the Glock and fired back, the crack of the pistol loud in the empty lot. He grunted and staggered back.

His gun came up again. I ducked around the corner of the comic store, and half a second later, there was another *paf paf*, and a spray of brick dust stung my face.

For a moment, I stood there, back pressed against the brick, heart pounding and breath coming in ragged gasps. When I peered around the corner again, he was gone.

Nausea roiled over me and through me. I leaned a hand against the wall to steady myself. Why hadn't I shot him when I had the chance? Maybe I could have hamstrung him, forced him to tell us where Tuyet was.

Of course, I might have killed him instead, and we'd be no closer to Tuyet than we were now. This might not even be related to Tuyet. Maybe it was sheer coincidence that a guy in a mask tried to kill me the same week I was turning the city upside down, looking for the man with the manticore tattoo.

I forced my gorge back down and hobbled back to Salazar's parking lot. Khanh was picking herself up, brushing dirt and gravel from her pants. One knee of her trousers was torn, and a bloody scrape covered most of her good arm, from elbow to palm. Blood seeped from a gash on her forehead.

"You all right?" I said. My left arm throbbed like . . . well, like someone had bashed it with a lead pipe.

She nodded. "One week America, already mug."

I picked up my keys and poked one at the lock on the driver's side. It wouldn't go in. I pressed a button on my key chain and shone a beam of blue light on the lock. A clear bead glinted in the keyhole. It looked like a droplet of water, but a tap of the key said otherwise. Super Glue. I checked the passenger side. Same thing.

I said, "We didn't get mugged."

Her eyebrows lifted, but I didn't elaborate. Instead, I pressed my injured arm against my stomach, took Khanh gently by the upper arm, and limped to Salazar's front door. The *Closed* sign was up. Not good business, considering the hours most of his customers kept, but probably a good idea when you'd just arranged for one to be murdered. I pounded on the door.

No answer. I pounded some more.

By the time he answered, my right hand felt bruised.

"Jesus," he said. "You can't read the sign?"

"Who did you call?" I said.

"I don't know what you're talking about."

"You went into the back, and when you came out, you wanted to sit around and tell war stories. You were stalling us to give him time to get here."

"Give who time? You're not making any sense."

"You set us up. It's just blind luck we're not in a hole in the ground."

His sooty skin blanched. "Wait a minute. I don't know nothing about no killing."

"What? You thought he wanted to take us out for a beer?"

He rubbed his hands over his head. It looked like he was petting the snake. "You gotta believe me, man, I didn't know—"

I leaned in close. "Your shit better be in order, Salazar, because cops are gonna be so far up your ass, you're gonna think you got a colonoscopy."

His shoulders slumped. "Why you gotta jam me up, man? I mean, how was I supposed to know what he was gonna do?"

"Because you have half a brain? Okay, maybe a quarter. Some fraction of a brain, anyway." I nodded toward Khanh. "The lady's bleeding. You got a clean towel? Emphasis on clean. Maybe some hydrogen peroxide and a bandage?"

"Do I look like a Doc-in-a-Box?"

"You look like a shitheel with a snake on his head. But I figure, this neighborhood, you've gotta have a first-aid kit."

"No call to get personal. Let me see what I can find. You gonna keep pounding on the door, you might as well come in and wait."

While he hunted down a first-aid kit, I dialed 911 and then a twenty-four-hour locksmith. The police said they'd send someone right away. The locksmith said he'd be there within the hour. I wouldn't have made book on who'd get there first. I debated calling Frank, decided it was too late to bother him, then changed my mind and tapped in his number. If it were my case, I'd want to get the call. It went to voice mail, and I left a detailed message.

Salazar came back with a roll of medical gauze and a bottle of peroxide. Khanh winced as the peroxide bubbled in her wounds, but by the time I taped the bandages on, she'd reclaimed her stoic expression.

Thirty minutes later, a patrol car pulled up to the curb, and a young guy who looked about a year out of college football climbed out. Khanh and I met him on the sidewalk, and he gave us a quick once-over. "The dispatcher said you didn't need an ambulance. You kind of look like you need one."

I looked at Khanh. "You need a hospital?"

She touched a finger to the bandage on her forehead and shook her head. "Like say in movie, only flesh wound."

I wasn't sure I could say the same, but I put on a brave face and looked back at the young cop. "We'll run by the ER after we get things straightened out here. You might want to fax your report to Frank Campanella and Lieutenant Malone at the West Precinct. There's a good chance it's related to a homicide they're working."

A line formed between his eyebrows. "Maybe you should tell me what this is all about."

Before I had to explain it, Frank's Crown Vic rounded the corner and rolled to a stop behind the patrol car. Frank climbed out and stumped over, hands jammed into the pockets of a baggy trench coat. Beneath the coat was a wrinkled gray suit with a loosely knotted tie. After he'd greeted and dismissed the kid, he said, "You want I should drive you to the hospital? Get that arm looked at?"

"I can drive. But thanks."

"You both look like you could use some rest. You up for making a statement?"

"I'm up. But I don't know how much I can give you."

"Let's start with whatever you remember about the guy who attacked you."

"He was dressed in black and wearing a mask. There's not much to remember."

"Your message said he spoke to you. Anything distinctive about his voice?"

"I think he had an accent. It was hard to tell. He hardly said anything. Just that he didn't think I'd shoot him."

"Probably just as well you didn't. You don't have another link to the girl, do you?"

"Apparently, I don't have this one."

"Would you recognize his voice if you heard it again?"

"I doubt it. He was . . . not whispering, exactly, kind of rasping."

He rubbed a hand over his stubbled jaw. "You didn't see his face, and you wouldn't recognize his voice. That's going to make it hard for us to identify him."

"You have Salazar's phone records."

"Which I'm running even as we speak, thanks to the wonders of modern technology. And now I'm gonna go in and check his cell phone. But what do you want to bet there's nothing on it?"

"Sucker bet," I said. "But we might get lucky."

He laughed, but there was no humor in it. "That would be a nice change. You know what I'm wondering?"

"Same thing I am. Why use the pipe when he had a gun?"

"Million dollar question. Maybe he didn't want to kill you."

I thought of the burst of brick dust inches from my head. "When he started shooting, I don't think he was missing on purpose."

"So he changed his mind. But what changed it?"

"When I find him, I'll ask him."

He reached out and took my left arm gently in his hands. It throbbed at the touch, but it was bearable. "It's swollen," he said. "Make sure you get this looked at. Your sister's head too. I'll call you when I find something."

"Or when you don't."

"Either way," he said. "And keep your eyes open. He didn't get what he wanted. Which means, whatever it is, he still wants it."

17

Frank had gotten it right: the only call on Salazar's cell phone was to a throwaway phone that couldn't be traced. It had probably already been ditched. Frank gave me the news with a weary resignation. It was what we'd both expected.

"Sure you don't want me to wait until your guy shows?" he said.

"We'll be okay. He should be on his way."

"I'll keep the phone by the bed. Call me if you need a ride."

I waggled the phone at him, repeated the line he'd given me at the murder scene. "Got you on speed dial. Go home and get some sleep."

We went back inside to wait. Salazar, somehow managing to look both contrite and put-upon, brought us two cups of coffee in Styrofoam cups. I took a sip and set it on the counter. It tasted like dirt. "You just blew a shot at three hundred and fifty dollars," I said. "So he must have offered you more."

He went around to the cash register, puttered with the receipt printer beside it. "Man, I got him here. It ain't my fault you couldn't hold onto him."

"Some warning would have helped. But that aside, how was he going to pay you?"

"I didn't—"

I reached across the counter. Grabbed the front of his T-shirt with my good hand. "Don't fuck with me, Salazar."

He raised his hands and shrank into himself like a salted snail. "His woman, man. She's supposed to bring it here."

"What woman? Tell me about her."

"I don't know nothing about her, don't even know her name." I tightened my grip, and he let out a squeal. "I only met her once, at the tattoo shop."

"She was a customer?"

"It was his idea, I think, but yeah. She got some kind of bird. Yellow, I think. With a broke wing."

"Name of the shop?"

"Place called Art & Souls. Dude . . . Let go."

I did, and he sank back against the wall, rubbing his chest. He said, "You find her, am I gonna get my three fifty?"

I bobbed my chin toward my aching arm, still cradled across my stomach. "If we find her, maybe I won't come back and stuff that shirt down your throat."

The cell phone in my jacket pocket buzzed. No name, unknown number. I flipped open the case and pushed the *Answer* button.

Ms. Ina said, "Bridget didn't come to work tonight."

"I take it that's unusual."

"If it weren't, I wouldn't be calling. No, she has a very good work ethic. She rarely misses, and when she does, she always calls."

"But not this time."

"No, and she doesn't answer her cell phone. I even tried texting her. Nothing."

"When's the last time you heard from her?"

"Three days ago. She was off yesterday and the day before."

Technically, she'd only been missing for a few hours, but I had a bad feeling all the same. "Have you told the police?"

"And say what? A stripper didn't show up for work? Don't be naive."

I pinched the bridge of my nose, ignored the quizzical looks from Khanh and Salazar. "What time was she supposed to come in?"

"Two hours ago. Could you go and check on her? And let me know what you find?"

"Is this the favor?"

"Certainly not. This you'll do because you're a decent human being." She rattled off an address. "It's off the beaten path. She's living with her grandmother while she gets on her feet."

"Could she be with a guy?"

"I doubt it. Her divorce was ugly. I got the feeling she's sworn off men for a while."

She'd barely looked old enough to be married, let alone divorced, but then, thanks to nature, makeup, and cosmetic surgery, I found it almost impossible to pinpoint the age of any woman between sixteen and forty.

It was too soon to be worried. Maybe she'd had a flat tire. Maybe she'd let her cell phone die. My niece Caitlin was always running down her battery playing Angry Birds or Bubble Witch, or whatever the latest, hottest, game was. "Can't talk long, Uncle Jared," she'd say. "My phone is about to die. I just wanted to call and say hi. And . . . well, you know."

I shook my head to clear it. This wasn't about Caitlin. It was about Bridget. I said into the phone, "I'm waiting for a locksmith, but I'll run by after he's done. I'll call you when I know something."

Khanh said, "Trouble?"

I filled her in, and she lowered her eyes and said, "This bad, yes?"

"Maybe. Maybe she fell asleep watching a movie. Maybe she was bumping bellies with a new boyfriend and lost track of time."

"You think?"

"No. But I'd like to."

❧

IT WAS twenty more minutes before the locksmith arrived. By that time, I'd had enough of Ray Salazar, and it was a relief when he closed and locked the door behind us. The locksmith was a wiry guy about five feet tall, with stringy brown hair and eyes the color of mud. The name tag on his chest said *Waylon*, and he thrummed with nervous energy. He moved lightly on the balls of his feet, his footsteps quiet on the broken asphalt. He looked us over as he climbed out of his van. Lifted an eyebrow but didn't ask why we looked like we'd been spat out of a meat grinder.

"This the truck?" He gestured toward the Silverado. Prison tats covered his forearms and the backs of his hands.

A real trust builder.

I showed him the lock, and he shook his head and said, "You're gonna need new locks. Take a few minutes."

He quoted me a price that wasn't quite highway robbery and set to work. His hands were deft, and I figured he'd done his time for burglary. It did my heart good to see him pursuing an honest profession.

I would have smiled at the thought, if it weren't for Bridget. Instead, I looked over his shoulder until he turned and squinted back at me with a raised eyebrow. "You get much closer, you're gonna have to buy me dinner."

I held up an apologetic hand and stepped away, pacing the blacktop until he straightened up and pressed a fist to the small of his back.

He handed me my shiny new key. "Better 'n new."

I paid him, and he climbed back into his truck, whistling. When he'd gone, I looked at Khanh. "Let's go find Bridget."

18

The house Bridget shared with her grandmother was on the outskirts of Antioch, a small clapboard farmhouse with peeling paint and a sagging wire fence. A pale light streamed from the lace curtains in the windows. The air smelled of rain and marigolds. Someone had planted a double row around the mailbox and along the length of the gravel driveway.

A dog on a chain gave a series of half-hearted barks, then whined and settled onto his stomach with his muzzle between his paws. Khanh hung back as I walked over and stroked his head. He thumped his tail on the ground and pawed at the empty bowl in front of him. Not far away was another bowl, a few nuggets of kibble scattered in the dust around it.

I took a bottle of water from the cache behind my front seat and poured it into his water bowl with my good hand, keeping my left pressed against my stomach to stabilize it. While he lapped eagerly, I scratched his head again and looked at the windows. No movement from inside.

Khanh followed me to the front door, and when no one answered my knock, trailed behind me to the back, where the air took on the musty smell of chickens. A sagging coop lolled behind the house, where a few bedraggled hens scrabbled in the dirt. They scattered, clucking protests, as we rounded the corner.

No answer at the back door either. I wrapped my good hand in my shirttail and jiggled the doorknob. Locked. No scrapes or chipping paint around the lock, no broken glass or forced entry.

I wiped dust from the rear window with the sleeve of my shirt. It was dim inside, but a thin light streamed from the front room into a tiny kitchen. On the floor lay a white-haired woman in a pink housedress and a single pink slipper. The other slipper lay a few inches from her bare foot. A small pool of blood had collected beneath her head.

"Shit," I said. "Wait here."

I fetched a pair of rubber gloves out from the truck, used my teeth to tug the right one on, then took out a credit card and went back around to the rear of the house. The card slipped easily between the latch and the doorframe. The door creaked open a few inches, and I nudged it the rest of the way. Smelled a musty odor, the scent of early decomp. A pair of dirty plates sat on the counter, piled with chicken bones and a few sad sprigs of rotting broccoli.

I kept my mouth shut. One of the first things senior homicide detectives delight in telling rookies is that all odor is particulate, which meant we were breathing in bits of decomposing broccoli, along with bits of decomposing woman. Something it was better not to think about.

"Stay here," I said again, and stepped inside, hands in my pockets, keeping to the edges of the walls. Like the rest of us, criminals take the most direct path to where they want to go. If the killer had left evidence, the edges of the room were the least likely places to find it.

Khanh slipped her hand into her pants pocket and edged in behind me.

I blew out a sigh. "Fine. Just don't touch anything."

I had to step over the dead woman's lower legs to get into the living room. Behind me, Khanh moaned softly, then sucked in a sharp breath and stepped across.

The living room was cramped, with mud-brown furniture and Elvis collectible plates on the walls. In the center of the room, Bridget slumped in a wooden chair, bound to it by her wrists and ankles, held upright by the rope that clamped her naked torso to the chair back.

She'd been there awhile.

Her face, upper body, and the tops of her arms and thighs were white. Her lower legs and the parts of her thighs and buttocks that weren't touching the chair were a livid purple where the blood had settled. Her lower abdomen was tinged with green. Small circular burns pocked her breasts and inner thighs, and just below her collarbone was a burn in the shape of a double helix. Bruises and thin cuts marred the rest of her torso.

Her hands looked malformed, and it took me a moment to realize why. The crocheted rug beneath the chair was soaked with blood, and some of it had pooled around what looked at first like Beanie Weenies. Then my mind registered the chipped purple polish and the occasional flash of bone. In the center of one bloody fingernail, a bit of rhinestone glittered.

Khanh clapped her hand over her mouth and stumbled backward, over the older woman's body and out the door. A moment later, I heard her retching.

I turned back to the body. Careful not to step in the blood, I pressed a finger to the side of Bridget's calf. Living skin would blanch, leaving a pale, fleeting impression of my fingertip as the pressure displaced the blood beneath. The skin on Bridget's calf remained a deep purple. Dead at least eight to twelve hours, enough time for the lividity to fix.

Her wrist was cold and stiff, but her head lolled forward and her facial features were beginning to relax. Somewhere between twenty-four and thirty-four hours, then. Much more, and the smell of decay would be stronger. Much less, and she'd still be in rigor.

My mouth tasted sour. While I'd been showing his picture around, he'd been here, torturing the girl. Wanting answers. Tying up loose ends.

This kind of torture, either he enjoyed it, or he wanted something from her. Maybe both. I stepped away, breathing fast and shallow, and tried to put it together.

Why Bridget? The news reports had said she'd found the body in midafternoon, which meant he should have no reason to think she could ID him. But if he'd seen Lupita, he might have reasoned that a young woman coming to the office at that hour almost certainly worked for Strip-o-Grams. After that, how hard would it be to stake out the place and, when the girl he'd seen didn't show, snatch Bridget? Either he'd decided that Bridget knew more than she was telling, or he thought she could lead him to Lupita.

My temples began to throb. If I hadn't spread his picture around, Bridget might still be alive.

I retraced my steps out to the back porch, where Khanh sat with her head between her knees, breath coming in ragged bursts.

"You okay?" I said.

Without lifting her head, she said, "We do this?"

"We didn't do this." It didn't sound convincing, so I said it again. "We didn't do this."

"Tuyet—" Her voice broke.

I sat down on the steps beside her. Laid my good hand between her shoulder blades. "She's going to be okay. We're going to bring her home."

It wasn't Malone's jurisdiction, but I called her anyway, then dialed Frank's number. Patrice answered, her voice thick with sleep.

"Is it an emergency?" she asked, voice low.

"It's nothing the night crew can't handle, but they may call him in anyway. I've got a homicide here, and it's related to a case he's working."

"If you don't need him right away, I think I'll let him sleep until they do."

All the years I'd worked with Frank, she'd never let him sleep through a call about a case. "What's going on, Patrice?"

Her breathing changed, and for a moment, I thought she'd tell me. Then she sighed and said, "He's fine, Jared. But come by and see us soon. We miss you. *He* misses you."

∝

We went back to the Silverado to wait for the police. I wanted to pace, but if there were footprints, I didn't want to obliterate them. Instead, Khanh sat in the passenger seat hugging her knees while I used my good hand to pull out my phone and punch in Ms. Ina's number with my thumb. She answered on the second ring. Waiting for my call.

"I don't know how to tell you this," I said.

"Oh no." Her voice was soft, sad. "Is she . . . ?"

"I'm afraid so. You need to call Lupita. Get her someplace safe. Anything Bridget knew, we have to assume he knows."

"She didn't know much," Ms. Ina said. "Not about Lupita. Lupita is a secretive girl. I doubt any of the others knew where she lived."

"Lived?"

"She's already gone. Back to Mexico, at least for the foreseeable future. Poor Bridget." Her voice caught. "Did she . . . suffer?"

My hesitation was answer enough.

"Oh, no," she said again. And then, "I hope you kill this bastard. I really do."

I closed my eyes and saw the playful smirk on Bridget's face, the blonde ponytails swaying as she danced across Ms. Ina's hardwood floor. Had she bargained for her life? Pleaded? Made up answers when she realized she didn't have the information he wanted? Had he left her alone while he checked her story and come back to punish her when he realized she'd lied? My mind raced, imagining things I didn't want to imagine.

Khanh lifted her head, still pale. "Why he do this?"

"He wanted information. She didn't have any to give."

"She tell, he let her go?"

"Probably not. But maybe he'd have killed her quicker."

I shifted in the seat, trying to ignore the throbbing in my arm. I pressed a finger to it, and a slice of pain shot through it, sharp enough to make my eyes water and my stomach churn. Maybe I wouldn't try that again. I touched it again, more gently, with my palm. It was swollen, hot to the touch.

Headlights swung into the driveway, and tires crunched gravel. The dog barked twice, and a few moments later, Malone pulled up beside me and got out of her car, looking like she'd swallowed a frog. "You have a knack for finding trouble. How'd you get in?"

"Back door. I popped it when I saw the old woman's body."

"Jesus Christ, McKean."

"There was a chance the girl might be alive."

She held up a hand—*stop talking*—and went around to the back. A few minutes later, she came out the front door and said, "Start from the beginning. How'd you come to be here, anyway?"

"She didn't show up for work."

"So the old lady called you."

"She couldn't very well call you. What would she say?"

"Oh, I don't know." She reached into her purse, pulled out a pack of cigarettes. "How about, the strongest connection we have to a witness in your murder case is missing?"

"And you'd have said, she's an adult, she's a stripper, so what if she's a few hours late for work." She glared at me, and I said, "I'm not busting your chops, Malone. I know how it works."

She heaved a sigh. "I guess you tromped all over the crime scene too."

"I didn't disturb anything."

"Didn't check her pulse? Try CPR?"

"It was pretty clear she was beyond CPR."

She looked at Khanh. "How about you? You touch anything?"

Khanh shook her head.

Malone tapped a cigarette out of the pack. "We'll wait here for the local cops and CSI. Not in any hurry, are you?"

"Truth to tell," I said, "I'm about tapped out. Khanh too, I guess."

"You saw the DNA spiral on her collarbone?"

"I saw it. You think Helix is the guy?"

"I don't know. It's kind of heavy-handed, but we have to check it out."

While Malone puffed at the cigarette, I told her about the attack in Salazar's parking lot. A little furrow appeared between her eyebrows. "I don't like this," she said. "You know what this was, right?"

"I know what it was."

"An interrogation." She ground the cigarette out on her heel, field-stripped it, and put it in the pocket of her slacks. "If he'd knocked you out with that pipe, there'd be two more chairs in there, and you and your shadow would be tied to them."

19

The local police arrived, followed a few minutes later by the forensic tech van. Khanh and I watched the flurry of activity from my truck. CSIs in disposable jumpsuits gathered evidence while a deputy with a buzz cut waved his arms and blustered into his phone. A young guy in uniform untied the dog and put it in the back of a patrol car with a reassuring pat.

It was after two by the time we'd made our statements and been dismissed. Two more hours before the doctor at Summit Hospital's ER rebandaged Khanh's wounds, put six stitches in her forehead, and told me to wake her up every few hours and ask her some simple questions. Concussions could be tricky, he said. You'd think you felt fine and then, boom, you were dead. With that cheery pronouncement, he turned his attention to me.

After a couple of X-rays of my forearm, he diagnosed a hairline fracture and applied a bright blue cast that started at my palm and went up to my elbow, leaving only my thumb and fingers free. He sent us home with two prescriptions for pain pills. I took a perverse pleasure in noting that mine were better than hers.

She dozed against the passenger door on the way home, stirring only briefly when I went in to fill the prescriptions. Twice, my eyes snapped open as the tires of the Silverado juddered on the shoulder, and I gave a little prayer of thanks when we finally pulled into the driveway. I shook Khanh gently awake, ran through the checklist the doctor had given me to make sure her brain hadn't ruptured, and steered her upstairs to the guest room. A sliver of light streamed from under Jay's door. Burning the candle at both ends.

I was supposed to wake Khanh up every two hours and run the checklist. I was supposed to take a pain pill for my throbbing arm. Instead, I lay down on top of the covers and let my eyes close. A stream of images passed in front of my eyes, things I should be doing, people I wanted to see, questions I wanted to ask.

Then there was nothing until the buzzing of my cell phone woke me. Lying on my stomach, I reached to turn it off with my left hand and hissed in a breath as a knife of pain cut through my forearm. I rolled over and fumbled for it with my other hand. Flipped it open and mumbled, "Yeah?"

Frank said, "You're not going to like this."

Before I could form a coherent sentence, he gave me the punch line. "We picked up Helix for questioning early this morning."

"Is that the part I'm not going to like?"

"No, that's the good part. The bad part is, we can't hold him."

"One of his ladies alibi him?"

He gave a humorless laugh. "How'd you guess? Not to mention, as his attorney kindly pointed out, there are plenty of people who know about that double helix symbol. Any one of them could have killed the girl and marked her with the spiral."

"He have any ideas who might have done a thing like that?"

"Says there's plenty of people want a shot at his action. But I was thinking, if he had a partner . . ."

"Or partners. They might be shifting the blame to him. But why do that, knowing he might give them up?"

"Maybe he can't. It's the Internet age. Maybe they do it all online."

"Or maybe one of the people I talked to this week decided he'd make a terrific red herring. I put his name out there."

"You didn't have to do much to get it there. He didn't exactly keep a low profile."

We spent a few minutes chatting about the case. Then, from the front of the house, Patrice called his name. "Gotta go," he said, and after weighing the virtues of sleep versus breakfast, I slid out of bed and reached for a pair of jeans.

"Thank God," Jay said, when I finally stumbled downstairs. It was almost noon, but he stood at the stove, stirring a pot of steel-cut oats. The butter, brown sugar, and cream were already on the table, a bowl of sliced bananas on the side. Khanh sat at the table, looking bleary-eyed. A bruise darkened one cheek, and one eye was ringed with purple. More bruises pocked her arms. A gauze patch covered the scrape on her forearm. Presumably, there was another beneath the knee of her black pants.

Jay ladled a scoop into a bowl and set it in front of Khanh, who gave it a dubious look. "Look like . . ." She cast about for an appropriate comparison, came up empty. "Nothing good."

I shook my head. "This from a woman who eats duck fetuses."

Jay ladled out another dollop of oats, looked back over his shoulder. "I'm not fixing duck fetuses."

"Too bad." Khanh forced a smile. "You learn make very good food, come Vietnam."

Jay set another bowl in front of me. "What happened this time?"

I held up the cast. "Bone meets pipe. Pipe wins."

Khanh said, "What we do now?"

"Now you stay home and rest while I go have a talk with our good friend Helix." At her baffled frown, I said, "That part about being good friends, that was sarcasm."

"Why I not go?"

"Somebody already tried to kill us. No point tempting fate."

She stared down at her bowl, pushing the oatmeal around with her spoon until the sugar made brown swirls in the cereal. After a few moments, she lifted her gaze and waved her stump toward the scars on her face. "You know what happen me?"

"Not my business," I said.

Jay took the pot off the stove and set it in the sink to soak, then slipped out of the room.

Khanh said, "I ten year old. My sister, Trinh, only eight."

As she spoke, she toyed with the spoon. She didn't look at me, and I didn't look at her, but as she wove the story, it unspooled behind my eyes like a movie.

⁂

THEY'D GROWN up in a small village not far from the Red River. Before the Communist takeover, her mother's family had owned a small plot of land where they grew rice and other vegetables, and where her grandmother made a meager living as a soothsayer. Then they found themselves on the wrong side of the government.

A lot of women in their mother's position had abandoned their Amerasian children, but Khanh and Trinh were lucky. They were embraced by their mother and her parents. While they spent much of their early childhoods in education camps, scrabbling for handfuls of rice and scouring the riverbank for mussels and snails, their family treated them with kindness. One neighbor, Min, made toys from the river clay, and they earned a few coins gathering clay for him in chipped pots. They learned English from their mother, who insisted they would need to know it when their father returned for them. He was trying to get them out, she said, but it was too hard. There were too many obstacles.

When Khanh was ten, her grandfather died, and the family moved to a nearby village to live with a cousin and her husband. Their first day there, their cousin pointed to an overgrown field on the south end of the village and then to an old man sitting on a reed mat, the legs of his trousers knotted beneath the stumps of his thighs. *That is a dangerous place*, their cousin said. *A field of ghosts.*

Two days later, while their mother went to the river for mussels, Khanh and her sister went out to gather bamboo to make baskets. *Take care of your sister*, Phen said to Khanh. *Keep her safe.*

The girls wandered toward a stand of bamboo at the south end of the village, Trinh's damp hand clasped in Khanh's. *Stay close,* Khanh said, and at Trinh's nod, turned to the bamboo stalks.

The sun streamed through the canopy of the trees. The air was damp and steaming, smelling of muddy water. The older girl, engrossed in her task, looked up, realized the child was no longer at her side. She scanned the landscape, saw her sister, hand stretched toward a brilliant yellow flower in the middle of the minefield.

The bamboo clattered to the ground, forgotten. Khanh ran toward the field, hand flung up in warning. "Don't move!"

The smaller child froze. Turned her head and opened her mouth to protest, then saw something in her sister's face and took a tentative step in her direction.

"No!" Khanh said. "Stay there. I'll come for you."

While Trinh stood frozen, ten-year-old Khanh picked her way through the field. The earth was soft from the recent rains, and she could see Trinh's small footprints in the grass. She stepped carefully into the impressions left by Trinh's feet. She reached the smaller child, took Trinh's hands, and placed them on her own waist. "You walk where I walk," she said, and turned to retrace her careful steps.

If a mine exploded, she thought, she would be torn to pieces, but her body would shield her sister's. Maybe, just maybe, Trinh would be all right. Khanh felt a sudden chill, though sweat stung her eyes and trickled down her neck. *I should have been watching her. She was mine to watch.*

One step. Two. The vegetation crunched beneath her feet. Trinh, realizing where she was, began to cry. Her small hands dug into Khanh's sides.

Halfway there.

Khanh tried not to think of the old man with no legs or of the others she'd seen, women, children, some missing limbs, some missing eyes, some crippled, some ripped apart, their startled spirits doomed to haunt the countryside as hungry ghosts. So many ghosts.

Almost there.

She felt it a heartbeat too late, a lessening of pressure as Trinh's hands slipped from her waist. Sensing safety, the little girl bolted around her sister and rushed forward.

No!

Khanh lunged, planted a hand on each of her sister's hips and lifted and shoved with all her might. Trinh flew up and forward as Khanh fell, hands flung wide.

There must have been a noise, a flash of white, a rush of red across her face, but those moments were lost now, perhaps blessedly lost. There was no memory of pain. But there was pain later, when she awakened, and for many months after. Pain when the bandages were changed and her wounds abraded and cleaned, pain in her stump, pain in the arm that was no longer there. The ghost of an arm. The ghost of pain.

And pain in her heart when she learned that she had not saved her sister after all, had not even been able to help their mother wash and wrap the remains or prepare the incense and offerings to keep the girl's spirit from rising as *ma doi*—a hungry ghost.

You were lucky, everyone told her. Lucky to be alive.

She wondered about that, especially when fire spilled from her pores and the weeks and months ahead seemed like nothing but endless, relentless pain, or when visitors glanced at her face and averted their eyes. Was it luck that had taken her sister and left her with a scarred face and half an arm?

She expected ridicule from the village children, who for years had taunted Khanh and her sister for their lighter skin and the trace of Western Europe in their features. She expected them to throw stones, to call her names and tease her about her scars. Instead, they kept their distance, eyeing her with a mixture of awe and apprehension.

What she had done was so huge they couldn't find a way to turn it against her. Her scars, which might have made her an object of ridicule, had become a symbol of self-sacrifice.

❧

Khanh fell silent, head lowered. The air in the kitchen seemed thick, a few motes of dust swirling slowly in the light that streamed through the window. After a moment, I said, "And you were never sorry you'd done it?"

She lifted her head and gave me a level look, then turned her face to the window. "Sometimes . . . I see people look my scars . . ." She shrugged. "I imperfect human."

20

I wanted to protect Khanh, to keep her in the shadows while I followed threads and searched for her daughter, but I understood now that, even if she'd had reason to trust me, she needed to play a part in bringing Tuyet home. She'd walked into a mine-field to save Trinh, but she had failed. That failure made her doubt herself. It made her doubt me. It made her doubt the possibility that Tuyet—that anyone—could be saved.

I went back to Helix's website, *Pimp It Up*, and showed Khanh the forum, books, and webinars dedicated to advising other upstanding young businessmen on the finer points of targeting, grooming, and turning out vulnerable girls. A prominent donate button on each page reminded visitors that their dollars subsidized the valuable free content.

Khanh, perched beside me on the couch, shook her head. "You think he kill Bridget?"

I clicked the *Log Off* button. "I think the manticore killed Bridget. Whether Helix is involved or not . . . Let's go see."

It was another gray day. The rain held off, but the air was thick and wet. It felt like breathing slush.

After a quick stop at the bank I stashed my ID, credit cards, the receipt, and all but three hundred in cash in a lock box behind the front seat. I tossed a space blanket across it. Then we crossed the Cumberland River and passed from downtown to East Nashville, a crime-infested patchwork of low-income housing, crack houses, and meth labs pocketed with funky artist hangouts, Victorian cottages, and the occasional jazz club.

We rolled past the bombed-out skeleton of a meth house we'd seen on the news, then passed a group of kids with skateboards. One boy jumped off a homemade ramp, one hand free for balance, the other holding up a pair of oversized pants. I pulled up and rolled down the window. "You know a guy named Helix?"

They exchanged amused looks. The kid on the ramp, lean and wiry, with skin the color of burnt cocoa, cocked his head and smirked. "You buyin' what he sellin'?"

"Depends on the price. And the goods."

He flipped his board up with his toe and caught it with one hand, then strolled over and leaned close to my window, baring his teeth in a dangerous smile. "You a cop? 'Cause you kinda look like a cop."

"I look too much like a cop to be a cop. Anyway, I tried it for a while. It didn't suit me."

"Don't know why. You the type, for sure." He jerked his head up the street, the way we were headed. "You'll know it when you see it, you got any brains at all."

Apparently, I had some brains, because, two blocks down the street, I saw it. One-story cracker box with a small front porch and gabled roof. Chipping purple paint. Sagging chain-link fence. Windows curtained with heavy black cloth. From the porch eaves hung a rainbow-colored windsock, intersecting spirals like a DNA chain.

A woman leaned against the fence, elbows propped on the top bar, emphasizing small breasts and a bony chest. Short skirt, hazel eyes, skin the color of a boiled pork chop. She smiled when I pulled up, almost like she meant it, and patted her hair, which had been dyed orange and teased into frizz. It looked like she was wearing a Pomeranian.

I got out of the car, and she pushed herself away from the fence, tugging at her skirt. "I ain't done nothin' wrong," she started, then stopped as Khanh climbed out of the passenger side. Her gaze flicked over the scars, the stump, the oversized Titans poncho, then swung back toward me. She looked at the bright blue cast jutting from the sleeve of my coat, and her mouth twitched. "You're not cops."

"No," I said, and made an offer to prove it. "Fifty bucks for a blow job."

"It's extra for two."

I glanced at her neck, where, just above her collarbone was a scar shaped like a DNA helix. "Truth is, I don't really need a blow job."

"Nobody does. It's what you might call a luxury. You wanna get luxurious with me, baby?"

It was probably the biggest word she knew, and she'd probably learned it from a hand-lotion commercial. "What I need is to talk to your pimp. Helix, right?"

"He don't like to be called a pimp."

"What does he like to be called?"

"A entrepreneur." She pronounced it with a *y* in the last syllable and not enough *r's*, but I knew what she meant. "Whattaya need with Helix?"

"I just need to talk to him." I pulled a twenty from my wallet, held it up between two fingers. "Tell him it's about the dead girl with the double spiral on her collarbone. Tell him I'm the one who found her."

She stared at the bill for a moment. Then she pushed herself away from the fence and plucked the twenty from my hand. "Just a minute."

She took her time sauntering to the house and up the porch steps. Lots of hip action going on beneath the short skirt.

Khanh nudged me with a finger. "She think you look, you buy."

"Not my type," I said. "Besides, a place like this, you don't buy, you rent."

An elderly black man came out of the house next door, smacked the screen door open, and mopped his broad face with a grimy handkerchief. He leaned on the porch railing and sipped at a Corona, watching us with hostile eyes.

A few minutes later, the woman with the orange hair came back. Jerked a thumb toward the purple DNA house. "You wanna talk, it'll cost you."

"How much?"

"Two hundred."

Khanh's mouth dropped open.

I said, "Steep."

"Talk ain't cheap. The blow job was a better bargain."

"Depends on what you need, I guess."

We followed her into a living room crowded with oversized leather recliners and a matching sofa that looked like it had been built for a family of Yeti. High-dollar brands. A big-screen TV filled one wall, and a high-priced speaker hung in each corner. The air was heavy with the stench of cigarettes, marijuana, fried fish, and stale beer.

Somewhere in another room, a baby cried, long, inconsolable wails.

The baby changed things. I glanced into the kitchen, wondering if, given the neighborhood and Helix's line of work, the covered windows meant sex wasn't all Helix was selling. Blackened or covered windows were signs of a meth lab. Images flashed through my mind. A two-year-old with burns over most of his body, an eight-month-old who'd died in convulsions after swallowing the rat poison his parents were using to cut their meth. In scope, prescription drugs were a bigger problem, but meth was a scourge. Sooner or later, it killed everything it touched.

I took a deep breath, nostrils flaring at the sour smells, but there were no smells of ammonia, ether, or rotting eggs, as there would have been if someone had been cooking meth. Through the open doorway, I saw dirty dishes, empty pizza boxes, crushed beer cans, and empty liquor bottles. No tell-tale plastic tubing, stained coffee filters, plastic gloves, or lithium batteries.

It didn't make Helix the father of the year, but at least it lowered the kid's risk. A gruff voice turned me back toward the living room. "You lookin' to buy the place, or what?"

The man from the website sat on the couch, legs spread, arms draped across the sofa back, making a point of filling the space. He was a big man, broad in the shoulders but soft in the middle. Mulatto skin, short-cropped hair, gray linen suit with a pale blue shirt and a striped tie. Lots of gold. Rings, chains, a gold hoop through one eyebrow. The tie was loose and the shirt untucked. He looked like a banker, except for the woman who perched beside him, one hand stuffed into the waistband of his pants, tugging without passion. Alpha male posturing. He might as well have pounded his chest and banged two garbage can lids together.

"You looking to sell it?"

He hunched a shoulder. "Right price, maybe. You got the right price, everything be for sale."

"Helix, I presume."

"You look surprised. You thought maybe I be wearin' a snake-skin suit and a hat with ostrich feathers? Hell, I got a business degree."

"I read that on your website. Color me impressed."

"You should be. Bet I make more money in a day than you make in a month."

"Yeah, but look what you have to do to get it."

His eyes slitted. Then he grinned, flashing gold incisors. He made a *hand it over* motion. "Time's money, Cowboy. You want to talk, pay up first."

I pulled out my wallet again and, keeping it tilted toward myself so he couldn't see the contents, peeled out ten twenties. He folded the bills into his palm, then plucked the wallet from my hand.

The baby wailed, and Helix gave the woman with orange hair a stern look. "Yo, Simone, shut that kid up."

With a sour glance at the girl on the couch, Simone stalked out of the room.

I introduced myself as a private investigator, and interest sparked his eyes. I didn't introduce Khanh. He hadn't introduced his women, would probably see it as a sign of weakness. Instead,

I said, "A woman was killed last night. She had your symbol burned into her."

"Simone say you the one who found her. Thing like that, I guess it mighta damaged your fragile little psyche."

"My psyche's pretty tough. How's yours?"

"Titanium." He cupped a massive hand behind the girl's head, lifted his hips in rhythm with her hand. "What I care about some dead ho? She ain't one of mine."

"Then how do you know she was a ho?"

"They all hos. What's your jones for this one?"

"I'm looking for a girl. A Vietnamese girl. Whoever marked the dead girl has the one I'm looking for. Or can get me one step closer to whoever does."

He flashed a predatory grin. "Hell, you want some Asian pussy, I get you some."

"Not just any girl. A particular girl."

"What I'm tellin' you is, they all the same. You had one, you had 'em all. What's so special about this one?"

"She's family. So she's not interchangeable." I pulled a business card out of my wallet and a pen from my pocket and scratched out the Chinese character Khanh had called the eye of the dragon. "You ever see a mark like this?"

I handed it to Helix, who looked at it briefly and shook his head. "Never seen it."

"Somebody's marking women with it. Same place you mark yours."

His lips tightened. "What's that they say? Imitation is the best kind of . . ."

"Sincerest form of flattery."

"Screw that." He closed his eyes. Gave a little grunt of pleasure. The girl slipped her hand out of his pants and wiped her palm on her jeans. He tugged his shirt down over his crotch. Somewhere in the back, the baby fussed, and Simone's voice, soft and cooing, shushed it.

I said to Helix. "If you're not involved in this, somebody's going to a lot of trouble to make it look like you are."

He gave a brittle laugh. "I gone kill some bitch, I'm not gone put my mark on her. How long I be breathin' free air, a bunch of dead hos start showin' up wearin' my signature?"

Simone came out of the back room jostling a mocha-skinned baby in a dingy pink romper. A pink bow stood out against a head of black curls. So much promise. No future. I saw her fifteen years from now, maybe less, a spiral-shaped scar above her collarbone. Just one more kid who couldn't be saved.

Helix fumbled with his zipper, fastened his belt. "Somebody tryin' to set me up for sure, but don't tell me you come here to do me no favors."

"Not directly, no. But our interests might intersect."

"I save you some trouble. I never seen your girl, and I never seen your mark, and I don't know who be doin' all this. Hell, how I know you not the one behind it?"

"If I were, why would I be here?"

He got up and shambled over to the TV, pushed aside a rack of DVDs, and took a thick stack of banded bills from the wall safe behind it. He tossed it to me, and I caught it one-handed and flipped through it. All hundreds.

"That's ten thousand dollars," he said. "I bet you never seen ten thousand cash dollars all in one place."

"Not true. I was Monopoly champion in third grade."

He gave me a sideways glance. "Naw, you not the Monopoly type. You the dodgeball type."

"Dodgeball was okay. My favorite was Manhunt."

"Yeah, I can see that. Not much money in Manhunt."

"Depends on who you're hunting."

He nodded toward the wad of bills. "My point."

"I'm not that stupid. All I want to know is, who might be trying to set you up? You got any partners? Asian-looking guy? White guy with a manticore tattoo?" I showed him the drawing of the manticore.

"Ain't got no partners. Don't believe in 'em." He looked at Simone, then at the girl on the couch. Jerked a thumb toward the hall. "Y'all get on up out of here now."

As the women trooped out, Helix gave Khanh a pointed stare. She looked straight ahead, not acknowledging his non-verbal message, and when it became clear that she never would, he shrugged and turned his gaze back to me. When he spoke again, most of the gangsta schtick was gone. "I have a good lawyer, Mr. P.I. Had me out of jail before lunchtime. We beat this one, he says. But what about the next one? Some asshole kills a girl and puts my mark on her, he's got a beef with me. You think he's going to stop?"

"Maybe. If it did what he wanted it to."

"I ain't behind bars, which means the cops still be looking for him. So how could it do what he wanted it to? You in tight with the cops, Mr. P.I.?"

"Pretty tight, some of them."

"Our interests intersect, you said." He nodded toward the wad of cash in my hand. "You want to prove it, go to work for me. Five thousand now, five thousand when you bring me the guy who setting me up. Hell, you don't even have to bring him to me. Just give me his name and address."

I tossed the money at him. He wasn't ready and had to scramble for it, tipped it with a finger, then got his palm under it and clamped his fist around it. He took two steps toward me, thunder in his eyes. "Something wrong with my money?"

"I don't want to work for you."

"I get it. You some kinda white knight. Think you better than me." I didn't answer, but he didn't seem to notice. He loosened his tie, shrugged out of his jacket, and tossed it over the back of the couch. "Couple ways this can go, bro. One, I kick your ass, shove this money down your throat, and turn out your ugly-ass woman. Not many guys into that shit, but I know a few that are. Two, you kick my ass. Not likely, but you could get lucky. Three, you take the money and bring me the name of the guy who set me up. Everybody be happy."

I shifted my weight forward and rolled my shoulders to get the kinks out. The arm in the cast throbbed. "I wouldn't be happy."

Helix bounced on the balls of his feet, clenching and un-clenching his fists. "You find your girl, you gone find this ass-hole anyway, right? Then you gone get him arrested, and his name and address be public record."

"You've got it all figured out. So why do you care if I take your ten thousand dollars?"

"Hell, I lose more than that between the sofa cushions. Ain't nothing."

Khanh touched my sleeve. "Ten thousand dollar, buy plenty medicine."

I clamped my teeth until my jaws ached. It wasn't my job to buy her mother medicine.

From the back of the house, the baby mewled. Helix and I studied each other from two feet apart. He spread his hands, his grin an arc of white and gold. "Say I been to your office last week and axed you to find out if my lady was cheatin' on me. What would you have done?"

"I'd have taken your money. And then, when I checked you out, I'd have given it back."

He shrugged. "Then you seriously stupid, man. Look, you can't be a good person and do what I do. I know that. I'm okay with it. But I'm a nice guy, Mr. P.I. People like me. Hell, you spend a hour with me, you gone like me too. But you, you sure you're so much better? You gone let your pride keep your lady here from getting her medicine?"

I handed him my card. "You think of anybody who might be setting you up, give me a call. Might be another wallet in it for you."

"A man can always use a new wallet." Smirking, he sum-moned Simone, who led us out, baby slung on one hip.

"That girl on the couch," I said, as she walked us down the sidewalk. "How old is she?"

Simone's smile was wry. "Twenty-one."

"Sure she is." I pulled another card from my pocket. "In case you think of anything that might help. Might be a reward in it. You could get out of all this."

She gave a bitter laugh, but reached for the card. "Why would I want out of all this?"

She shifted the baby to the other hip and leaned against the fence again. Took a long drag from her cigarette. I watched her in the rearview mirror as we pulled away. She was blowing smoke rings at the baby's face.

Khanh shook her head. "Ten thousand dollar."

"It's a lot of money."

"You rich American. Easy say no."

"Not so easy. But you work for a guy like Helix, pretty soon you only work for guys like Helix." I put it from my mind and glanced at Khanh. "I'm sorry about what he said. When he was talking about turning you out."

"You think I care some *hậu môn* say ugly? He nothing man. I not care what he say."

I didn't believe her. Small hurts could grind you down the same as big ones. They just took longer.

21

Art & Souls tattoo parlor was a well-kept secret, tucked at the edge of an East Nashville residential neighborhood. A neon sign above the door flashed the name, along with a wisp of blue light winding through the outline of a heart. In the front window, photos in thin black frames showcased the artists' work—detailed renderings of wildlife, landscapes, and mythological creatures blended into custom artwork. Beneath each photo was a strip of white paper with a typed description of the traits symbolized by the tattoo. I found Salazar's on the second row, the coiled snake looking curiously more alive than when I'd seen it in person. The tag beneath said: *Unpredictable. Dangerous when threatened.*

Beside it was a picture of a woman's shoulder and upper arm. A spray of butterflies rose from just above the elbow to the top of the shoulder, then spilled across the shoulder to the neck, back, and collarbone. The tag said: *Vibrant and ephemeral.*

Inside, it reeked of antiseptic. More photos lined the walls, interspersed with cases filled with piercings. In one corner stood a workstation with a computer and a stack of papers. In another was a thick leather photo book on a podium. A vinyl-covered reclining chair dominated the center of the room, and beside it, on a rolling cart, was a collection of inks, tips, and disposable needles. A pudgy, balding man in a Comic Con T-shirt stood wiping the chair down with a paper towel and some pungent disinfectant in a spray bottle. As we came in, he glanced up, blue eyes looking bulbous behind thick lenses.

"Perfect timing," he said, smiling. He stared intently, first at me, then at Khanh, as if he were memorizing us. "Which of you is here for the ink?"

"Neither, actually."

"Too bad." He glanced at Khanh again and opened a drawer on the cart. Pulled out an orange pencil and a sketch pad. "I know just what I'd do for you."

A few sweeping gestures, and he exchanged the orange pencil for a blue one. Working swiftly, he laid in outlines, then the broader strokes. Finally, he turned the pad so we could see a partial portrait of Khanh's right side, beginning at the tip of her stump and ending just below her hairline. He'd drawn in the tattoo, a swirl of flames emerging from the stump and sweeping up toward the elbow, where a beautiful Asian woman with outstretched wings rose out of the flames. Her wings were ablaze, and fire raged around her, the rising flames entwining with a spray of morning glories. The final flower rested at Khanh's temple, just above the place where her scars ended.

Rough as it was, it was stunning.

Khanh stared at the page, mouth open, as if she couldn't decide whether to be pleased or offended.

I frowned. "That's not—"

Ignoring me, he said to Khanh, "You been through the fire, and it made you strong. Or maybe you started strong, and that's what got you through it. Either way, it tempered you."

"Very observant." The brittleness in my voice surprised me. "You'll have to do better than that if you want us to believe this is some kind of psychic bullshit."

He tore out the drawing and handed it to Khanh. "I never said it was psychic. It's all there, the way she moves, the way she holds her mouth."

I reached for the drawing, but Khanh turned away, moving it out of my reach.

"Beautiful," she said. "Not like me."

"It's you, all right," he said. "What I do, I help people see it."

She held it out toward him, and he said, "Keep it. You decide you want to get it done, you know where to find me. One of a kind. I never do the same design twice." He put the pad and pencils away and said, "If you didn't come in for a tattoo, what are you here for?"

I showed him my license. "I'm looking for a guy who got a tattoo here. A manticore. He had a woman with him, and she got some ink too. A bird with a broken wing."

"I remember," he said. "It was about a year ago, but I still remember. Tell me he didn't kill her."

"Why would you think he might?"

He pulled off his glasses, rubbed at the lenses with his shirt-tail. The glasses had left deep gouges in the sides of his nose, but without the thick lenses, his eyes looked normal. "There was a coldness in him. You could see it in his eyes, the way he looked at her, the way he kind of put himself in her space. She didn't want a tattoo, I could tell, but I was afraid of what he'd do to her if I didn't go along. You know—if I let him know she'd given it away that she wasn't completely on board."

"You thought he was abusing her. Did you report it to anybody?"

"It was just a feeling I had. She didn't have any bruises or anything." He shoved the glasses back onto his face and sank onto the tattoo chair. "He did something to her, didn't he?"

"I don't know. We think he killed another woman, maybe two. And we're looking for a third. Someone he or a partner might be holding captive."

"Oh, jeez. She was a nice lady, too. But low self-esteem. You could tell she'd been through a lot."

"It would really help if we knew where to find him."

"I have a contact list. You know, for specials and stuff." He pushed out of the chair. "I can pull it up on the computer, but he's not on it."

Beside me, Khanh let out a disappointed sigh.

I said, "Of course he's not. That would be too easy."

He held up a hand. "He's not on it, but she is. She came back a few days later, looking scared out of her mind. Asked to be put on our mailing list. I asked if she was sure, and she said she was, that looking at the photos made her happy. She asked me to address it to Occupant, but I remember which one it was. If he finds out where you got it, though . . ."

"He won't find out from us."

"This girl you're looking for . . ."

I pulled Tuyet's picture up on my phone and held it up. A sharp breath whistled through his teeth. He glanced at Khanh, then back at the photo, then back at Khanh. "Similar bone structures. Your kin?"

Khanh nodded. "My daughter."

With a wordless nod, he went to his computer, pulled up a database, then plucked a Post-It from a handy pad and scrawled an address. "By the way, the guy's name is Karlo," he said.

"A year ago, and you still remember his name?"

"He was kind of a joke around here for a while. Like, don't steal my fries, man, or I'll sic Karlo on you."

"He made an impression."

"Mister, he would have made an impression on granite. You know what I drew for him?"

"A manticore."

"I showed him the picture, kind of worried because, you know, what if he didn't like it? But he did. Ran his finger over it a few times and got this nasty grin on his face. Said, 'You got it right. This is the soul of a *man*.' That sticks with you, you know? 'Cause the whole point of a manticore is, it isn't a man."

"Part man," Khanh said.

"Only the thinking part. The rest is all beast."

"That tells us something about him," I said.

"You got that right," he said. "Only thing is, it's nothing good."

22

According to my reverse phone directory, the woman's name was Leda Savitch. A quick background check revealed no visible means of support. She lived near midtown, a few blocks from Hillsboro Village, in a two-bedroom brick house with a peaked roof and cobalt shutters. A whitewashed railing ran along the front porch, and a set of tubular wind chimes hung near the door. A wooden porch swing swayed in the breeze. Rose bushes lined the front walk.

As I pulled the truck up to the curb, an itch started on my left elbow. I tapped the cast just over the itch, which moved a few inches to the right. I slid a finger into the cast with no appreciable effect, finally popped open the glove compartment and fished for a pen. Too short. I got out of the truck and rummaged behind the seat until I found my weather radio, then snapped off the antenna, slipped it into the space between the cast and my skin, and scratched vigorously. Ah.

The corners of Khanh's mouth quirked. "You feel better?"

"A little."

"Good. We go talk Leda Savitch now?"

I tucked the antenna into my pocket for future emergencies and said, "You sure you want to hear this? What if she thinks this guy Karlo walks on water?"

"I be very strong. Want hear what she say."

We walked up the cobbled sidewalk to Leda's front door and rang the bell.

A heavyset woman in her early forties answered the door, wiping flour from her hands onto a white lace apron. Her blunt features and solid build were reminiscent of Eric's sketch of Karlo. Peasant stock. She might have been pretty once, but never beautiful. With her dyed blonde hair and her yellow sundress, she looked like a Marshmallow Peep.

The sleeveless dress showed the tattoo on her upper arm, the bird's expression an unsettling combination of adoration and resignation.

Through the screen door, Leda Savitch said, "You are selling something? Magazines? Chocolate bars? I have no need of either." Her eyes were wary, her accent heavy, Russian maybe, or one of the Balkan countries.

I held up my license. "We need to talk about Karlo."

"Karlo?" The suspicion in her eyes turned to fear. "My brother is a good man."

"I think we all know better than that." I held up my phone with Tuyet's picture on it. "This girl is missing. At least two others are dead. Don't you think it's time somebody stopped him?"

Her gaze shifted away from the photo. I moved the phone back into her line of vision. Her mouth trembled. She pressed a hand to her lips and closed her eyes. After a moment, she sighed, blinked, and fumbled with the latch. "I suppose you should come in. My apologies for the mess. I was making Kremšnita."

"Never heard of it."

"Custard cream cake in puff pastry, powdered sugar on top. Karlo is careful with his weight, but he loves my Kremšnita."

Despite her apology, there wasn't much of a mess. The house was clean, bright, comfortable. It smelled of sugar and warm vanilla pudding.

I said, "You and Karlo are close?"

"We came to America together during the troubles. He has always taken care of me."

"You aren't married?"

"I was engaged once, back home. He died in the troubles." She gestured toward the living room. "Please. Come sit down. I'll make coffee. Then we can talk."

While Leda puttered in the kitchen, Khanh and I settled ourselves on the living room sofa. The walls were pale yellow, splashed with fractured light from a row of prisms hanging in the window. A curio cabinet displayed a collection of blown glass sculptures, handcrafted wooden carousels, and several sets of Russian nesting dolls.

From the doorway, Leda said, "We left so much ugliness behind, I want only pretty things. Beautiful things, but fragile. Like life. Karlo thinks it's silly."

"Karlo is a practical guy?"

She carried a silver tray with three steaming cups and a china coffee service to the table, then dropped two sugar cubes into one and stirred in enough cream to turn the coffee the color of caramel. Sinking into the chair across from us, she set her cup on the table beside her and said, "Dead girls. A missing girl. This is a matter for the police, no? You are not police. So why are you here?"

I nodded toward Khanh, whose fist was clenched against her thigh. "Please," she said. "He take my daughter. You tell me where he take her."

"Why would Karlo take a woman?"

I said, "We think he sells them. He and some other men. From what you know about him, is that possible?"

Leda closed her eyes, steadied her cup and saucer on her knee. "These other men. Who are they?"

"An Amerasian. Maybe a black guy, calls himself Helix."

Relief flooded her features, and her eyes opened. "Karlo would not work with a black man. This I know."

"But an Asian, he might?"

"Perhaps. He would not like it, but he might. But . . . selling women?"

"That doesn't sound like something he would do?"

She raised her hands, palms up. After a long moment, she said, "He has much anger in him."

"Toward women."

"Toward everybody. But yes, toward women. I will tell you a story."

Khanh opened her mouth, and I held up a hand. *Wait.*

"We were very young. Karlo had a wife then, Sonia, and a baby girl. He loved them very much. It was a happy time. You would not have known him."

She was right. I tried without success to reconcile the man she'd described with the one who had snapped a girl's neck and shoved her into a dumpster. She went on. "I was engaged to marry a boy named Pyotr. We loved each other since we were children. One day, there was bombing in our village. Karlo was in the field, plowing, and when the bombing stopped, we all ran to see who was hurt, who needed help. Karlo's house was destroyed, and in the rubble we found the bodies of his wife and baby girl. His wife . . ." She lowered her gaze. Her hand tightened around the cup. "She was naked. And Pyotr . . . he was with her. They had been . . . together. Karlo changed after that. He joined the military the next day, fighting the Serbian oppressors."

"That war's been over for a long time."

"There is always war somewhere."

"And with war come the spoils of war."

Her cheeks pinked. "You think he rapes women, but no. I think he has never touched a woman after that. Not that way."

I must have looked skeptical, because she took a deep breath and leaned forward, punctuating her words with staccato jabs of her finger. "He thinks sex is filthy. Disgusting. And women who do it are the same. He is proud of his control, that he does not lower himself to this."

It fit what we'd learned from Amber. He hadn't tried to sleep with her. He'd jerked off while she danced and called her nasty names. Angry at her for being a whore. Angry at himself, maybe, for wanting what she offered.

I said, "Is that why you never married?"

"When we first came to America, I met a man. We went out a few times. Dinner, a movie. One day that man disappeared. No body, nothing like that, but nobody ever saw him again."

"You think Karlo did that?"

"I love my brother. But I think it is safer for everyone if I stay away from men."

I said, "Some of the people we spoke with . . . they thought Karlo might be hurting you."

"My brother loves me. He uses his fist sometimes, but that is the way of things, no?" Her fingertips brushed absently at her jawline. There might have been a shadow there, a healing bruise beneath her makeup, but I wasn't sure if it was really there or if I was only seeing what I expected to see.

"No," I said. "That is not the way of things."

"I will tell you another story," she said. "It happened last spring, Karlo finds a bird under my maple tree. It's a young bird, fallen from the nest. I see in my brother's face he intends to rescue it. It is still dazed, its little mouth gaping. Karlo cups it in his hands to lift it back into the tree. It begins to struggle. It's frightened, poor thing, and it pecks him, pecks his finger. And just like that, he snaps its neck." She looked down at her lap. "I am an intelligent woman. I do not peck."

"You're pecking now," I said. "Just by talking to us."

Khanh stood up, walked to the window and looked out through the prisms to the yard outside. The rosebuds were splashes of color against the green leaves. She said, "You man disappear. Why you not tell police?"

Eyes averted, Leda set her cup and saucer carefully on the tray. "What would I tell them? There was no evidence of foul play. He was just . . . gone. My brother is very good at being a soldier."

I said, "He's not being a soldier now. He's just hurting women."

She stared down at her hands, clasped so tightly that the knuckles were white. Then, "Maybe this is possible. If he sees these women as whores. He would not think of them as people who matter. And . . . I think he does not think rape is wrong if it happens to an enemy."

"And women are the enemy."

"Not all women." She looked away, but not in time to hide the sudden moisture in her eyes. "A girl who was pure . . . if it happened through no fault of her own . . ."

I thought of how the Serbian soldiers had systematically raped Bosnian and Croatian women in order to break them and demoralize their men. Thought of something she'd said earlier—*Beautiful things but fragile. Like life.* She gave a strained laugh, made a dismissive gesture. "Anyway, as you said, that was all a long time ago. This woman you think he took . . . is she good girl?"

Khanh's head snapped around. "She have good heart."

"But maybe a little bit wild, yes? I do not like to think my brother would do these things, but I think . . . if she is a little bit wild . . . it is possible."

I said, "Who are his friends? Who does he hang out with?"

"His friends are all dead. He has no friends."

"How about business associates?"

"He never talks business with me."

I blew out a frustrated breath. "Does the name Mat Troi mean anything to you?"

"No. Why? Is he one of these traffickers of women?"

"We think so." I leaned forward, elbows on knees, and said, "Is there anything else you can tell us? Anything at all?"

"No. Not about these men, the selling of women. But if this is true, you should know this about Karlo . . . he can turn his heart off, like a machine. You know he was a mercenary. What you do not know . . . his specialty was breaking prisoners."

A small sound came from the back of Khanh's throat.

"Tuyet is strong," I said to Khanh, though I had no idea if this was true. "She'll find a way to hang on until we find her."

Khanh moaned. "She not know I come for her. She think she all alone."

"Does she know about your arm?" I said, "About the mine-field?"

Khanh nodded.

I put my arm around her, felt her shoulders tremble. "Then she knows you're coming."

Tuyet

*T*he punishment pit was dank, half a foot of brackish water lapping at the feet and haunches of the three women who squatted there. Each had claimed a separate wall of the pit for her own, Tuyet on the south, Hong across from her on the north, Beetle between them on the west. A flash of pink caught Tuyet's eye—the rippling flesh of an earthworm lacing itself into the earth beside her face. She stretched toward it, dug her fingers into the dirt and came away with a handful of black earth. She rifled through it with a forefinger until the worm lay naked and wriggling in her palm.

"Hey," she called to Hong, who huddled silently against the opposite wall. "Hey!"

Beetle watched from across the pit with flat, reptilian eyes. A predatory stare. Tuyet tore her gaze away from Beetle and said again, "Hey!"

Hong didn't answer. She hadn't answered for the past two days, sinking deeper and deeper into herself. She no longer went to the farthest corner of the pit to relieve herself, choosing instead to soil herself where she lay. Perhaps she had a point—the rainwater around their feet was rank with their waste anyway—but Tuyet, perhaps still clinging to some shred of humanity, perhaps in the grip of an irrational stubbornness, refused to foul herself.

She sloshed over to Hong, keeping to the center of the pit. Away from Beetle. Away from the shallow cleft on the opposite wall, where a mound of jumbled skulls and bones rose from

~ 154 ~

the dark water, shadows curled around them like burial rags. It seemed darker there, as if the sun itself feared to disturb the dead.

A breeze caressed her cheek. Like the fingers of dead women, she thought, and shivered.

She stretched out a hand and brushed the hair from Hong's face. The older girl moaned and covered her eyes with her hands. A pang of guilt shot through Tuyet's chest. Hong should not be here. The kindest of them all, she had been taken because Tuyet's confession had not come quickly enough. That knowledge was a weight in Tuyet's stomach.

"Look," Tuyet said, opening her fist. "You have half."

Hong made no move toward the worm. Across the pit, Beetle came to her feet.

Tuyet plucked the worm from her palm and bit it in half, felt grit and slime and the slight resistance of the worm's flesh between her teeth. There wasn't much taste, nothing but earth and rain and a sudden rush of energy she knew was all in her mind. For days, she had lived on worms and grubs and the occasional scrap that sailed into the pit from above.

Those scraps gave her hope. She told herself they meant the men intended to keep her alive, and if they meant to keep her alive, they would feed her soon. Starvation aged a woman, made her old before her time. A used-up, shriveled husk would bring a poor price. The men would want her to be beautiful again, and so there would be a limit to her punishment.

An image of her grandmother haggling over the price of octopus came to her, and tears sprang to her eyes. She shook her head to banish the memory, but it was as if that moment in Mat Troi's bed, that moment when she had summoned up her loved ones, had broken the walls she had built in her mind. Other memories flooded in, so strong they drove her to her knees.

Her mother's hand on her forehead, her grandmother's cracked voice singing a ridiculous folk song. Good memories followed by a rush of shameful ones, a harsh word to her mother, an argument about her life in the bars, the time she'd stolen her grandmother's earrings, the time she'd tossed her hair and called her mother ugly and her grandmother a traitor. She was an ungrateful daughter. Probably, their life was better without her. Probably, they were glad she was gone.

A wave of heat surged up her cheeks, and suddenly she leaned forward and shook Hong's shoulder roughly, forced the worm between the other girl's teeth. "You eat, you hear, stupid girl? We stay strong or we die."

No response. Then, slowly, Hong's jaw began to move.

From above came the rattle of boots on gravel. Then a shadow passed in front of the sun and fell across the pit, and an obscene joy coursed through her. His name burst from her lips, and she wasn't sure if it was a plea or a curse: "Mat!"

"Guess again." The thick European accent made her stomach sink. The tattooed man tossed a rope ladder over the edge of the pit and laughed. "Come up."

She shook her head. It was too far. She had no strength. And he would only hurt her if she came to him.

Beside her, Hong moaned. "No."

"No?" He pulled out a pistol, something ugly and military-looking. "Come up or die. It makes no difference to me."

Tuyet squinted up at him and saw the truth in his face. He would leave them there forever, and their bones would join those at the edge of the pit. She shook Hong again. "Come on."

Hong wrapped her arms around her knees and curled into a ball. "No," she whimpered. "No, no no no no no no."

"Still no?" The laugh from above was harsh. "Okay."

The pistol bucked in his hand. There was a crack, and Hong slumped forward, a thin stream of blood trickling from her forehead and staining the water at Tuyet's feet.

The pistol muzzle swung toward Tuyet. "Now you," he said.

She swallowed a sob and pushed herself to her feet. "No, I come! I come."

She slogged through the water and mud and stretched one hand toward the ladder.

"Wait." He tugged the ladder upward, just out of reach. "I have a better idea."

His leer sent a shiver of fear through her stomach.

From his waistband, he drew a long-bladed knife with a serrated edge. He pointed it at Beetle. "You. You want to live?"

Beetle's lips twitched upward. She nodded.

"One girl live, one girl die. You decide." The knife splashed into the water between them. Beetle plunged after it.

For a moment, Tuyet stood frozen, muscles trembling with exhaustion. Then, too late, she leapt for the knife.

23

We left Leda's with a Tupperware dish full of Kremšnita and her promise not to tell Karlo about our visit. I thought she'd keep her promise, if only because learning about us would make him unhappy, and an unhappy Karlo was something she would want to avoid. If I'd had to make book on it, I'd have said 98 percent. Not bad odds, but it was the 2 percent that would kill you.

I texted what we'd learned about Leda Savitch and her brother to Frank and Malone, then waited for Khanh to ask what came next.

She didn't disappoint. "What now?"

"Now we let this simmer. I've got my son tonight. His mom has probably already dropped him off at the house."

She opened her mouth as if to protest, then closed it again.

"I'll work on it from home," I said. "While Paul's asleep."

"You do favor, who am I say what you do, not do?" Her tone said she had a definite opinion about what I should and shouldn't be doing, but I didn't rise to the bait. In her place, I would have felt the same way. We rode home in silence, and by the time I had the truck in *Park,* Paul had launched himself from the front porch and was halfway down the sidewalk.

I scooped him up with my good arm and introduced him to Aunt Khanh. He buried his head in my shoulder and gave her a shy wave, then coughed into my shirt collar, his breath smelling of eucalyptus.

Jay stood on the front porch, the remote control in his hand. "Maria says Paul has a cold. She sent Benadryl, Vick's, a bunch of other stuff. And his Scout project."

Paul's final Wolf Cub task was a collection of Tennessee leaves and wildflowers. Maria had sent a glass-covered display case, and inside it were index cards, two fine-point markers, a can of liquid acrylic, and three times more press-on labels than we could use in a century. My job was to help Paul find the plants and assemble the display, but since it was almost sunset, it seemed wiser to make the labels tonight and collect the samples in the morning.

Paul helped me lay the case out on the living room table, where Jay and Eric came in and praised it effusively before heading out to Eric's latest art show.

"Make something fabulous," Jay said, giving Paulie a quick peck on the forehead, "and we'll see you in the morning."

Paul grinned and gave him a high five. Then, while Khanh sulked in front of the TV, I wrote the name of each plant on an index card and handed it to Paul, who painstakingly copied them onto labels.

We'd gotten five made when my cell phone buzzed. I checked the ID, saw it was Frank, and picked up.

"That drawing you gave us," he said, "Karlo Savitch. We got him."

"That was fast."

"It's a good drawing, and that's a distinctive tat, and it helps we had a name to go with it. Guy has a record. Assault with a deadly weapon, but it didn't stick. Witness got cold feet. I'd have liked a little more leverage before we brought him in, but with your girl missing, we figured we'd better give it a shot. Anyway, I wondered if you might want to come down here and watch the interrogation."

"Seriously?"

"Call it a consultation. There's something off about his affect. He isn't acting like a guy whose DNA might be under a dead girl's fingernails."

"And you want to brainstorm about why?" It was how we'd often worked, one of us handling the interrogation, the other taking note of anomalous responses and making suggestions for the next round of attack.

"I do. But leave your shadow at home."

"Hold on a minute." I looked down at Paul, whose head was bent, tongue stuck out in concentration. I sighed. "I'll be right there."

Khanh looked up. "Be right where?"

"They picked up Karlo Savitch. Frank wants me to watch the interrogation. Can you take care of Paul until I get back?"

Her chin came up. "I go you."

"Either you watch Paulie, or we both stay here."

She lowered her head, but not before I saw the flash of anger—or maybe desperation—in her eyes. "Okay," she said, finally. "I stay Paul. You find out where Tuyet."

"I just watch. I don't get to ask questions. Don't worry. We're getting close." I knelt beside Paul, whose face was puckered with disappointment.

"Police stuff?" he asked.

"I'm sorry, buddy. I'll be back as soon as I can. Your Aunt Khanh will help you."

He turned his face away, laid his head on the table, and coughed. "Don't want Aunt Khanh."

"I know, Sport. I'll be back as soon as I can." I ruffled his hair, kissed the top of his head, and left them to their mutual disappointment.

KARLO SAVITCH was built like a tent peg—big head and broad shoulders tapering down to a narrow waist and long, thin legs. While I watched through the two-way mirror, he shook a tangle of mud-brown hair out of his eyes and smoothed his mustache with a thick finger. That done, he folded his hands on the table in front of him. His sleeves were rolled up, the skin of his forearms unmarked. It had been more than a week since the Asian girl's murder, but I would have been happier to see the tracks of her nails in his skin.

Savitch lowered his head. Picked at a nail. Wiry black hairs crept down the back of his neck and into the collar of his wrinkled button-down shirt.

Frank went in and sat across from him. Savitch unfolded his hands and leaned back in his chair, teeth bared in a mocking grin. A man barely pretending to be civilized. Even taking into account that he had gamed the system before and won, he was too cocky for a guy who'd left DNA at a murder scene.

Frank said, "We can end this right here, Karlo. We have skin and blood under the dead girl's fingernails. So all you have to do is let us do a little DNA swab, and we can rule you out. No reason not to, right? Unless, of course, you're guilty."

Savitch shrugged. In a thick, Eastern European accent, he said, "Go ahead. Take your DNA. You will find nothing. I did not kill this girl."

"You were recognized, identified by a witness."

Savitch leered. "Little blonde stripper I see on TV? No one believe that little whore. Especially when she say she did not get good look at face. Especially since no proof man she saw is even killer."

Especially since she's dead, I thought. And wasn't that convenient?

Frank said, "We know you were there, Karlo, and we know the girl was killed around the same time." He looked down at the file in his hand. "Says here 'aggravated assault.' 'Assault with a deadly weapon.' 'Assault and battery.' Looks like you have a temper, Karlo."

"I am a passionate man. So what does that matter? I was never convicted of these things."

"Because the victims were afraid of you. This here is what we call a pattern, a pattern of losing control. So maybe this woman did something that ticked you off, made you lose control. We've all been there with our women, right?"

Frank's voice was solid, but one eyelid twitched, and I knew he was thinking of Patrice and the forty years of marriage in which he'd never raised—or wanted to raise—a hand to her.

Karlo said, "I never lose control."

"The guy who killed her put his forearm around her throat, like this." Frank pantomimed the action with an invisible victim. "Picked her up off the ground so she couldn't breathe and squeezed so hard the bone in her neck broke. You were in control when you did that?"

"I did not kill this woman."

"If you didn't kill her, maybe you saw something that could help us find the guy who did."

"I mind my own business. Why should I care who kill this girl?"

"You don't think a woman's life is worth a few minutes of your time?"

Karlo shrugged again. "World is full of women. Always more where that one came from."

"You realize that's not exactly the viewpoint of a morally evolved human being. Or even just a human being."

"I see news report. This girl is nobody. Is not like somebody kill doctor making cure for cancer." Savitch leaned back, tipping up the front legs of the chair. "You take DNA now. You see. Then I want lawyer."

And just like that, it was over.

24

Back in the observation room, Frank said, "What do you think?"

"You were right. He's too calm."

"You think he's the guy?"

I looked at Savitch, who sprawled in the uncomfortable chair, humming something that might have been a Ukrainian folk song. Smug smile, butcher's hands, the tattoo Lupita had described cutting across his face.

World is full of women. Always more where that one came from.

"Yeah, I think he's the guy."

"I think so too. We got a search warrant based on the picture and his past history. It was iffy, but we got a sympathetic judge, and Malone pushed hard on the way the victim had been tortured and the possibility that he might have another girl stashed somewhere."

"Malone? You're kidding."

"She's a pain in the ass, but she takes kidnapping and torturing women as seriously as the rest of us."

"Point taken. Find anything?"

"Couple of beers in the fridge, a few skin magazines lying around. Mostly run-of-the-mill stuff, with one Bondage & Domination rag thrown into the mix. Nothing to link him to our victim or your missing girl. But he had a veritable arsenal. Guns and knives in every room, and I'm not talking your grandma's BB gun."

"Does he live in a house or an apartment?"

"Apartment."

"He isn't going to stash the girl there."

"So if he's the guy, he's got another place. But we couldn't find any record of one."

"The guy who took Tuyet is part Asian, so there are at least two of them. Maybe they use the other guy's place. And maybe the DNA belongs to him."

"If it does, you'd better come up with that witness. Because without that DNA, we've got nothing."

While I was trying to figure out how to convince Lupita to come back from Mexico and testify, the observation room door banged open and Malone burst in. When she saw me, she stopped short and jerked a thumb toward the center of my chest and said to Frank, "I don't remember saying you should sell tickets."

"I'm bouncing a few ideas off him, that's all. He has good insights. And he knows how to keep his mouth shut."

"He got fired for not keeping his mouth shut." That was both untrue and unfair, but now didn't seem to be the time to say so. She stalked over to the glass. Scowled at Savitch even though he couldn't see her. "But as long as he's here . . . how about it, McKean? Is this the guy who tried to kill you?"

"It's the guy, 99 percent."

"Ninety-nine percent won't hold up in court. You've got to be 100 percent."

"It was dark. He wore a mask. I could swear it on a stack of Bibles, and any prosecutor worth his salt would tear me to shreds."

She blew out a disgusted breath. "So basically, you're no help at all."

My face burned, and I felt my nostrils flare. "What do you want me to say? The build is right. The accent sounds right. But even if he hadn't been whispering, he didn't say enough to get a good handle on the voice."

"I wish to hell you hadn't lost that witness."

Frank said, "A scared illegal sees a guy for half a minute in the dark? She'd crumble like tissue on the stand."

Malone shot him a glare that could have melted glass. "So if this DNA thing comes up bad, we've got nothing, and he walks."

"So we sit on him awhile, until he leads us to the girl."

"Only we tipped our hand early. He'll be more careful now."

"It was a gamble," Frank said. "We knew that when we brought him in."

Malone slapped the wall in frustration. "Yeah, well, we lost."

The door to the observation room burst open, and a young cop in uniform blurted, "We got a call from Channel Three, they got a message from the *For Justice* guy and are filming live from the crime scene."

"Hold on," Malone said. "There's been another bombing?"

The officer looked sick. "Not this time."

↾

THE ADDRESS Channel Three had left was in another district, well out of Malone's jurisdiction, so we crowded around the TV in the break room while the blonde who'd shadowed Ashleigh at my office stood in front of a modest suburban ranch house and described the unfolding events in a breathless, solemn tone. A ribbon of text scrolled across the bottom of the screen, identifying her as Portia Ross.

The screen split, and Ashleigh, perched behind the anchors' desk, said in a brittle voice, "So, Portia, what can you tell us about the series of events that led you to this gruesome discovery?"

She looked flawless, as always, but the stiffness in her shoulders said she was upset. Probably felt she should be the one on the scene, where all the action was.

Portia was saying, ". . . a call received by this reporter just twenty minutes ago. A man claiming responsibility for the *For Justice* bombings said there had been another killing."

She'd rushed to the address he gave her, expecting to find the smoldering husk of a dope factory. Instead, she found a well-kept home in a well-kept neighborhood, front door unlocked with an envelope taped to it. Inside, she found the victims shot at close range and laid out in the living room like railroad ties. This time, they weren't disenfranchised dope dealers. They were a Metro police officer and his family. Wife, three kids. The oldest was fourteen. The usual message had been scrawled across the officer's forehead: *For Justice.*

Malone said, "Just when I think I know how bad things can get, somebody goes and does something worse."

"He's changed his M.O.," Frank said. "Bombs for the meth heads, bullets for the cops?"

The name of the murdered officer—Kevin Bannister—scrolled across the bottom of the screen, and my stomach did a little flip. "Jesus."

Malone's eyebrows lifted. "You know him?"

"We met." I shook my head, trying to dispel the images that flashed across my mind. "Once on a case and once at a precinct picnic. We were both still uniforms. Played a couple rounds of Frisbee golf."

He'd won both rounds, a stocky guy who jumped like a pit bull, overcoming gravity by sheer determination.

I closed my eyes, tried to imagine how it could have happened. How *For Justice* had managed to overpower an entire family, including an athletic young cop.

Portia Ross went on. "Inside the envelope was a manifesto accusing Metro Nashville's police department and court system of corruption and vowing to bring the wrongdoers to justice. The document included a list of names . . ."

We stared at the screen as the list scrolled down it. Portia must have snapped a photo with her phone and sent it to the station before dialing 911.

It was a long list. Two or three more dope dealers. A couple of defense attorneys. A couple of prosecutors. And cops. Lots of cops.

"She's finished," Malone said. "Obstruction of justice at the very least. Tampering with evidence."

Frank scrubbed his palms across his face. "She'll say she had to check it out before she called. She'll say she opened the envelope because it was addressed to her, or she thought it might be a prank, or . . . Who knows what she'll say, except that she'll be full of shit."

"Shit," Malone repeated, sourly. "It's what's for dinner."

I reached over and tapped Frank's bicep with the back of my hand. Pointed to the screen.

Two names below the murdered cop's was Harry Kominsky's, and right beneath it: *Frank Campanella.*

25

Frank went pale. "I gotta get home."

Malone gave a sharp nod. "Your wife. Of course."

I tried not to picture Patrice and Frank lying on their living room floor, small round holes in their foreheads, arms crossed over their chests or maybe pressed along their sides.

I said, "You want me to go with you?"

He forced a smile and shook his head. "You just find that girl of yours. I need you, I'll call."

He left at a trot, and when he'd gone, Malone said, "Who the hell is this guy?"

"It's in the names," I said. "Find the connection, you'll find him."

She rolled her eyes. "Thank you, Obi-Wan."

"Sarcasm is the sign of a weak mind," I said. She held up her middle finger, but there was no real anger in it. I returned the gesture and left, already envisioning the chaos the manifesto would cause. The scope of the thing ensured that the police, already spread thin, would be spread even thinner as they tried to protect their own.

I stepped out of the precinct into a strong breeze. By the time I got home, the dark clouds had rolled in again, and rain was in the air. I pulled my antenna out of my pocket and gave my arm a satisfying scratch, then fed the horses and went inside, where Khanh sat in the recliner reading one of Jay's books: *The Shining, Shining Path*, about a young roadie who goes on tour with a busload of Buddhist monks.

She looked up and nodded toward the couch, where Paul was sprawled, still dressed in jeans and an Avengers T-shirt. His cheeks were streaked with tears, and a line of drool trickled from the corner of his mouth. My heart twisted. I shouldn't have gone. Nothing had come of it anyway, which meant I'd disappointed him for nothing.

Khanh said, "He want wait for you."

I nodded, scooped him up. His eyes fluttered open, then closed again, and I carried him up to bed. His breathing was labored, and I didn't like the sound of it. Not life-threatening, but still it worried me. He woke up long enough to take some Benadryl and let me slather his chest with Vick's, then sank back into a fitful sleep, arms and legs splayed like a starfish.

When I came back downstairs, Khanh said, "You good father. Many men not want imperfect child."

"There's nothing imperfect about Paulie." My voice was brittle.

"My country, some people think child like Paul bad luck."

"Some people are assholes. What do you think?"

"Think like you."

The heat on the back of my neck receded.

"Besides . . ." She held up her stump. "I bad luck child too. What you learn from police?"

"Savitch isn't cooperating, but if the DNA matches, Frank can squeeze him about Tuyet, offer him a deal if he tells us where she is."

"It match, right? Lu-pee-ta say he kill girl."

"It should match, but . . . I don't know. He's acting hinky."

"Hinky mean strange?"

I nodded.

Her eyes welled. "You say find Tuyet. But every day, not find."

"I know. I'm sorry."

"Every day, less chance we find. More chance you give up."

"If we're going to be related, there's something you need to know about me," I said. "I might get sidetracked sometimes, but I don't give up."

She let out a small breath, as if she'd been holding it, waiting for my answer. "I not give up either," she said. "You, me, same same."

⌒∕⌒

THE NEXT morning, Paul and I went to the woods to search for native leaves, seeds, and flowers. His breathing was a little better, but he tired quickly, and I carried him most of the way, pausing occasionally to pluck a sarsaparilla leaf or a promising wildflower. We shared a cheese pizza with Jay and Khanh. Then I left him with Jay while Khanh and I went out to find our Good Samaritan.

I boosted Khanh into the passenger seat, then went around to the other side. She held up the list, thumb pointing to the owner's name. "This woman. We look for man."

"We can't rule out the women. Our Good Samaritan might have been driving his wife's car."

"What mean Good Sama-ri-tan?"

"Good Samaritan. It's from the Bible. Rich guy goes out walking, gets robbed and beaten up by a bunch of bandits. So there he is, lying half-dead by the side of the road, and all these people pass him by and don't help him. People like his neighbors and the wise men of the church. They all pass by on the other side and act like they don't see."

"Know people like that. Most world, maybe."

"Then this Samaritan comes along. The Samaritans were people from another religious group, and they were considered the scum of the earth. But this Samaritan saw the man lying there and picked him up and took care of him."

"Man in car. You call him this, why?"

"He gave her a ride to my place. Lot of people wouldn't have picked her up, wouldn't have wanted to get involved."

"Why he not take to doctor?"

"Maybe she didn't want to go."

~ 170 ~

I held out my hand, and she put the list into it. Beatrice had been thorough, including names, addresses, phone numbers, and makes and models of vehicles. Jay and Eric had already marked out the pickup trucks, a couple of SUVs and a VW Bug. They'd checked out the first few pages without luck. That left us three. The bumper sticker we were looking for wasn't one-of-a-kind, but in conjunction with the partial plate and the general type of car, it narrowed the field. I used my phone to search online for the slogan Lupita had referenced. It said, *Be nice to nerds. Chances are, you'll end up working for one.*

As we worked our way through the list, we found a lot of bumper stickers—*4 out of 3 people have trouble with fractions*; *I childproofed my house, but they still get in*; *What if the Hokey Pokey really IS what it's all about?*—but not the one we were looking for.

At five o'clock, on the last page of the list, we found an architectural wonder owned by a guy named James Decker. He lived a few miles from downtown, between West End and swanky Belle Meade, in a stacked-stone mansion inspired by a French country manor. Peaked gables, copper gutters, board-and-batten shutters, antique-style lanterns.

The circular drive was empty, no sign of anyone outside. I drove up to the garage, where a quick peek through the window confirmed that no one—at least no one with a vehicle—was home, so I parked half a block away and waited for Decker to come back. While we waited, I pulled my Nikon out of the camera bag behind my seat, put on the zoom lens, and snapped in a new video card.

At five thirty, a woman in a powder blue Miata pulled into the driveway. A little after six, a man in a silver Mercedes pulled in. The rear of the car was toward me, and I aimed the camera. Pressed zoom. The rear bumper expanded in the lens, and the bumper sticker came into view.

Be nice to nerds. Chances are, you'll end up working for one.
Bingo.

I showed Khanh the close-up of the bumper sticker. "It's him."

"You go talk him?"

"Let me check with Frank first."

He was number four on my speed dial, just behind Maria, Jay, and my brother. I punched it in and asked after Patrice, asked how they were holding up. Doing fine, he said, but chafing at being under guard.

"I want to be at work," he said. "Or, barring that, at Myrtle Beach with my wife."

"That might not be a bad idea. Take yourself out of the equation."

"I don't know. Running . . . it's not really my style."

"What does Patrice think?"

After a long silence, he said, "She has some business here to attend to. I guess we're in it 'til the end."

He had enough on his plate. I hung up without asking him about Decker, called Malone instead. "That partial plate I gave you. You run it yet?"

"I'm a little busy, here, McKean. Why do you want to know?"

"'Cause I'm looking at the guy's driveway, and I don't want to tip him off if you haven't talked to him yet."

"That's considerate of you."

"Common courtesy. I don't want to walk all over your homicide case if I don't have to."

"And if we haven't talked to him?"

"Then I give you twenty-four hours before I go knock on his door."

"Generous."

"I thought so, considering Tuyet's life's at stake. His name's Decker. James Decker."

"As it happens, we have talked to him. Bumper sticker notwithstanding, he's not the one."

"Who talked to him?"

She blew out a frustrated breath. "I know where you're going with this, but you're wrong. He was on the road the night it happened, gave us the name and number of the coworker he was traveling with—a coworker who, you might want to know, vouched for him 100 percent. He even let the detectives take samples from his car. No blood, no hairs that might have matched the victim's. It was as clean as my grandmother's soap dish."

"Too clean?"

"Nothing that tripped anybody's radar. Your witness, either she didn't see what she thought she saw, or she remembered it wrong."

"She could have missed the color of the car. Maybe misread a number. Probably got the bumper sticker right, though."

"Odds are. But that's a dead end. There's no way to track how many people might have that same sticker or who they might be."

"Did you Luminol the car?"

"Jesus, McKean. We have a witness placing Decker someplace else. We have a passenger side floor mat with no trace of blood. And according to your own witness, even if he was the guy, the victim was alive when he left her. He didn't even see the suspect. Why would we Luminol the car?"

I laid my forehead against the steering wheel. "What about the flight manifests and the video footage at the airport?"

"If she was on that flight—or any flight that week—he brought her in under a fake ID. The video is worthless. We can see a girl who *might* be your girl, but the man she was with is a cipher. He's either the luckiest man on the planet, or he knew where the cameras would be."

"He's a pro, then."

"Stating the obvious is sort of a hobby of yours, isn't it?"

"Just keeping things clear."

"Besides, she looked willing enough. Kind of gooey-eyed and smiling."

"Yeah, that's how it is until they tie you up and sell you to the highest bidder."

"Is that all? Because we really have our hands full right now. There was another one this morning."

"Shit. Bomb or bullet?"

"Bullet."

"Oh no."

"Another cop on the list and two more in the blue-and-white out front. You didn't see it on the news?"

"I haven't turned the TV on today."

"Only the die-hard antiestablishment types are still calling this guy Mr. Clean."

"What's everybody else calling him now?"

"The Executioner."

He would have liked that. "Sexier than Mr. Clean," I said.

"Yeah, I bet he got a hard-on when he heard it."

I thanked her and signed off. Told Khanh what Malone had said and watched the hope drain out of her face. "Mr. Decker not man in car?"

"Sounds like no."

"Say have alibi. Mean what?"

"Somebody says he was somewhere else at the time."

"She say no blood. You say cut feet, plenty blood."

"I know, but . . . I'm still gonna talk to him."

⁊

JAMES DECKER answered the door with his tie loosened and the top button of his collar undone. He was in his mid-to-late thirties, with dark hair beginning to thin and a tan that looked like it had come out of a bottle. His handshake was firm, his build athletic. From the way he moved on the balls of his feet, I'd have guessed tennis, but a row of trophies on the wall behind him said his sport of choice was fencing.

In one hand, he held a light beer. It seemed an unnecessary sacrifice, in light of his physique, but maybe it wasn't a sacrifice. Maybe he liked a little beer with his water.

"We're following up on a statement you made to the police," I said.

"Ah. About the dead girl." He took a swallow of his faux beer, as if for reinforcement, and said, "I can't add anything to what I said. I wasn't there. I didn't pick anybody up, certainly not a bloody young woman in her underwear."

"Her underwear?"

"A slip, I think the police said."

"Would you mind if we looked at the car?"

He cocked his head, looking us over. "You're not police."

We'd left our rain gear in the truck, but I guess my jeans and Khanh's yoga pants didn't look official. "I never said we were."

"So what's your interest?"

I gave him the short version. Missing girl, connected to the dead girl in the dumpster.

A quick hunch of shoulders. With an affable smile, he said, "What the hell. It's a waste of your time, but I guess you won't feel good unless you check."

He was right, but I didn't feel any better afterward, either. I didn't spot anything the police hadn't seen. As far as I could tell, the car was clean.

I thanked him for his time, and he walked us to the edge of the driveway and watched while we pulled away. Wordlessly, Khanh picked up the list from the seat beside her, read off the next name.

We went quickly through the rest of the page. No one had a bumper sticker like the one Lupita had described. Maybe our man had removed it. Maybe he was from out of state and wasn't on the printout.

Maybe Lupita had just been wrong.

We rode home in disappointed silence. When we got there, Paul was asleep, and the project sat on the living room table, leaves and wildflowers sealed in acrylic, labels written in Paul's crooked scrawl and affixed beneath each plant. The cards Jay had written for him to copy were stacked neatly to one side. I imagined them working at the kitchen table, plastic cloth and aluminum pie tins to minimize the mess, Paul dropping globs of acrylic onto each plant, and Jay painstakingly removing the excess and leaving each leaf encased in a thin acrylic glaze.

A sliver of light came from under Jay's door. Tweaking his newest game, I guessed, a battle for Santa Land between elves and ice zombies. The elves wielded glitter guns, cookie dough cannons, and hot marshmallow catapults. Each hit turned a zombie into a sugary ally. Paul was a beta tester, and if his enthusiasm was any indicator, the game was destined for success.

Khanh came to stand behind me. "I know you want time with son, wish Tuyet never come here. I wish, too. But now . . . we big trouble, need you."

"I promised him," I said.

She looked through me at something I couldn't see. "When Tuyet little girl, I promise keep her safe. Some promise, nobody keep."

26

With the search for the Good Samaritan at a dead end, Savitch was the only connection we had to the dead girl, and the dead girl was the only connection we had to Tuyet. On Monday morning, after Maria had picked up Paul and his Wolf Cub project, I got on the computer and pulled up a database I used for background checks. A few minutes after typing in *Karlo Savitch*, I had his address and phone number, along with his marital status (single), occupation (security consultant), and finances (few expenses, but an income exponentially greater than mine). Maybe I should triple my fees and call myself an investigative consultant.

Savitch lived on the second floor of a four-story brick tower apartment building near Hillsboro Village, within walking distance of the historic Belcourt theater, a mom and pop bookstore, and an eclectic assortment of shops and restaurants. With Khanh riding shotgun, I passed the dragon mural on the wall across from the theater, and a few turns later parked a block from Savitch's apartment building. It was called Four Towers, even though it was shaped like a cracker box and didn't even have a turret, let alone a tower. Four stories, forty units, ten on each floor. A pair of Bradford pear trees flanked the front door, someone's pitiful attempt at landscaping.

"Come on," I said to Khanh. "Let's see what the neighbors think of our boy Karlo."

"You not afraid he find out you ask about him?"

"I want him to know. Might rattle his cage a little."

It was still too early for most of the restaurants, but we showed Eric's drawing at all the area shops. Savitch was a memorable man but not a personable one, and people were eager to talk about him. No one knew him well. No one had ever seen him with an Asian man or woman. No one knew who his friends or lovers, if he had any, might be.

The owner of the Bookman Bookwoman bookstore, a kind-looking woman wearing wire-rimmed glasses, looked at the drawing and said, "He comes in once a week, mostly interested in history books. Strictly nonfiction. He always comes alone."

We crossed the street to Fido, a trendy little restaurant that had been a pet store in a previous life. The bone-shaped sign above the door was a relic of its past. Inside, a waitress with pink highlights in her hair said, "Who could forget him? He gets the roasted apple and onion sandwich with blue cheese. He doesn't tip, which is fine by me. I'm just happy when he leaves."

"That's an unusual perspective," I said, "from someone who makes her living from tips."

"I'm telling you, he's creepy. Something about the way he looks at me. Like he thinks I crawled out of a sewer."

"He probably does," I said. "He's that kind of guy."

It was almost noon when we went back to the Silverado. I pulled my laptop out from behind my seat.

"You have many thing there," Khanh said, pointing to the storage space behind the cab.

"Be prepared, that's my motto," I said. "I was a Boy Scout too." I pulled my sleeping bag over the rest of the equipment in the storage space—ammunition, camera, surveillance equipment, dog carrier—then opened the laptop and pulled up my skip-tracing database. Thank God for mobile broadband.

A few clicks got me the name of an elderly woman named Wentworth, who lived on the second floor across from Savitch.

"Watch and learn, Grasshopper," I said.

Khanh lifted her eyebrows but didn't ask, and I didn't even try to explain.

We went back to his apartment tower. The door had a no-solicitation sign, but it opened easily, no key lock, no need to be buzzed in. Trusting folk.

Or maybe not. A bored-looking security guard sat at the front desk, reading a Batman graphic novel and sipping from a coffee mug shaped like a chimpanzee. The badge on his shirt said his name was Geoffrey.

He looked up from his book and grunted. "Help you?"

"I'm here to visit Georgina Wentworth. Second floor."

"Sign in and go on up."

Not much in the security department, but his presence alone was a deterrent to violent crime. Criminals like soft targets. The smash and grab guys would pass by Four Towers in favor of easier marks, and the charm and weasel guys, the ones who scammed elderly widows out of their savings, didn't worry about things like security guards.

I scrawled my name on his list and handed the pen to Khanh, who signed in small, neat letters. Then we took the elevator to the second floor, where Mrs. Wentworth lived across the hall from Savitch. At my knock, a quavering voice from inside said, "Who is it?"

"I'm a private investigator, Mrs. Wentworth. I wonder if you could answer some questions about your neighbor, Mr. Savitch."

"An investigator? But not with the police?"

"No ma'am, but I'm working a case with them. I'm licensed."

"Slide it under the door."

I wondered if she'd seen that in a movie. I pulled my license out of its case and slipped it through the crack between the door and the dingy carpet.

Footsteps shuffled on the other side, followed a few moments later by the click of the dead bolt and the rattle of the security chain. Then the door opened, and a woman with a dowager's hump and a helmet of steel-gray hair opened the door. She handed back my ID and smiled up at me, wrinkles webbing her face. The top of her head came to the bottom of my breastbone.

"Mr. Savitch is a very private man," she said. "He keeps to himself. Why are you interested in him?"

There are times when a lie is the only way. This wasn't one of them. I told her the truth. Then I showed her Tuyet's picture and said, "Savitch is involved. We just can't prove it yet. What can you tell us about him? Likes and dislikes, who he hangs out with?"

She ran a finger gently over Tuyet's picture. "He likes music. Classical. *Swan Lake. The Snow Maiden. Francesca da Rimini.* I hear it through the walls."

"I know *Swan Lake.* The other two, not so much."

"They're not as common, but I studied classical music when I was young. I wanted to be a concert pianist." She held up a gnarled hand. "Time is a cruel master."

"It is that."

"That's all I really know about Mr. Savitch. He's a very . . . self-contained man."

"Have you ever seen him with a woman? Or with an Amerasian man?"

"Never. He's always alone."

"Ever hear him talk about a friend or coworker?"

"We pass in the halls sometimes. Occasionally we speak. Civil enough, but nothing of substance. Sometimes he looks at me, and I think . . ." She made a dismissive gesture. "It may be my imagination."

"I'd like to hear it anyway."

"It's the way he looks at me sometimes . . . like he's thinking I've outlived my usefulness. *Old battle axe, why doesn't she just go ahead and die?* Maybe I'm projecting."

"Or maybe not. He's not a nice man."

She made a little clicking sound with her tongue. "I think he has a sister not far from here. If he has any friends, I've never seen or heard of them."

We took a rain check for her offer of coffee and homemade cinnamon rolls and thanked her for her time. Then Khanh and I went door to door, showing my license and asking the same questions. Fifty years ago, they would have been able to tell me everything from his favorite foods to the names of his childhood pets, but that was a different time. What would once have been taken as concern would now be considered an invasion of privacy. We came away with nothing more than Mrs. Wentworth had given us.

I nodded to the guard as we passed. We walked to Provence bakery and were halfway through our blackened chicken salads when my cell phone buzzed. I looked at the caller ID.

Malone.

I punched *Connect* and said, "I thought you weren't talking to me."

"Savitch's blood type doesn't match the DNA under the victim's nails."

It wasn't exactly a surprise. We'd known there was a chance Savitch had partners and that the girl had scratched one of them before she escaped. Still, it felt like a punch to the gut.

I said, "That explains the cockiness."

"So you need to cough up your witness, or we're going to have to let this guy go."

I cleared my throat. "I can't cough her up. She's gone back to Mexico."

"I went out on a limb on your say-so, McKean. I called in a favor and got a half-assed search warrant because you were sure this guy was the one."

"He is the one."

"But we can't prove it. Look, I know you've been cowboying around the last couple of years, but you remember how it works. It doesn't matter what we know. We need real proof. Courtroom proof."

"It matters what we know," I said. "Because that's how we get the proof."

For a moment, there was silence on the other end. Then she gave a dry laugh and said, "Maybe so, McKean. So call me when you get some."

That night, when the horses had been fed and brushed, I went upstairs. Too wired to sleep, I cleaned my rifles and my shotgun, then laid out all three Glocks on the table beside my bed. I cleaned and oiled them, then closed my eyes and practiced disassembling and reassembling them by touch.

A little after midnight, Khanh padded by on her way to the guest room. She stopped in the doorway and watched for a moment, then said quietly, "I think maybe you dangerous man."

"I hope so," I said. "Because the guys we're going up against are bad news."

27

I called my friend Mean Billy and said, "Hey. You got a couple guys who can help me pull surveillance on an apartment building over near Hillsboro Village?"

Billy ran Kaizen, a homeless shelter and rehab/job training center for veterans. He'd been Special Forces in Vietnam, and while he was a good sixty pounds heavier, he still moved like a panther. He was an affable man. Gentle, even. But beneath the grizzled beard and the paunch was a heart as solid as an iron bar.

"You paying?" he said.

I hesitated. "The usual."

"Dangerous?"

"I don't think so. They pull out if it looks like the guy wants to engage."

"Maybe I'll come myself. It's been awhile since I had any excitement."

"It's a stakeout, Billy. It's the opposite of excitement."

"Well, maybe somebody'll come out and shoot at us. That'd be exciting. Anyhow, I'll see what I can do."

He pulled up two hours later in a black sedan. Beside him in the passenger seat was Tommy Harmon, a pale redhead with a freckled face and a pair of high-tech artificial legs in place of the ones he'd lost to an Iraqi bomber.

Billy rolled down the window of the sedan, and stuck his shaggy head out. "Hey."

"Hey, yourself. Hey, Tommy."

Tommy grinned and raised a hand in greeting.

Billy's smile faltered when he saw Khanh. Then his gaze skimmed her scars and the stump of her right arm. His eyebrows lifted.

"This is Khanh," I said.

"Any friend of yours is a friend of mine."

"Actually, she might be my sister."

His mouth dropped open, and I added, "Half-sister."

I said it like it didn't matter. Then I filled him in on the dead girl and Tuyet's disappearance. Showed them Eric's drawing of Savitch. "Khanh and I are going to take the front. You guys got cell phones?"

Billy held his up and waggled it. "Locked and loaded."

"You got a zoom on it?"

"Such as it is."

"Get a shot of everyone who comes or goes; if our Amerasian shows up, we'll have a picture. If Savitch leaves out the back, you call, then follow him. If he goes out the front, we'll do the same. Whichever way it goes, we'll keep in touch with the cell phones and tag team him so he doesn't make the tail."

"How long you think we're gonna be watching this guy?"

"Until he leads us to Tuyet."

༶

I CALLED Jay, brought him up to speed.

"I'll take care of the horses for you," he said.

"Thanks. And . . . thanks for what you did for Paul."

"I was happy to do it."

"I'm sorry you had to."

"I'm sorry a woman might be being tortured somewhere and no one can seem to find her. You do what you need to do."

When I hung up, Khanh said, "He good man."

"The best."

"But many ghost."

"Again with the ghosts."

"Both you. Many ghost."

"You can't live thirty-six years and not have a few ghosts." I said it lightly, but she was right.

I set the Nikon on the seat beside me and we settled in to wait. She was good at waiting. Most people have to fill the silence with chatter, but she seemed comfortable in it. Maybe sustaining a conversation in English was a strain, or maybe she'd just spent a lot of time in her own company.

A woman in a green jogging suit came out wearing headphones. I zoomed in and snapped her picture. A man in a rumpled brown suit went in carrying a briefcase. Zoom and snap.

A little after two, Savitch pulled up in a Yellow Cab and went inside. People came and went, and my Nikon recorded them all. By eight that evening, it was clear Savitch had settled in for the night. I taught Khanh how to use the camera. Then she and I spelled each other, one watching while the other dozed or walked down the block for coffee or a bathroom break. Out back, Billy and Tommy did the same.

Monday night passed, and all day Tuesday. Every few hours, I turned on the news, and we listened to the escalating hunt for the Executioner. One pundit suggested putting everyone on the list under the same roof and under heavy guard. Another said that would just give the Executioner a single target. Another suggested putting the cops and attorneys under guard and letting the drug dealers fend for themselves. There was something appealing about that option, but it wasn't civilized to say so.

On Wednesday morning, I got a text message from Maria's cell phone. It said: *[Heart] Daddy.*

My son had discovered emoticons.

I texted back: *[Heart], Paul.*

A moment later: *[Heart, smiley face] Daddy.*

I texted back: *[Heart, smiley face], Paul.*

Then: *[Heart, smiley face, horse, sheep, cat, balloons, fireworks] Daddy.*

I wasn't sure if he was trying to send a meaningful message or just sending icons that appealed to him. I sent him a string of Emojis I thought he'd like. A few minutes later, another text came in:

At the pediatrician's. Not serious, just a little worried about this respiratory thing. Will keep you posted. [Heart]. Maria.

The heart made my pulse quicken.

At noon, Billy called and said, "Hell, Cowboy, Howard Hughes got out more than this guy. We bailing or staying the course?"

I looked up at Savitch's window. Curtains closed. No movement. I hadn't expected any, but I had a bad feeling all the same. I said, "This guy didn't have much of a social life. Could be that's all this is. Or getting arrested spooked him and he's hunkered down."

"You're the boss." After a moment, he said, "How you taking all this?"

"I'm taking it fine. Boredom is my life."

"You know what I mean," he said. "It was a different world over there. Sometimes you needed someone to get you through the nights, you know? Some reason for getting out of the bunk in the morning. It wasn't that you didn't love the girl back home. It was just that she was . . ."

"Back home?" I finished for him.

"Exactly. You get what I'm saying?"

"I get it."

"When all this is over, come by. I'll crack us open a couple of beers."

"When all this is over."

Khanh shifted in the passenger seat. "Over soon," she said. "I hope."

At seven, Billy called again. "You sure this guy is going to lead us to Tuyet? 'Cause he don't seem to know it."

"Maybe he slipped out and we missed him."

"We didn't miss him on our end. Somebody stacked some boxes and crap in front of the back door. It's still there."

"Must make for a very interesting surveillance."

"I ought to charge you double for boredom. I haven't even gotten to use my fancy phone camera."

I called Malone. "Something's wrong here at Savitch's place. He went in Monday around two and he still hasn't come out."

"You're sure you didn't just miss him? Maybe he's just out getting laid somewhere."

"We didn't miss him."

"Look, he's not under arrest anymore. He can go anywhere he wants or stay home under the blankets if that's what he prefers. I can't go barging into his apartment just because you have a bad feeling."

"Are you guys even watching him?"

"What guys? Half the force is on that damn list and the other half is trying to keep them alive. Besides . . ." She heaved a heavy sigh. "I'm getting a lot of flak from upstairs. The DNA debacle really hurt us."

"He knows where Tuyet is."

"And he's going to lead you there. Yeah, yeah. I hope you're right."

"But you don't think so."

"No, I think you probably are. But don't do anything stupid. If you do find her and she's not gift wrapped and waiting on the sidewalk for you, I want you to call me and let me know."

"Gift wrapped and waiting on the sidewalk, we'll probably need the bomb squad. But don't worry. I won't do anything stupid."

Her laugh took the sting out of her words. "That would be a great favor, if you can manage it."

After I'd hung up, Khanh looked at me. I answered before she could ask. "Give him until tonight. If he still hasn't come out, I'm going in."

28

Darkness fell. The sliver of moon shed little light, but the street lamps lit the block with a pale glow. Just before nine, I walked down to Fido and picked up four coffees and four pieces of carrot cake. I ate mine on the way back, then gave one of each to Khahn. While she nibbled at the cake, I tucked my gloves and a set of lockpicks into my jacket pocket.

"Be careful," she said. "He very bad man."

I gave her a reassuring grin. "Maybe he should be careful. Weren't you the one who said I was dangerous?"

"Be careful anyway. Dangerous not same as lucky."

"Neither is careful. Maybe you should tell me to be lucky."

GEOFFREY THE security guard was sitting in his usual place. This time he was reading a Philip K. Dick novel and munching from a bag of Hot Fries. He picked up a bottle of Tabasco sauce and splashed it on a fry, popped it into his mouth.

"Mrs. Wentworth?" he said, around the fry.

I held up the bag and the cups. "I brought her these. Thought you might like some too."

"What is it?"

"Coffee and carrot cake."

"Oh, Lord. Carrot cake." He rubbed his belly. Eyed the bag. "Fido's is the best."

I left the coffee and cake on his desk, then took the stairs up to two. I left Mrs. Wentworth's in front of her door, glanced around to make sure the hall was empty, and knocked on Savitch's door. No answer. Tried the doorknob. Locked. I pulled on my gloves and took out my lockpicks.

Savitch had four locks—the doorknob lock, the dead bolt that had come with the apartment, and another pair of dead bolts. I picked the doorknob lock easily, found all three dead bolts unlocked.

Inside, the smell of blood and shit was strong, and beneath that, cigarette smoke and the smell of a body just beginning to ripen. It was dark inside, the only light streaming through the slats of the living room window, but I didn't need light to know someone had died here. I slipped inside, pushed the door closed, and glanced around.

A man slumped on the sofa, presumably the source of the stench. I touched two fingers to his neck. Cold to the touch. I pulled my key chain out of my pocket, used the tiny LED flashlight on my key ring to shine a light on his face. Thick brows, heavy jaw, manticore tattoo running from just above his right eye to the edge of his jawline. Karlo Savitch.

The LED light showed a deep wound to the base of the skull. Gunshot wound, from the look of it. Blood had soaked into the shoulders of his shirt and made a saddle-shaped stain along the back of the sofa.

I pulled out my phone and dialed the first two digits of 911. Stopped. With Frank and Harry under guard, odds were that the scene would be processed by a couple of guys who'd never even seen a corpse. They might miss the thing that could lead us to Tuyet, or—more likely—find it and fail to recognize its significance. Besides, they'd be working a murder scene. I just wanted something that would push me in a direction.

I did a quick walk-through of the apartment, careful not to disturb anything. Savitch's furniture was functional but worn, his clothing unremarkable. Work boots. Work pants in khaki, navy, and gray. Solid-colored button-front shirts. Three pullover sweaters, one gray, one blue, one brown. Wool pea coat with lined gloves stuffed in the pocket.

Obviously, a man who didn't care about appearances. But he indulged himself in other ways. Top-of-the-line CD player with an extensive collection of classical and baroque CDs. On the kitchen counter, a bottle of Auchentoshan Scotch single-malt and a bottle of Pear Williams Eau de Vie Pear Brandy, along with a basket of Asian pears. In the fridge, shrimp cocktail, a couple of Kobe beef steaks, a porterhouse, some top-of-the-line fillets. In the cabinet, a bottle of ice wine and an expensive French white.

On the coffee table in front of the body were a box of gourmet Danish chocolates and a pack of Ronhill Croatian cigarettes. Car keys. Cell phone.

I moved to the next room, the library. Ran my gloved finger lightly over the titles—on one shelf, books on history, weapons, war, and mercenary life; on another, psychology books on brainwashing and mind control.

His workout room was extensive. Weight machines, free weights, treadmill, NordicTrack, rowing machine.

In every room, always near at hand, strapped beneath a table or tucked into a drawer, was a combat knife or a pistol. The one in the drawer of the bedside table took my breath away—a Korth semiautomatic, tactical model, high-polish blue. Its German manufacturer called it raw steel transformed into precision and priced it upwards of six thousand dollars. I'd never seen one outside of a gun show, and for a moment, the temptation to slip it into my waistband was almost overwhelming. I put my hands in my pockets and moved on.

There was nothing there that would tell me where Tuyet might be. But it did raise the question: how did a man with a weapon in every nook and cranny end up shot in the back of the head in his own living room?

I went back into the living room and picked up the dead man's cell phone, careful not to smudge any prints that might be there. It was the old fashioned kind with buttons. Using a pen to push them, I pulled up the call history. There wasn't much, just a series of calls to his sister and a few to a nearby Chinese restaurant. Probably, like Frank said, he used a throwaway phone for business.

I turned off the phone and put it back where I'd found it, glanced around to make sure I hadn't left anything behind, then stepped into the hall and closed the door. Across the hall, a stream of light came from under the door and lit the plastic cup and the bag with the carrot cake inside. I pulled off my gloves and put them in my pocket, then picked up the cup and bag and knocked on the door.

When it opened, I held out the bag and the cup. "I wanted you to have this, because I sort of used you to get in here. But things are about to get exciting around here, so . . ."

"Mr. Savitch?" She peered around me at the door across the hall as if she could see through it. "You didn't . . . ?"

"Of course not."

"But someone did."

"I'm afraid so."

I called 911, then Malone. Texted Jay. Then I went downstairs.

Geoffrey looked up from his book. "Mrs. Wentworth like her carrot cake?"

I showed him my license, and a flush crept up his neck and toward his hairline. "So that carrot cake—"

"—was a genuine gesture."

"So what was it you were doing here?"

"Guy named Karlo Savitch. Second floor."

"Right across from . . ."

I watched him put it together. "That's right. He hadn't come out in a couple of days, so I went up to check on him, and when I knocked on the door I smelled it."

"Smelled . . . oh, my God. Oh, my God." He sank back in his chair, color seeping from his face. "Tell me it was a heart attack."

"Gunshot." At his dismayed expression, I added, "It wasn't your fault. Whoever did it, it was someone he knew. Someone he let in. Can you think of anybody like that?"

"He never got visitors. Never." The shock on his face gave way to indignation. "If I'd known you were here about Mr. Savitch, I wouldn't have let you in."

"Of course you wouldn't. Why do you think I didn't tell you?"

"I can't believe this." He blew out a long breath, then yanked open a desk drawer and scooped in the empty cake box, the Hot Fries, and the Tabasco sauce. I left him brushing crumbs from his desk and went out to the pickup to fill Khanh in, then called Billy and said it all again.

"Me and Tommy might go ahead and bug out," he said. "It ain't like we saw anything."

"Go ahead. I'll explain about the crap in front of the back door, how we knew he hadn't gone out that way. And thanks, Billy."

When I shut off the phone and looked up, Khanh had gone pale.

"What is it?" I said.

"This man all we have. Now . . ." Her eyes glistened. "Nobody left take us Tuyet."

"Whoever killed Savitch knows where she is. We just have to find them. Nothing's changed, except they're spooked, and that could be a good thing. Maybe it'll make them careless."

"Maybe make them kill her."

"We can't think about that. Picking her up in Vietnam, offering her a ticket here, like Frank said, that sounds like trafficking, and if it is, it's just business to them. They'll keep her alive as long as she has value to them."

She looked up at Savitch's window. "We make trouble. What happen we make more trouble than Tuyet worth?"

I couldn't answer that. We sat in silence, waiting for the sirens. Then I got out of the truck and went to meet them.

❦

FIRST CAME the emergency vehicles, then the police cars, then the coroner's van. Malone squealed to the curb in a sporty little red car and pushed her way through the crowd until she stood nose to chin with me. "What the hell did you do?"

"I didn't do it, Malone. I called it in. I told you something was wrong."

"And I told you to call me."

"You told me to call you when I had something. Well, now I have something."

She blew out an exasperated breath. "I'm going up to look at the scene. When I come back, you're going to spill your guts to me. Is that clear?"

"Crystal."

"Am I going to find pick marks on the locks?"

"Probably," I said. "It depends how good you are."

There were four steps in front, and she took them two at a time. I went back to the truck to wait and found Ashleigh Arneau leaning against the front bumper of the Silverado. No entourage, not even a cameraman. Khanh was standing beside her, and Ash was handing Khanh a linen business card with gold lettering.

"You don't need that." I plucked it out of Khanh's hand and walked around to the driver's side, fishing my keys out of my pocket.

Khanh reached for the card.

"No." I crumpled it into a ball and tossed it into the bed of the truck.

Her eyes slitted. "How you know I not need?"

"Years of experience." To Ashleigh, I said, "What are you doing here? Don't you have a story to butcher?"

Ashleigh pushed herself away from the bumper and said, "Are you going to stay mad at me forever?"

"At least."

"I don't blame you for being upset. I took advantage of you."

"You have an infinite capacity for understatement."

"I know it was wrong. Sometimes I start thinking about us, the good times, you know, and I can't believe I let things get so out of hand."

"Nice speech, Ash. Must mean you want something."

Her cheeks pinked. "There's a story here, maybe a big one, and you know what it is. The dead woman in your dumpster, the murder here tonight. Is this related to the Executioner? And why is Frank Campanella on the Executioner's list? Is he dirty?"

"Frank Campanella is the most honest cop—the most honest man—you're ever going to meet. Leave Frank the hell out of this."

"He's on the list for a reason."

I blew out a frustrated breath. "Where's your shadow?"

"My shadow?"

"Cute blonde. She got the break on the Executioner story."

Her lip curled. "Portia. She's a speed bump, that's all, barely a blip on the radar. But if there's anything you can tell me . . . Jared, I really need this."

"Stay away from Frank," I said, and climbed into the truck.

Ashleigh's jaw tightened, but the smile held. "You've got the number."

Khanh stood on her tiptoes and stretched her arm over the side of the truck bed until her fingertips brushed the crumpled card. She rolled it toward herself and curled it into her palm.

"Don't use that," I said, as she clambered into the passenger seat. "Or I swear I'll-"

"What? Not find Tuyet? You not find her anyway."

The words hung between us for a moment. There was no echo in the cab of the truck, but the sound seemed to reverberate all the same. A hundred responses swirled through my mind, a hundred chances to say the wrong thing. I clenched my teeth until my jaws ached.

She lowered her head. "Not mean that," she whispered. "I very grateful your help."

"That's the trouble with words," I said. "You can't unsay them."

"I not-"

I held up a hand, cutting her off. "Just stop," I said. "Before we both say things we don't mean."

But what I meant was, *before we both say things we mean but shouldn't say.*

This time, the silence was uncomfortable. The air felt thick and heavy, and I was glad when Malone came down forty minutes later and made a beeline for my truck. I got a couple of paper clips out of the glove compartment, straightened them out, then told Khanh to stay and climbed out to meet Malone, who stopped, crossed her arms, and said, "Okay. Tell me what happened."

"We'd been staking this place out since Monday. Yesterday, we started thinking something might be up. Today when Savitch still hadn't come out, I called you."

"And I told you he was probably out getting laid. Christ, what a nightmare." She rubbed at her temples. "Go on."

"When he still hadn't come out by nine, I went up and knocked on the door. There was no answer, so I put an ear up to the door and caught a whiff of decomp."

"You should have called right then."

"I figured you'd say it was just a dead rat in the walls or something."

A muscle in her jaw pulsed. "You've had a hard-on for Savitch since before we knew who he was. How do I know you didn't kill him?"

"Because you have a brain. The guy could have held the Alamo with the firepower he had in there. He would never have let me get behind him."

"God." She ran her hands through her hair. "We pick up this guy on your say-so, and no sooner do we let him go than somebody offs him. We might have gotten this guy killed, McKean."

"We didn't get him killed. He got himself killed when he started dealing with killers. That's the problem with being a villain. Your partners are all bad guys."

She wrinkled her nose. "You homicide guys . . . you don't let anything get to you, do you? What did you do when you smelled the decomp?"

"I thought again about calling you, decided I didn't have enough to go on. So I picked the lock instead." I showed her the paper clips. Misdirection, but not an outright lie. "You can see it would take awhile."

"It didn't occur to you to ask the security guard to let you in?"

"No, actually it didn't."

"You picked the lock. Then what?"

"I saw a guy on the couch. Confirmed it was Savitch and that he was dead. I did a quick pass through the apartment to make sure there were no more victims and that the killer wasn't still there."

"And then . . ."

"I went across the hall and gave Mrs. Wentworth some coffee and a piece of carrot cake."

Her mouth dropped open. "Dead guy on the couch, and you did what?"

"He wasn't exactly going anywhere."

"When did you finally decide to call it in?"

"Right after the carrot cake."

"Jesus." She reached into her pocket and pulled out an evidence bag with a couple of buckskin-colored hairs in it. Each was about two inches long. "Same length and color as yours. Found it in the bedroom."

"I just told you. I cleared the apartment."

"And then you delivered carrot cake. I swear, I'll put you away for obstruction. Breaking and entering. Maybe worse, if I find out you're lying to me."

"Courtroom evidence, Malone. As a wise woman once said, call me when you've got some."

29

"She like you," Khanh said, when I got back into the truck. "But not much."

"She loves me like a brother." I grinned. "She just hasn't figured it out yet."

Still wired from finding Savitch, I turned on the radio and punched through the channels until I found a local talk station. The good news was, the Executioner had racked up no more victims. The bad news was, they still hadn't caught him. No one mentioned Savitch's murder. Too soon to have made the airwaves, or maybe just not sexy enough.

It was after midnight when we got home, but the downstairs lights were all on, and Eric's car was parked beside Jay's. Khanh beat me up the porch steps and pulled open the door, and the smell of seafood and spices poured out. Jay stepped out of the kitchen, wiping his hands on a towel, and said, *"Cua Rang Me*. It means Tamarind sweet crab. I had a little trouble finding the tamarind, and Eric had to clean the crabs, but somehow we managed."

Eric gave him an indulgent smile. "He doesn't have the stomach for mayhem."

"True." Jay's smile seemed genuine, but his eyes looked tired. "Anyway, I hope I got it right."

Khanh's mouth broke open in the first genuine smile I'd seen. "Smell very fine. Like home. Thank you."

It had been days since we'd had more than coffee and takeout in the truck, and suddenly, I realized I was ravenous. We sat around the kitchen table, cracking crab claws and dipping the meat into little bowls of lime juice and chili salt.

"Better than a cheese sandwich," Eric said, grinning. "Maybe even better than pizza."

Khanh smiled. "American food no taste. This . . . very good. Almost good like Vietnam."

"The chef is honored," Jay said, "having never been to Vietnam."

When supper was finished and the dishes done, Khanh went upstairs to bed. Jay and Eric exchanged meaningful looks, and Eric retreated to the living room. Jay said to me, "There's something I need you to see."

I picked up the Papillon pup and followed Jay to his room, where he tapped something into his computer. A website came up: Chinese dragons and cherry blossoms on a red background. It asked for a password, and he typed one in. A second later, a welcome page filled the screen.

He turned it toward me, and I skimmed the text. *For discerning men . . . for centuries, Asian women have been renowned for their lovemaking . . . treated with the respect and deference a man deserves . . . sample a variety or enter into a recurring relationship. Ultimate fantasy, ultimate discretion.*

He clicked on *Catalog*, and a page of photographs sprang up, all Asian women and girls, each with a number and a veiled description of each woman's special attributes and the fantasy she supplied. I pointed at a picture of a girl who couldn't have been more than ten. The tag below her number said, *Available for adoption to LOVING parent.*

"They don't have names," Jay said, "in case there's a special name you like. Then you can call her that and not spoil the fantasy."

"Where did you find this?"

"I've been looking ever since you told me you suspected trafficking, but it took me a long time to find the right one and hack in."

"Good God. There are more of these?"

"Enough to make you sick. A lot of them are just a slapped-together catalog of crappy photos. This one's pretty elaborate—professional photos and layout, a chat room for the members. The fantasy's a big thing with these guys, and they have these opaque ways of saying things, kind of like a secret code. I've found some of these guys on other sites, and from what they say there, I'm starting to figure it out. I haven't been able to track it back to the source yet."

"Is this what you've been working on every night? I thought it was the Christmas game."

"I put that on the back burner, but I didn't want to tell you in case I came up empty."

"How close are you to finding the source?"

"Hard to say. They've diverted through a lot of different servers in different states and countries."

"I'll get the web address to Malone. She can get their guys on it too."

"Of course." He looked back at the screen and clicked to the next page. "There's one more thing."

He scrolled down, clicked on the center photo, turned the screen so I could see.

Tuyet.

30

The next morning, I left Khanh at home and drove across Percy Priest dam to Frank's place on the lake. The water was a muddy umber, swollen and white-capped by wind. From the driveway, I could see Frank's fishing boat pitch and tug against its tethers. Patrice's flowers rimmed the yard, Heirloom and English Legend Roses with names like Blushing Bride and Danny Boy and Coronation. White wooden trellises covered in climbing roses flanked the front door.

Frank's Crown Vic sat in the driveway between Patrice's faithful Honda Accord and a patrol car with two uniformed officers in front.

I showed the officers my ID, and went to the front door, where I punched the bell with more force than was necessary. Patrice answered the door dressed in baggy jeans and a loose sweatshirt. Her face looked drawn, her complexion sallow. A pale blue bandanna was wrapped around her head, but no wisps of hair curled around her ears or along the nape of her neck. Her eyebrows were gone.

I kissed her on the cheek and smelled shampoo and lavender, and beneath it a slightly sweet, slightly acrid smell that reminded me of nursing homes. I said, "What's going on? Besides the two guards out front."

"And two more in the back." She hugged me a little longer than usual. "He hasn't told you?"

"You know Frank."

"Breast cancer." She stepped out of the hug, gave her scarf a self-conscious pat. "With everything that's happened lately, he probably didn't want to worry you. Go talk to him, lovey. He's downstairs fussing with his trains."

"Wait a minute, wait a minute. How long have you known? What's the . . . ?" *What's the prognosis?*, I wanted to say, but the words stuck in my throat.

"I have an enzyme that makes the cancer more aggressive. But they say I'm doing well."

"What does that mean, doing well?"

She forced a laugh. "I think it means I'm still above ground. Don't look so stricken, lovey. I have a long road ahead, that's all. I have to be able to laugh about it."

I gave her another squeeze. Then she shooed me down to Frank's basement, where he stood at his worktable holding a miniature red maple in place while the glue dried.

I pulled a metal folding chair over and said, "You should have told me."

He hunched a shoulder. "You've had a lot on your plate. Besides . . . talking about it . . . it makes it seem real."

I nodded. That, I understood. "Need me to do anything? Mow your grass? Trim your hedges?"

"We're doing okay." He lifted his finger, and the maple held firm. "Get you a beer?"

"Sure."

He went to the fridge, grabbed a couple of Czech brews, and handed me one. "I'm going crazy here. I thought about what you said. About taking Patrice off the board."

"You should take both of you off the board. This guy—this Executioner—he's either very good or very lucky."

"Maybe both. I'm thinking of sending her to her sister's in Knoxville for a few weeks. Just until this is all over. But she has chemo on Wednesdays. There are logistics involved."

My mother had gone through three surgeries and two rounds of chemotherapy and radiation before the cancer beat her. They'd poisoned her, then carved her up a little at a time, and still the disease had eaten her alive.

I said, "What can I do?"

"There's nothing you can do. There's nothing anybody can do. It's up to God, and he doesn't share his plans with me." He set his beer on the table and took a pine tree from a plastic bin on the floor. "Let's talk about your missing girl."

"There's nothing to talk about. I'm running out of leads."

I told him about Savitch. He clicked his tongue against his teeth and said, "The problem is, your suspect pool is basically everybody in the world."

"It's not everybody in the world. Just the ones who came through Nashville by way of Vietnam in the last few weeks. It shouldn't be that big a pool."

"We checked the manifests for a full week on either side of Tuyet's disappearance, just in case the grandmother got the date wrong. No Mr. Mat, no Mr. Troi, no Mr. Mat Troi. No Mr. Matthew Troy. No Tuyet. But if you widen the net to any flight that might have connected to a flight that might have connected to a flight that originated in Vietnam . . ." He spread his hands in a helpless gesture.

"I'd still like to get my hands on those manifests. Khanh might recognize something."

"And Malone would kill anybody who gave them to you."

"Malone has her hands full." I took a sip of beer. "We could do each other some good."

He touched the pine tree to a patch of open turf, picked it up and moved it a few inches to the left of an acrylic pond. "Use that silver tongue of yours. Maybe you can convince her."

The thought of tongues and Malone took my mind in an unwelcome but not unpleasant direction. I banished the image and said, "She's immune to my charms."

He laughed. "Go figure."

"What are you going to do, Frank?" I asked. "About Patrice? About the Executioner?"

He opened his beer. Took a long swig. "Patrice is tough. We'll get through. As for the Executioner, he has a long list. They'll catch him before he gets to us."

"Unless he goes alphabetically. 'C' is pretty close to the beginning of the alphabet."

"I'm ready for him, Mac. Those other guys, they didn't know he was coming, but now he's tipped his hand."

"Why you? What case could you have worked on with all those other people?"

He reached into the box and pulled out a couple of little plastic deer. "There's not one. We're thinking maybe it's one perpetrator, not one case. We're narrowing those down."

"They cross precincts. So either some of the cops on the list have moved or whatever he's pissed about happened before the restructuring. Or you've got one issue that carries over."

"Some of each, maybe. And whatever happened, he thinks it was a miscarriage of justice. Maybe somebody he thought was innocent went to prison."

"Or maybe somebody got off he thinks shouldn't have."

"Scumbags get off every day." He touched a bead of glue to the deer's feet and placed them carefully beside the pond. "That would be a long list, for sure."

"For Justice," I said. "I knew a guy named Justice once. Billy Justice. He was a sculptor."

"This guy thinks he's an artist, the way he poses the bodies."

"Performance art?"

"Be something if that was it, wouldn't it? Your friend Billy ever get himself arrested?"

"Not that I know of."

"Too bad. Wouldn't that make things a lot easier?" He touched his beer bottle to mine. "To catching the sons of bitches."

31

On the way home, I stopped at Office Depot and picked up a map of Nashville, pushpins, a three-by-five-foot whiteboard, and a set of dry-erase markers. The whiteboard went on one guest-room wall, divided into columns: *time line, Mat Troi, Karlo Savitch, trafficking*. The map went on the other wall, pushpins marking Karlo's house, the airport, and my office.

Khanh came in while I was working. I handed her the pen. "You write down everything we know about each of these things. Maybe something will come together."

While she made notes, I went upstairs and printed out the photos of everyone who'd gone into or out of Karlo Savitch's house since Monday afternoon. Savitch had been killed by someone he trusted enough to let in his apartment. Someone he'd trusted enough to turn his back on. Someone who was probably in one of these photos. I spread them out on my bed and started sorting. When I was finished, I had several possibles and one that made the hairs on the back of my neck stand up.

A man in jeans and a windbreaker, sunglasses, cap. Just like the man Malone had described from the airport security footage. Average build, athletic. Average height. Age could have been anywhere from midtwenties to forty. The hair that fell over his ears was dark, the skin tone golden. The sunglasses obscured the shape of his eyes, but he might have been Amerasian. He'd gone in with the woman who lived in Apartment 421, and their body language said they were intimate. But there was a hesitance in her manner, a curiosity in the way she looked at him, like whatever was between them was still new. Maybe he'd culti-vated it to give himself an excuse—an excuse besides Karlo—to be there.

I felt a familiar vibration in my chest.

We were closing in on him.

My fax machine began to hum. Over the next few minutes, it spat out a sheaf of airline manifests—page after page of pas-senger lists, along with the flights they'd been on. On the cover sheet, Frank's hasty scrawl read: *Guess I'm the one with the silver tongue.*

I texted a thanks and went back into the bedroom, where Khanh stood in front of the poster board marked *Time line,* purple marker in her hand. Below the header, she had scrawled, *Tuyet call from America.*

I said, "Look what I have."

She turned, and I held up the manifests.

"Let's see what we can find."

We pored over them, every incoming flight to Nashville with a connection that had originated in Vietnam. As Frank had said, there was no Tuyet. No Mat Troi and no permutation thereof.

I ran my finger down the column, estimating how many men were on the list. It would take time to investigate them all, but it could be done. What did we have but time?

Khanh's finger stabbed at the page. A man's name. Harold Sun.

"Mat troi," she said, a quaver in her voice. "It mean 'sun.'"

32

There were eleven Suns in the Nashville white pages, a few more in the surrounding areas, but only one with the first name Harold. I punched him into background database and found the thirty-two-year-old owner of an Asian import store, Imperial Sun Imports. The company website had a photo of a smiling Sun in a suit. I compared it to the photo I'd taken at Savitch's—the one of the man in the ball cap and sunglasses.

The cap and glasses made it hard to tell if it was the same guy, but the age and build were right, and the mouth and jawline looked the same. I sent Sun's profile picture to my phone and laptop, then printed it out and put it in the folder with Tuyet's photo and Eric's drawing of Savitch.

A quick call to Beatrice gave me Sun's tag number, along with the make and model of his car. Then I called Malone and read off the information Jay had given me about the website.

When I told her about the connection Khanh had made to Sun, she said, "I don't know. It's thin. Kelly means church, but that doesn't mean if I'm looking for a Kelly, I pick up all the Churches too."

"I know it's thin. I'm just calling because I promised to keep you posted."

"You know what you're asking me to do? What if Lipschitz means sun in Yiddish? Do I pick up all the Lipschitzes too?"

"Was there a Lipschitz on the plane?"

"No, but—"

"Then why are we talking about him? This guy Sun is in the import business. Gives him a legitimate reason to go back and forth to Asia."

"Every guy on that plane had a reason to be in Asia. Most of them do business there. That's why they were *on* the plane."

"You're not exactly making me chomp at the bit to keep you in the loop."

"I don't want you in the loop. I especially don't want you in the loop with hunches and intuition."

"You told me you wanted everything I found."

"Do you know what things are like around here? Everybody who's not on that fucking list is protecting the guys who are on the fucking list or hunting down the guy who wrote it."

"And everybody else can go screw themselves?"

"He's not just targeting our guys, McKean. He's killing their families. Wives. Kids. Everybody. What would you do?"

"Exactly what you're doing. But that's why you should work with me on this trafficking thing."

"Work with you."

"You guys are spread thin. I can throw everything I have at it. I have sources you can't get to. You have resources I can't access. Quid pro quo."

"Quid pro quo." She gave a sharp little laugh. "Who said that?"

"Hannibal Lecter," I said. "But don't let that influence you."

❧

WHILE WE waited for Malone to think it over, Khanh and I went back and pushed through the doors of Hands of Mercy. We could have gone straight to Sun Imports, but Hands of Mercy was closer. Besides, I would have liked a stronger connection to Savitch than a bad photograph and a hunch.

The lobby was empty, no one behind Claire Bellamy's desk. I left Khanh in the waiting area and wandered around the corner, where I found Talbot on his office phone. He held up a finger: *Just a minute.*

I stepped back into the hall, and a few minutes later, he came out and shook my hand. "Sorry for the delay. Fund-raising is a never-ending job. Sometimes I feel like Sisyphus, pushing the eternal stone. Any luck finding the girl?"

"Not yet, but we have a new lead." I held up the folder. "Any chance we could talk to Marlee again?"

"Sure. You can speak with her in here." He gestured down toward the conference room where we'd met him before.

While he went upstairs to get Marlee, I went back for Khanh, who sat in one of the stiff plastic chairs, reading a booklet from the rack beside Claire's desk. *Trafficking in America: The Brutal Truth.*

"You sure you want to read that?" I said.

She looked up, eyes wet. "No. But I read anyway. Make me strong for Tuyet."

"You're plenty strong already." I took the booklet from her, put it back on the rack. "Some things you don't need to think about."

"Think about already," she said, and picked it up again. "Nothing so bad I not think about already."

∽

MARLEE CAME into the conference room alone, wearing a wary expression and an oversized Tweety Bird T-shirt over denim cut-offs. She slid into the chair across from Khanh and me and said, "Mr. Talbot said you want to see me."

"We have a picture I'd like you to look at. See if you saw this man when you were with Helix."

"Like a john?"

"Or someone Helix did business with. Maybe a partner."

"He don't believe in partners. Says you can't trust 'em."

"He's right about that," I said. Karlo Savitch had turned his back on a partner and been rewarded with a bullet to the head. "But could you take a look anyway?"

I opened the folder to the picture of Sun and handed it to her.

She looked at the photo. Drew in a long breath and touched her index finger to her lower lip. "No. No, I've never seen him."

"You're sure?"

She slapped the folder shut and slid it across the table at me. "I told you, I've never seen him. You got any more guys to show me?"

"No."

"Then I can't help you."

Khanh turned her head away, covered her eyes with her hand.

I stopped back by Talbot's office, where he sat behind his computer, hard at work again.

"Any luck?" he said.

"She didn't know him." I held up the folder. "Can I leave this with you? It's a picture of the guy who brought Tuyet to America. Maybe you could post it with the others?"

"Of course." He stood up and held out his hand for the folder. "I'll leave it for Claire to post."

He walked us out, and as we passed Claire's desk, he laid the folder in the center of the desk. "So she'll be sure to see it," he said. "Let us know if there's anything else we can do."

33

Imperial Sun Imports was in a Brentwood strip mall near Interstate-65 and Old Hickory Boulevard, an area with an eclectic blend of high- and lowbrow-businesses and restaurants. Sun Imports exemplified this by selling expensive Asian furniture and accessories, along with an assortment of cheap toys, spices, and souvenirs.

His car, a pale green Cadillac with vanity plates that said SUN, was parked in front, at the edge of the lot nearest the road. According to the website, Thursday hours were ten to seven, so if he worked the full shift, he should be there for at least four more hours.

I parked a few spaces away from his car and pulled my Fast Trak Pro GPS tracker out of my equipment bag. A sweet little device with a ninety-day battery and forty-pound magnets for serious holding power. Foot traffic was light, and when the coast was clear, I curled the device into my palm, climbed out of the truck, and sauntered past Sun's car, pausing just long enough to attach the tracker inside his rear wheel well.

Back in the Silverado, I pinged the Fast Trak from my cell phone and got a strong signal in response. A few minutes later, we were out the other side of the lot, and fifteen minutes after that, I pulled onto his tree-lined street. Between my database and Google Earth, I'd gleaned that Sun lived alone in a two-story Tudor mansion with an eight-foot privacy fence and a kidney-shaped pool in the backyard.

I parked a few doors down and on the other side of the street. Checked to see if anyone was watching. For once, the weather was in our favor, the damp chill keeping the neighbors in the house.

"Nice house," Khanh said, wryly. "Big money in Asia import."

"I guess it depends on what you're importing."

"You think Tuyet inside?" Her left hand moved across her lap toward the door handle. "Tuyet inside, I go with you."

"If you're with me, who's going to warn me if he comes home?"

"Store close seven P.M."

"And if he gets a stomach ache and decides to come home early?"

"Why we not go in, he come home, we grab him?" Khanh asked. "You make tell where take Tuyet."

"Because that's called kidnapping, and we tend to avoid it, unless we want to go to prison."

"Break in house, go prison too."

"A guy has to draw the line somewhere."

⟡

I LEFT her with my laptop, the Fast Trak's satellite map on the screen. Sun's position was a red X on the map. "He starts to move, you buzz me on my cell."

She nodded.

"He's probably got a security system, so I'll only have a few minutes before the cops get here. He'll know somebody's been inside, but that's okay. He's been comfortable a long time. We shake him up, maybe he'll jump. Lead us to Tuyet."

"You not think Tuyet here."

"If it were me, I'd have another place. Someplace that would be hard to connect to me. If it's a big operation, that's definitely how they'd do it, but if it's only him and Karlo . . . they could have the women in a crawl space or a cell of some kind in the basement."

"Be careful." She touched the back of my hand lightly with her fingertips. "Be lucky."

I loped across Sun's lawn and let myself into the backyard. He had sliding glass doors in the back, easy to pick, and a sticker that named the security company he used. It was a good system, hard to disarm. I could get in, but after that . . . it was a different story.

I took a deep breath. Rolled my shoulders to release the tension. Less than a minute later, I was in. I moved fast, checked the basement, attic, closets, opened each door to see if there was a prisoner inside. Remembering a pair of killers who kept their captives in a cabinet under the bed, I gave a quick glance under each bed and tapped the floor checking for hollow spaces.

On some level I noticed the high-end Asian artwork, the quality furniture, the books on Eastern culture, but there was no sign of Tuyet, and by the time I heard the sirens, I was out.

✑

On Saturday morning, a few patches of blue broke through the clouds. To the east was the promise of sunshine. To the west, the sky was a mass of roiling gray.

Sun still hadn't jumped.

He'd come home, gone to work, come home again. Grabbed a few meals at nearby restaurants. Nothing out of the ordinary, no movement at all since dinner Friday night. Khanh and I had gotten a motel room nearby, and I'd set up my laptop so we could take turns keeping an eye on the screen. My watch ended, and I nudged Khanh, who lay fully clothed on the bed closest to the window. She yawned and stretched, pressed her fist into the small of her back, then padded to the window, blinking the sleep away.

Her skin looked strained and gray in the diffused light.

"You okay?" I said.

"Too much wait."

"I know."

"You say make jump. He lead us Tuyet. Maybe he wrong guy."

"I don't think so."

Her chin quivered, and she fingered the jade monkey at her throat. "Maybe he sell her, we never find. Maybe he kill her already."

"Let's hang tight for a while longer. If he still doesn't lead us to her, I'll go talk to him. Stir the pot."

"What mean stir the pot?"

"It means change things up, make him uncomfortable. Make some trouble for him so he has no choice but to react."

"Stir pot," she said, and nodded. "Hope we stir pot soon."

34

Sunday and Monday were more of the same. Then, on Monday afternoon, my cell phone buzzed. The ID window said *Ash*. My thumb hovered over the *Cancel* button, but curiosity got the better of me, and I punched *Talk* instead.

Before I'd gotten out a greeting, she interrupted. "You've got to get down here."

"Get down where?"

"The girl who found the body in your dumpster. She had a scar like a double spiral, right?"

"More insider information?"

"Let that go, already, would you? The important part is that her pimp? D'Angelo What's-his-name? He just got blown to kingdom come."

"Whoa, wait a minute, hold on there. Who got blown where?"

"Just get down here, now. You know where it is?"

"I do. But why are you telling me this?"

"Call it a gesture of good faith."

"I'll be there in twenty minutes."

I killed two of those minutes telling Khanh about the explosion. She took a step back and said, "I stay here. Watch Sun. In case he jump."

"And if he does, what will you do? No, you're coming with me."

She crossed her left arm over her stump and jutted her chin. "I stay here."

"Think about it, Khanh. You don't have a car. If he did go somewhere, you couldn't follow."

"Why this matter? This explosion?"

"It's connected somehow. Just like Savitch. Why kill him if he wasn't involved? Somebody was afraid Helix—or one of his women—would talk. Which means at least one of them knows something."

She bent her head and put her hand over her face. "We go, maybe miss Sun. We stay, miss something else. Either way, miss something."

"We lose Sun, we'll pick him up with the tracker," I said. "We miss this, we miss it."

⁂

THE SMOKE guided me in, a dirty gray haze that hung in the air and reflected the flashing lights of emergency vehicles jamming the street. I parked the Silverado at the end of the block and Khanh and I wound our way through sidewalks crowded with gawkers. The air smelled foul and chemical, an unholy blend of charred wood, plastic, hair, and human flesh. An acrid smell like charcoal and burned beef liver, with an overlay of sulfur. It filled the nostrils and seeped into the skin, a smell so thick and greasy you could taste it. My eyes watered and my throat burned, and Khanh retched and covered her nose and mouth with her hand.

Ashleigh stood just outside the police line, mic in hand, her back to the smoldering ruin. A few feet away, the cameraman trained the camera on her, while the blonde reporter, Ashleigh's blip on the radar, watched with hunger in her eyes.

"Over to you, Rob," Ashleigh said, and flipped off her mic. She shouldered past the cameraman and came toward me. "They were cooking meth, and it went up like a volcano."

"Helix wasn't cooking meth."

"No, he was, that's what I'm telling you."

"And I'm telling you, I was in that house, and there was no meth lab there."

She glanced behind her, where Portia Ross was cocking her head to listen, then took my right arm and moved farther away. "This is bigger than a dead hooker in a dumpster. Jared, what's going on?"

"I don't know yet. Not completely."

"But you know something."

"I know I gotta talk to Malone."

"They aren't going to let you in there."

"We'll see."

I dialed Malone's cell, and after a few rings, she picked up. "Damn it, McKean. I'm pretty busy here."

"I just talked to this guy, Helix, a few days ago. Let me in, maybe I can shed some light."

"You don't want to see this. It's awful."

"I've seen awful before."

There was a silence while she thought about it. Then, "Hold on. I'll come and get you. Just you."

⁂

THE HOUSE had been reduced to rubble, ash, and a few charred beams.

I breathed in through my mouth and said, "Did they get out?"

"We recovered four bodies inside, two adult females and an adult male upstairs and another female in the basement. Sent one survivor to the burn unit. She didn't even make it to the hospital."

"Got a name?"

"No, but she had a lotus flower tattoo on her stomach."

"Ah, God. Marlee."

"What is it?"

"I talked to her at Hands of Mercy a couple of days ago."

"What about?"

"She was one of Helix's women. I showed her a picture of Harold Sun. She said she didn't know him." I thought back to the way she'd averted her gaze and pushed the photo back across the table at me. "But I think she was lying."

"Why would she come back here?"

"Maybe to warn Helix we were getting close? Or maybe she thought she could blackmail one or both of them. She said Helix didn't believe in having partners, but she might have lied about that too."

She took a pack of cigarettes from her jacket pocket and tapped one out.

"Jesus, there's not enough smoke in the air?"

"My little puff isn't going to make a difference. Here, give me a light." She handed me her lighter, and I lit the cigarette for her. We'd done this dance before, at her first murder scene.

She took a long drag and held it, then blew the smoke out her nose. "You said you were going to shed some light."

"I am, but I want to ask you a question first."

"Go ahead."

"How come you're such an asshole when other people are around, but almost human when I get you alone with a couple of dead bodies?"

She gave a funny little laugh and said, "You got me. It's the bodies. Makes me feel all warm and fluffy inside."

"I think you're not as tough and angry as you act."

"You're wrong. I'm tougher and angrier." She tipped back her head and blew a perfect smoke ring. "I know guys like you, McKean. Hell, I've dated guys like you."

I cocked an eyebrow. "You saying I'm your type?"

"Not even close. But now it's your turn. Enlighten me."

"You still thinking they were cooking meth in there?"

"That's what it looks like. At first we thought it was the Executioner, but there was no note."

"But this wasn't a meth lab."

I brought her up to date, and she said, "What, you have X-ray vision? We found the chemical residue and what was left of the gear in the basement. They were probably cooking it up there."

"I don't think so. The house smelled bad, but not meth bad. The girl on the couch had track marks on her arms, but nobody had meth mouth or bugs under the skin. And Marlee said Helix didn't let his ladies use meth. Said it made them ugly."

"Which it does."

"The timing's too coincidental. This has to be connected to Sun."

"If you're right, I don't like where this is going. You finger Savitch, and they kill him. You connect Sun with Helix, and they kill Helix too."

"You think this is my fault?"

"I'm not saying that. Though, you look at it one way, and you kind of painted targets on their backs. I'm just saying, these guys are playing for high stakes. You and your shadow . . . you haven't exactly been keeping a low profile."

I nodded toward the smoldering ruin. "They're already cleaning up. If they act true to type, either Sun is writing the list, or he's the next one on it."

She sucked in a lungful of smoke and held it, then slowly blew it out. "You've been watching Sun for the better part of a week. You might be wrong about him."

"Or someone—maybe Helix—tipped him off, and he's lying low."

"Could be." She took a long breath in through her nose. "There's something you need to see."

I followed her past the charred frame of the house to the body bags lined up neatly along the front fence. Three adult females, one adult male.

She paused. "You think you could ID these guys?"

I knelt and unzipped the first bag, eyes watering at the stench—the sulfur-and-charcoal stink of burnt hair and seared skin blending with the charred-meat smell of flesh and the sickening sweetness of cooked spinal fluid.

Beneath the blisters and the curling skin, it was easy enough to discern Helix's features. I zipped the plastic over his face and turned to the next body. It was a woman, a few tufts of Pomeranian-colored hair surrounded by puckered red skin. Simone.

The next was the young woman Simone had said was twenty-one. I looked up at Malone. "I don't know her name, but she was at Helix's house. These are the only three people I met here."

"Take a look at the other one anyway," she said.

I peeled it open and looked down into the face of an Asian woman. The heat of the fire had contracted her facial muscles and pulled her lips into a gruesome grin.

I pulled the zipper open a little more, saw the dragon eye brand on her collarbone.

Malone said, "It's not Tuyet, is it?"

"No."

"I didn't think so."

"She's the one you found in the basement?"

"Shackled to a table. I hope to God the smoke got her before the flames did. We found something else, too."

I zipped up the last bag and followed her to the van where the forensic evidence was being processed. She gestured for me to wait, then stepped inside and came out a moment later with a cloth-bound ledger.

"We found this in the basement, in a fireproof safe." She handed it to me, and I glanced down the columns, names on the left, dates and monetary amounts in the center, generic aliases—Mr. Smith, Mr. B, Mr. K—on the right.

On the last page, five lines from the bottom, was Tuyet's name, followed by last Tuesday's date, a six-digit amount, and the name Mr. J. There was one name below hers. No date, no sale amount. Probably the woman in the body bag.

I ran my finger down the columns again. "You think this book is the real deal?"

"We found three sets of shackles in the basement. Between that and the book, it looks like they brought the girls in groups of three."

"Any connection to Sun?"

"Not yet."

I looked back at the body bags. One man, three women. Four adults. I said, "What about the baby?"

"What baby?"

"Little girl, less than a year old. I saw her when I was here before."

"Maybe it was someone else's baby. A guest's."

We both looked toward the house, the queasiness on Malone's face echoing the churning in my gut. The fire had reduced the house to scraps, but some of the scraps were recognizable. A scorched refrigerator, a cracked toilet lid. And in what would have been the back bedroom, the charred slats of a baby's crib.

Her hands went to her mouth. "Ah, no, McKean. Not that." And then, "I guess I'd better go and tell the fire chief."

She was back a few minutes later. "There was no baby," she said, her face awash with relief. "Thank God for small miracles. No pun intended."

"Thank God," I echoed. "But if she isn't here, where is she?"

I LEFT Malone with the crime scene and went back to find Khanh and Ashleigh talking quietly beside the Channel Three van. Portia perched in the back of the van, complaining bitterly to the cameraman about something I couldn't hear.

"Let's go," I said to Khanh, stepping between her and Ashleigh. "I'll fill you in on the way back."

Ashleigh cocked an eyebrow. "After I called you here, that's it? You aren't even going to tell me anything?"

"I'll tell you everything when it's all over."

"I need something now."

I thought it over. "I already told you there was no meth lab here. But here's something else. Helix had a baby. She's missing."

Ashleigh smiled. "I like the baby angle. Viewers love babies, and nothing draws people in like babies and tragedy." She turned to Khanh and pressed another business card into her hand. "Call me if you want to talk."

35

Back at the motel, I checked the Fast Trak. Sun's car was at his house. I kicked off my shoes and turned on the television, flipped through the channels until I found a documentary on cane toads. Khanh went into the bathroom and came out in her pajamas. She curled into the other bed, reading *The Shining, Shining Path*.

The documentary showed a black-and-white photo of a girl pushing a doll carriage. Inside the carriage was a monstrous toad in a baby bonnet and a christening gown. Cute.

My cell phone buzzed. I looked at the caller ID. Maria.

"I don't want you to panic," she said, as soon as I picked up. "But there's a problem with Paulie. His heart. He's okay, for now. But can you meet us at Saint Thomas?"

"For now?"

"For the moment. He needs surgery. His body has been handling the murmur for a long time, but the resp—" Her voice caught. "They say the respiratory infection affected his ability to compensate. He's conscious, but . . . they're going to operate tonight."

"I'm on my way."

She gave me the room number, and we hung up.

Khanh looked up from her book. "On way where?"

I tried to steady my breathing, keep my voice calm. "Kids with Down syndrome are prone to a lot of other disorders. Leukemia. Heart defects. My son has something called a ventricular septal defect. A hole in his heart. It causes a heart murmur, which isn't life-threatening, but sometimes things happen to make it worse. Like overexertion, or a bad cold."

"He have bad cold."

"And it stressed his heart. He needs surgery. I have to go. I'm sorry."

She reached over, touched the back of my hand. "No need sorry. Of course, you need go." She turned her head away. "Not able watch Sun forever."

He'd led us to his house, to the import store, to nearby restaurants. Everywhere but to Tuyet. I wondered if Khanh had let herself realize that if Tuyet was depending on Sun for food and water, she was already dead.

I wrote my cell number on a pad next to the motel phone and promised to call when I knew something. Then I went back to the truck and brought back a Smith & Wesson .38 revolver. Full cylinder, extra box of ammo. Laser site activated by squeezing the grip. The laser was a mixed blessing, since a shooter could follow the beam back to you in the dark, but if you were a novice, it upped your chances of stopping the target.

Khanh listened carefully while I showed her how to use it, and when I left, she had it on the desk beside her, the grip just touching her left hand.

"I'll call you," I said again.

"I be here."

Saint Thomas Hospital was a few miles west of downtown, a twenty-minute drive from our Brentwood motel room. From the outside, it looked more like an office building than a hospital, but it was the best place in the state, maybe in the country, if you had something wrong with your heart.

When I walked into Paul's room, he opened his arms and grinned. "I have surgery, Daddy."

"I know, Sport."

His smile grew wider. "I gonna look like Frankenstein!"

Maria sat in the armchair beside the bed. "I told him he isn't going to get a big scar up the middle, just a few very tiny ones. He's too excited to listen to me."

I lowered the rail on one side of Paul's bed and scooted onto it. He slid into the curve of my arm and leaned his head against me. He looked good, but it worried me that they'd scheduled a night surgery. It meant they weren't sure it could wait until morning.

"I gonna get a needle stick?" he asked, brow furrowing.

"I don't know, Sport. We'll have to ask the doctor." I kissed him on the head, and Maria passed Paul the remote. We watched cartoons and talked about nothing until the nurses came and prepped Paul for surgery. Maria and I signed a sheaf of terrifying permissions. Then D.W. brought in three Styrofoam cups in a cardboard carrier, and the three of us went to the surgical waiting room, drinking bitter coffee and hoping for the best.

"He's going to be okay," I said. "Even getting a pacemaker is an outpatient procedure these days."

"It's heart surgery," Maria said. "A heart is a big deal."

"I'm just saying, this is a really routine surgery. We always knew he might have to have it one day. Virtually nobody has any complications."

"Virtually," she said. "One to two percent. That's one in a hundred."

"Those are good odds."

"Not when it's your child."

An hour passed. Two. The average surgery for ventricular septal defect was between three and four hours. At two and a half, I was pacing like a caged wolverine.

Maria rubbed her eyes and tossed the *Women's Fitness* she'd been reading onto a pile of dog-eared magazines. "I used to think, oh if only Paul didn't have Down syndrome, everything would be perfect. Now all I can think is, oh if only Paul didn't have this heart problem, everything would be perfect."

"Me too," I said. "It changes your perspective."

D.W. stood up and stretched. His eyes were red, with purple hollows underneath. "I'm going to go pick up some Jell-O. For when he wakes up. Either of you want anything?"

"Something decadent and chocolate," Maria said.

"Nothing for me."

He gave her a peck on the lips and left, shrugging into his Tennessee Titans windbreaker. Maria touched my cast, then gently closed her fingers over mine. "Does that hurt?"

"No."

"Tell me he's going to be okay."

"He's going to be okay, Maria. I promise you he's going to be okay."

An hour later, I went down to the lobby to call Khanh.

"I'll come with you," Maria said. "I need to stretch my legs."

When I turned on my phone, the voice mail and missed call icons flashed on the screen. I pushed the voice mail icon, and Khanh's voice said, "Me, you friend, we go stir pot."

Shit.

I dialed her number. No answer. Called the motel room. A canned voice invited me to leave a message since no one was available to take my call.

Double shit.

Maria rubbed her face with her hands. "What's going on?"

"She's not answering. Her message says she's gone to stir the pot."

"That sounds bad. Maybe you should go and check on her."

"She's a grown woman. I'll check on her when Paul gets out of surgery."

She reached for my hand again, pressed it to her cheek. "You have no idea how much I want you here, but I really think you should go."

36

The room was empty, as I'd known it would be. The Smith & Wesson was gone. A note on the pillow repeated the message: *You friend and I go now, stir pot.*

I only had one friend who would be willing to help Khanh stir the pot. I dialed Khanh's cell again, then Ashleigh's. Both went to voice mail, and I left them the same message, short and simple: *Call me.*

I texted Malone the basics, knowing there was nothing she could do. Khanh and Ashleigh had left under their own power to confront a man we couldn't prove was dirty. A man who wasn't even in Malone's jurisdiction.

Damn it, Ash. She should have known better.

I understood Khanh's impatience, though. I should have expected this from a woman who would walk into a minefield.

My tracking device said Sun was at home. I pinged it to make sure, and the response told me the device was still in place.

Impulse and adrenaline urged me to squeal up to his front door and kick it in. Common sense and self-preservation held me back. Instead, I took the time to pack my laptop and equipment. Glock in the shoulder holster. Colt .45 in a holster that fit snugly inside my belt. Beretta .38 strapped to my ankle.

I drove too fast to Sun's street, then slowed down and cruised the block. It was after ten, and traffic was light. The houses were empty and mostly unlit, except for the flicker of televisions. There were no streetlights, so the road was lit only by the crescent moon and the Silverado's headlights. No sign of

Ashleigh's car. I drove a grid, a half mile in each direction, in case they'd parked some distance away and walked in. Nothing.

They had to have come here. What else could Khanh have meant when she said she was going to stir the pot?

I parked on the next street and walked back, careful to stay in the shadows. Sun's house was dark, not even a porch light. The gate to the backyard creaked as I slipped through it. The pool was lit, a rippling blue glow in the blackness.

Cupping my hands around my eyes, I peeked in the garage window. Sun's car was there. No sign of Ashleigh's. I pulled out my LED light and scanned the ground beneath the windows and by the sliding glass doors. There, on the concrete patio was a footprint. It was small and slender, like a woman's, tread marks blurred but discernible. I listened at the door, heard nothing but my heartbeat and the wind, and bent to get a closer look. Something glinted in the grass beside my boot. I shone my light on it, and a chill sank deep into my bones.

A small jade monkey on a silver chain.

₿

I CALLED Malone and texted Frank, then drove to the Brentwood police station and made a missing persons report to a beefy detective who said, "I'll put out a BOLO on both women, but let's hope they show up embarrassed and hung over in the morning."

"From your lips to God's ears," I said, but I didn't believe God was listening. Or if He was, that He gave a tinker's damn about any of us.

My last call was to Harold Sun. It went straight to voice mail: *This is Sun. You know what to do.*

I waited for the beep and said, "You have something I want. I have something you need. Call me." I wasn't sure he would. Fifty-fifty, maybe. Events were spiraling out of his control, and by now he knew I was a threat. He'd want to take me out if he could get away with it, but he had no way to know if I was a lone gun or in contact with the police. Either way, we both had to assume that any arrangement either of us made was a trap.

There was no sense staying at the motel. I swung back to pick up the rest of my belongings, then realized Khanh's duffel was still there. I felt another stab of guilt as I unzipped it to put in her toiletries and soiled clothing.

There wasn't much inside. A few more photos of a smiling Tuyet—riding a motor bike, trying on a New York Yankees baseball cap, striking a ballet pose in front of a statue of Buddha. Another photo of Tuyet and an older woman sitting on the steps of a coffee shop, arms around each other. In the older woman's face was the ghost of her younger self, the woman who had stolen—at least for a time—my father's heart.

There wasn't much else. A passport, a wallet with a few wrinkled twenties, a small ivory Buddha. For luck, I guessed.

Quickly, I stuffed the clothing and toiletries inside and carried both bags to the truck. If she came back, she'd find the room empty, but she wasn't coming back. Not unless I went and got her.

On the way to the truck, I called Maria. "How is he?"

"Out of surgery. Still sleeping."

"What did the doctor say?"

"He said it went well."

I breathed out a relieved sigh. Then something in her tone registered. "It went well. But?"

"I worry about the 1 percent. Did you find Khanh?"

"She's gone, Maria." I looked up at the sky, the purpling bruise around the moon, and shook my head. "She's just gone."

37

By the next morning, Sun's car still hadn't left his garage. Ashleigh and Khanh hadn't shown up looking sheepish after a tumble with a couple of cowboys and a mechanical bull, and according to Portia Ross, the police were no closer to finding the Executioner. But when I stopped by the hospital, Paul greeted me with sleepy eyes and a thumbs-up, so things were looking up. He poked my cast with a gentle finger. "Hurt, Daddy?"

"A little. You?"

"Uh huh."

Maria said, "They're giving him Advil and Tylenol for the pain. And something else, in his IV."

I stayed with him while Maria and D.W. went downstairs for breakfast, then when they got back, kissed him good-bye and drove across town to Hands of Mercy. It had occurred to me that no one would have thought to notify them of Marlee's death.

Claire sat at her desk beside a young black woman in jeans and a red tank top. A spiral sketchbook lay open between them, along with a set of colored pencils. They took turns adding lines to a drawing that looked like a cactus giving birth to a pineapple.

Claire's smile faded when she saw my face. "Letisha, would you mind finishing this in the art room?" The black girl looked at me, then at Claire. She gathered up the art supplies and went upstairs with an exaggerated sway of her hips. Claire shook her head. "These girls are so sexualized. It's the only language they know. But you didn't come here for a lecture on the destructive nature of trafficking."

"I came here to give you some bad news."

"Oh. Oh no. Wait, let me get Andrew."

I followed her around the corner and found Talbot at his computer again. "One minute," he said. "I just need to finish this e-mail. There."

"He has bad news," Claire said. "I wanted us both to hear it."

"It's about Marlee," I said.

"She left," Talbot said. "We assumed she went back to her pimp."

"She did. And then someone blew them both up, along with everybody else in the house."

Claire sank into the chair across from Talbot's desk and covered her mouth with her hands. "Oh my God."

Talbot came around the desk, and she stood up so he could put his arms around her. She laid her forehead on his chest and clutched his jacket in one fist, her shoulders jerking in silent sobs.

"What happened?" Talbot said.

"That picture I showed her," I said. "We think she recognized it. Maybe she went back to warn Helix that we were on to his partner. Maybe she thought she could blackmail them. But then they decided to tie up the loose ends."

Claire lifted her head. Her mascara had left dark rings beneath her eyes. "What picture?"

Talbot said, "I put it on your desk so you could scan it in and post it with the other two. It was in a manila folder. Didn't you see it?"

"There was no manila folder on my desk." She looked up at me. "You don't think she took it?"

"Maybe. She'd need it to show him we were closing in."

"We'll need another one to post, then." She pushed away from Talbot, dabbed at her eyes with the tips of her fingers. "You had your pictures on a smartphone last time. Can you just share the file with me?"

I pulled it up on the phone and transferred it to her number. She looked at the photo and her mouth dropped open. "Oh my God, Andrew. Did you see this?"

"No, I was in the middle of something when they brought it. I figured I'd take a look when you posted it. Why?"

"It's Hal."

"It's not Hal. It can't be."

She handed him the phone. He looked at the screen, the muscles around his eyes tightening, then sank onto the desk as if his bones had turned to oatmeal. "This isn't possible."

"Who is Hal?" I said.

Talbot said, "My brother. Half brother. He took his mother's last name." He bowed his head and pinched the bridge of his nose between two fingers and a thumb. "How could he do this?"

"Your father," Claire said, softly.

Talbot turned to me. "Our father was a gunrunner. He had contacts all over the world. He used to take us with him, teaching us the family business. He must have branched out."

"You said your stepmother was trafficked."

"Dad bought her from a Saudi prince, who'd gotten her from a kingpin in the Japanese mafia. She used to tell us stories. Horrific stories."

"What about your real mother? She didn't object to all that?"

"She died when I was a child." He rubbed his eyes with the heels of his hands. "I can't believe Hal would put another woman through that kind of hell. But he must have started making contacts when we were working with Dad."

Claire said to me, "They were just boys. It was all they knew."

I looked at Talbot. "When did you get out of the gunrunning business?"

"I left home when I was fifteen and didn't look back. Hal and I reconnected at our father's funeral a few years ago. His mother had died by then."

"So you and Hal weren't close."

"As kids, we were inseparable, but I just had to get out of there. I was always sorry I'd left him. So when we reconnected . . ." His voice caught. "If I'd looked at that picture, Marlee might be alive."

My cell phone rang. Sun.

I looked over at Talbot and Claire, who looked like they'd just walked away from a plane crash.

"Where are they?" I said into the phone.

Harold Sun said, "I got your message. I have something you want, but what do you have that I need?"

"Freedom. I don't care about your little business venture. I just want Tuyet and the two women you took yesterday."

"You're saying if I give you three women—three specific women—you'll stop investigating. But it's a little late for that, isn't it?"

"The cops don't have anything on you yet. As long as I can keep the women quiet—and I can—you can go on buying and selling girls to your heart's content."

"How do I know I can trust you?"

"You pick the time and place. You bring your people, I'll come alone. However you want it."

"Tomorrow morning. Ten A.M. Indian Springs in Percy Warner Park. You know it?"

"I can find it."

"If there's so much as a single cop, I'll know."

"How will you know?"

"Trust me, I can smell a cop a mile away. I do, and I'm gone. Oh, and bring ten thousand dollars. That's a bargain. The ugly one's not worth much, but I can get that and more for the other two."

"Where am I supposed to get ten thousand dollars?"

"I don't care where you get it," he said. "Just get it. And if you try to screw me over tomorrow? I'll send those women back to you in pieces."

The call ended, and Claire and Talbot looked at me. I recapped the conversation, and Talbot put his head in his hands and said, "Of course you have to call the police."

38

Together, Percy and Edwin Warner Parks covered almost 3,000 acres, mostly heavily wooded. Driving through parts of the Warner parks, it was easy to forget the city was just a few miles away. Indian Springs was one of the most remote places in the parks—few hikers, few picnickers, no Frisbee golf stations. Presumably, that was why Sun had chosen it.

I got there at eight and settled in at the picnic shelter with a couple of bottled waters. A few scattered raindrops pattered on the roof of the picnic shelter. Malone came out of the woods to tell me she and her crew were already set up. They were good. A glint of light on a gun barrel and a shadow at the tree line that might have been a man were the only signs that I was surrounded by heavily armed guys in Kevlar. I told Malone about the glint and the shadow, and the next time I looked, they were gone.

I had a leather bag full of money from the Metro PD evidence room. I put it on the picnic table and paced and stretched, wondering how early Sun would get there and how he planned to scout the place.

At nine, Frank called. I was glad for the distraction.

He said, "I was thinking about your friend the sculptor."

"Billy Justice?"

"I was thinking, what if Justice is a name and not a concept? So I went down to the station and pulled up every Justice in the system, first name or last."

A tingle started in my stomach. "You found him?"

"Justice Hogarth. Honor student, eighteen years old, killed in a random shooting by a drug dealer, name of Cornelius Snow. Arrested and released more than a dozen times. The last time was for murder, but all the witnesses got amnesia."

"You worked the case?"

"All of us on the list worked one or more of Snow's cases, one way or another. Hogarth's old man made a stink with the media, accused the whole system of being corrupt. He was a big-time war hero, got some traction with it for a while, and then everybody moved on."

"Everybody but Hogarth's old man."

"We got him, Jared. We got the son of a bitch."

NINE THIRTY came and went. Then ten. A few more droplets fell. My neck began to ache. Ten thirty, a man in a baggy green jacket drove up and parked next to the picnic shelter. Malone jogged out of the woods in a pink tracksuit and hustled him away. She looked good in pink.

Ten forty-five. I dialed Sun's number. No answer.

Malone walked out of the woods again and said, "He's not coming. We might as well pack it up." She looked deflated.

"It was worth a shot," I said.

"We're treading water here, McKean. Nothing's making sense. You know what the medical examiner found about the Asian girl in Helix's basement?"

"No, what?"

"No smoke in her lungs. She didn't die in that fire. She was already dead. Knife wound to the stomach."

"There was no reason for Helix to keep a dead woman shackled in his basement. Which means somebody else put her there."

She nodded. "Which means he really was being set up. Sun and his people probably thought the body would be too burned for us to notice the knife wound."

I sat down on the picnic table, feeling numb. I had no grief to waste on Helix, but I'd liked Simone. And as Malone had pointed out earlier, I was the one who'd put the target on their backs.

"Helix was into a lot of bad things," she said, reading my mind—or maybe just my face. "He put himself out there. Maybe you gave somebody an idea, but it's just as possible he drew that attention all by himself."

"Maybe."

"You were getting close. They needed to point you in a different direction. If it hadn't been Helix, it would have been someone else. Go home, McKean. Get some rest. You'll feel better."

"I think I'll stick around a little longer."

"Suit yourself."

With Malone and her team gone, I felt vulnerable, exposed. Eleven thirty came and went. At twelve o'clock, my cell phone rang. I picked up.

"Sun? Where were you?"

"I told you I could smell cops a mile away."

"I don't know what you're talking about."

"Seriously? They might as well have been wearing neon signs."

"Listen, I—"

"No, you listen. You're lucky, I'll give you another chance, but you need to know how serious this is. How serious *I* am. Choose."

"Choose? Choose what?"

"What will it be? An earlobe? A whole ear? Maybe a finger? Yes, I like that. You get to choose which of these lovely—or not so lovely—ladies gets to lose a finger."

The veins in my temples pulsed until I thought they might explode. "You're crazy."

"If I were crazy, I'd enjoy this part of it, but I don't. Choose now. You don't have much time."

"I'm not going to choose, you psychopath."

"Then the stakes go up. Shall I cut off these pretty little nipples? You can carve a lot off of a woman before she dies. Karlo taught me that." A woman shrieked—Ashleigh, I thought—and he came back on the line. "That was just a taste of what will happen to these women if you fail to choose. One. Two."

"I'm not choosing."

"Fine," he said. "Then they both lose an eye."

Another shriek, and then both women were sobbing. Sun said, "Decide!"

Impossible. Ashleigh, I thought. Khanh had been through enough. And she was a better person. But Khanh was stronger. Ash seemed tough, but she was weak underneath. I wasn't sure she could survive it.

"Khanh!" I blurted. Then, "No! No, wait!"

"Too late." There was a thunk and another scream. "I'll be in touch," Sun said, and the line went dead.

✍

I CLIMBED into the Silverado, numb. I felt cold, as if I'd just been immersed in ice water. Another chance, he'd said. But when, and how? I wasn't good at waiting, but there didn't seem to be much else to do.

I drove to Saint Thomas and slipped into my son's room. Maria was asleep on a cot by his bed. Paul lay on his back, eyes closed, the monitor wires attached to his chest and the IV tube taped to his wrist. His breathing seemed normal. The monitors flashed and beeped at the right times. Careful not to wake them, I pulled a chair over to his bed and watched him sleep until my eyelids grew heavy.

The buzzing of my cell phone woke me.

"Don't talk," Sun said. "Just listen."

I looked out the window, saw an opaque sky and a sheet of rain against the glass. On the cot, Maria stirred, then rolled over and lay still. I slipped out into the hall, phone to my ear.

"No police," Sun said. "You got cute last time, and a lady lost a finger. You going to get cute again?"

"No."

"Good." He reeled off an address. I didn't need to write it down. It was Ashleigh's.

◇

I SHOULD have called Malone, or even Frank, but the memory of our last appointment stopped me. I kissed my son gently on the forehead and took the elevator down to the lobby, where a clot of concerned visitors stood in front of the glass doors, watching the rain.

"Flash flood warnings," a woman said, consulting her cell phone.

I pushed past them into the parking lot. Rain pelted my skin and plastered my hair to my scalp. I was drenched in seconds.

I found the Silverado and pulled out of the lot, hunched over the steering wheel, windshield wipers slapping the glass, my headlights making a bubble of light in front of me. Occasionally, another car emerged from the gray as I passed it or it passed me. Through sheets of rain, I caught an occasional glimpse of other vehicles lining the sides of the road.

Smarter—or less desperate—drivers, waiting out the storm.

It took about a century to get to Ashleigh's. I left the keys in the ignition and the driver's door open, drew the Glock as I pelted to the front door and kicked it open. It opened with a bang, and I realized too late that Sun had left it ajar. I stumbled into the foyer, skidded on the slick tiles.

"Ash?" I called. My voice sounded strained. My muscles felt taut, vibrating beneath the skin.

No answer.

The dining room was empty. So was the den.

I found her lying on the living room floor, in a puddle of muddy water. She was dressed in bikini panties and a torn blouse that clung to her skin. Her back was to me, a two-pronged burn below one shoulder blade. A length of cotton rope bound her hands. Her hair was matted with mud and rain.

"Ash. Ah, God, Ashleigh."

I knelt beside her, pressed my fingers to her neck and felt a thready pulse. A relieved breath burst from my lungs. She was alive.

I dialed 911, then used my pocket knife to cut the ropes. Rubbed her icy hands in mine until they warmed. Her eyelids fluttered open. Then her arms snaked around my neck, and I rocked her like a baby until we heard the wail of sirens.

"Stay with me?" she said.

"I'm not going anywhere. Did they—"

"They cut off her finger. God!" Her voice rose, tinged with hysteria.

"I know, I know. Do you know where you were?"

"I don't know anything. They used something . . . a taser, I think." She gave a little hiccupping laugh. "I guess I got the story this time."

"I guess you did."

She clung to me as they loaded her into the ambulance, one fist clenched in my shirt, the other squeezing my fingers until I thought they would break. As the paramedics wheeled her into the emergency room, a doctor with a craggy face and a bad comb-over peeled her hand from my shirt and injected a sedative into her vein. She whimpered once, then fell silent. A few minutes later, her grip on my hand loosened and he helped me lower her to the pillow.

When her breathing was even, he gave me a nod and I went out to the waiting room and watched the hands of the clock creep around its face. The big hand had inched its way around twice when my phone buzzed. Sun.

"Did you find her?" he said.

"I did."

"This was a gift. A gesture of good faith. You leave us alone, and we let this one live. If not . . . we know where she lives."

"I get it."

"This is the one you care about. You know it. I know it. *They* know it. Do we have a deal?"

I thought of Khanh, bound and gagged, maybe worse, hoping I would come for her, wondering if I would even try. My fists clenched, but I shook away the image and said, "We have a deal."

∽

By the time Ashleigh's parents arrived, she'd been settled in a private room. She gave my hand a final squeeze, and I slipped out as her mother slid onto the bed and wrapped Ash in her arms. Her father stood back, hands in his pockets, eyes red and a muscle in his jaw throbbing as if he couldn't decide whether to cry or hug his daughter or hit someone. I gave his shoulder a pat, then drove home through the deluge, where Jay met me at the door, bleary-eyed, holding up a sheet of paper. He looked like he hadn't slept all night.

"James Decker," he said. He rattled off a phone number and address.

"Decker? You're sure?"

"I'm sure. I've been tracking this son of a bitch through twenty different countries."

"James Decker. That's our Good Samaritan."

39

James Decker, thirty-two, brown/brown, married, two daughters. Both in elementary school. The thought made me angry all over again. He owned two cars and a boat, and he made a good income as a marketing director for a company that turned out to be a shell.

Malone had called me a cowboy, but I was not a stupid cowboy. I called her as soon as I'd finished the background check. The call went straight to voice mail, so I left a message and called the precinct, where I spent fifteen minutes listening to elevator music, the calming influence of which was lost on me.

Finally, my phone buzzed, and Malone's breathless voice came on the other line. "I can't talk right now. We've got this bastard. He took down two more of our guys, the son of a bitch, but we've got him pinned down in a shed a couple of miles outside town. He's got hostages. I'll get to you as soon as I can, I swear."

Frank's phone went to voice mail too. I said I'd call him later and told him to give Patrice my love. Then I called Mean Billy. He picked up, and I said, "Remember that time you said I ought to pay you double for boring?"

"How could I forget? You got some other boring thing for me to do?"

"It isn't boring. But it's not exactly legal."

"How not-exactly-legal is it?"

I thought of my conversation with Khanh:

That's called kidnapping, and we try to avoid it, unless we want to go to prison.

"I'm about to cross a line."

∽

JAMES DECKER, our Not-so-Good Samaritan, worked out of an office that didn't exist for a company made of thin air. His car wasn't in the garage, but the Miata was. While Mean Billy stood behind me looking like a constipated grizzly, I held up my license and knocked on the door. An attractive brunette in a red jogging suit answered. "May I help you?"

I waggled the license. "Could you tell me where Mr. Decker is, please? It's important."

"He isn't in. What's this about?"

"It's better if we talk to him directly. It's . . . of a personal nature."

"I'm not sure I know what you mean."

"Have you been tested for STDs lately?"

"Of course not. We've been married for eleven years." She crossed her arms across her breasts. "I'm not going to stand out here in the rain and talk about this."

"I'm not trying to alarm you. I'm just trying to find Mr. Decker, make sure he gets everything checked out. And you too, of course. Assuming you and he are still . . ."

A red spot bloomed in the center of each cheek. "I don't know who you are or who's been telling you these lies, but I assure you, that's all they are. Lies."

"Our sources are very good, Mrs. Decker. The young lady doesn't want trouble, just a modest settlement."

Her shoulders stiffened, then slumped. "I guess maybe you should come inside."

She closed the door behind us, and while we dripped on her carpet, she crossed her arms again and said, "Okay, what's going on?"

"A young woman has accused your husband of certain . . . indiscretions. She says she has a venereal disease she could only have gotten from him. If you could just tell me how to reach your husband, I'm sure we can get this all straightened out."

"He just left for the office."

I handed her a notepad, and after a brief hesitation, she scribbled an address.

I said, "It's better if you don't let him know we're coming. Makes his responses more authentic. If he knows ahead of time, I can't say anything in my report about how he seemed genuinely surprised. Harder for me to testify that he's telling the truth. You know, for the settlement."

"Of course."

She was muttering to herself when she closed the door behind us, and I thought, not without satisfaction, that even if Decker survived the day, he might not survive the night.

Back in the Silverado, Billy gave a dry chuckle and said, "That was just plum cruel."

"It's better than he deserves."

"Was that the part where we crossed the line?"

"No, that part comes next."

The address Mrs. Decker had given us was for a swanky office building in Belle Meade, a short drive from their house.

Billy said, "Tell me again why we're doing this."

"Because the police are tied up with the Executioner, and Sun is probably going to kill Khanh. If he hasn't already."

"Because she isn't marketable?"

"That, and she's been a pain in their collective ass."

"They could sell her for domestic service."

"Let's hope they think of that."

We took the stairs to Decker's office, our damp footsteps muffled on the plush carpet. Good acoustics, I noted. Sturdy walls. Lots of soft surfaces to absorb sound. The people who worked here liked their privacy, which was just as well for us. I was looking forward to a little privacy myself.

I pushed open his office door and said, "Hello, James."

He was sitting behind a big polished desk with a state-of-the-art computer on it. He pushed his glasses up with his middle finger and said, "You again? I already told you—"

"A pack of lies. So let's start over, Decker. Let's start with a dead girl in a dumpster. Or maybe we should start with Karlo Savitch and Harold Sun."

His hand moved toward the edge of his desk. Panic button underneath, I guessed. Or maybe a pistol. I pulled the Glock and pointed it at his head. "Hands on the desk."

Sweat beaded on his upper lip. "I . . . don't know what you're talking about."

Billy walked around the desk and pulled the chair, with Decker in it, to the middle of the room. Safely away from the panic button. "Lie number one," Billy said. "Can I shoot him now?"

"Not yet."

A dark stain appeared at Decker's crotch, and the air grew sharp with the smell of ammonia. "I have money," he said. "Lots of money. Just tell me what you want."

"The truth," I said.

"I told the police the truth," he said. "I was nowhere near when that girl died. I even let them take samples from my car carpet."

"Because you'd already replaced it. That's the only thing that makes sense. And your buddy who alibied you? One of the guys from your website?"

His tongue flicked across his lips. "I don't know what you're talking about. What website?"

"I'll pull it up for you. Billy, cover him?"

"Sure thing." Billy gave Decker a cheerful smile that didn't reach his eyes. He leaned forward, and rain dripped from his beard and onto Decker's forehead.

I went around the desk and pulled up the site. Tapped in the password Jay had given me. The color leeched from Decker's face as I turned the screen toward him and read the text aloud. I said, "This is your work, right? You're the . . . You're the procurer?"

"No, no. I . . ."

Billy said, "He's told so many lies, I can't even count 'em. Can I shoot him *now*?"

"*Not yet.*" I turned back to Decker. "Tell me about the dead girl. And you'd better tell the truth, because my friend is very good at knowing when people are lying."

Decker's voice cracked. "I told you before, I don't know anything about that girl."

"You dropped her off at an office near Vanderbilt, and right after you dropped her, Karlo Savitch killed her."

"No, I—"

Billy raised his pistol, and Decker stopped short and clapped his hands over his mouth. Billy said, "Try again."

"Okay, okay." Decker wiped tears from his cheeks with his palms and sat up straighter, apparently determined—finally—to die like a man. "She escaped. Nobody ever did that before, but there was a storm, and it knocked out some of the sensors, and also, a tree fell so that, if she could get across the moat, she could climb up it, get over the wall."

I looked at Billy and back at Decker. "The moat? Like with alligators and a drawbridge? That kind of moat?"

"The name's a joke. It's not water. It's glass. Twenty feet of broken glass, all the way around the walls, so even if they get away from the holding cells—" At the look on Billy's face, Decker squeaked and rushed through it. "If they get away, they can't get across the glass. Please, I'll tell you what I know. Only, I can't go to jail."

Billy thumped him on the head. "Pray you live long enough to worry about jail."

I thought of the dead girl, shards of glass in her feet. "You keep them barefoot."

Decker's gaze swung from Billy to me. He gave a nervous titter. "Karlo says . . . said . . . it's the best way."

"Karlo was in charge?"

"No, Karlo was a beast. His expertise is . . . was . . . torture. Psychological, physical . . . he keeps, I mean kept, the goods in line."

"The goods?" Billy snarled.

"The women. I mean the women!"

I said, "So Karlo is the punisher, and you're the procurer."

"No! Sun's the procurer. I'm just the marketing guy. I just find the customers."

"Big cog in a nasty machine," I said. "Without customers, there's no business."

He swallowed hard. "We just provide a service. If we didn't do it, somebody else would. And, like Sun says, we give them food, a place to stay, better than they'd get at home."

"Better than this?" I took Tuyet's picture out of my pocket and shoved it in his face. "Look at her face, how happy she looks. Is she ever going to laugh like this again? You fucking—"

I turned away so I wouldn't shoot him. Waited for my voice to steady. "So the girl escaped. What was her name?"

Head down, he whispered, "I don't know."

"Let's call her Li. Li's a good name. Li walked barefoot across twenty feet of glass because she had it so much better than she did at home. And then she climbed over a wall—"

"More glass," he whispered. "Embedded in the top layer. Works like razor wire, only it doesn't freak out the neighbors."

"Climbed over a glass-covered wall and walked . . . how far?"

"I don't know exactly, seven miles, maybe more."

"Why did she get in the car with you?"

"I don't have much to do with the goo—, I mean the girls. She wasn't my . . . my fantasy type, so I wouldn't have . . ."

"But you worked there."

"Not with the girls."

"So she didn't recognize you, and you were able to get her in the car."

"Normally, they wouldn't. It's part of Karlo's training, like at first, they'll ask some guy for help, and he comes across all sincere and like he's going to get her out, but then it turns out he's in on it. It's like a test, and if they fail, Karlo gets to . . . has to . . . punish them. By the time it's over, they think everybody's in on it. They wouldn't go with you if you were the Pope himself."

"But she did."

"All my life, I was able to sell things. Sandra, she's my wife, says I could sell wool to a sheep."

Billy said, "You sold her on getting into your car."

"She—"

"Call her by her name," I said through clenched teeth. "It's Li."

"Um . . . Li kept saying an address over and over. It was kind of near my house, and I couldn't take her back to the compound, because Sandra expected me at home, so I called Sun, and he said go ahead and take her there, but drive her around a little first. Maybe fifteen minutes."

"You didn't ask why?"

"I didn't want to know."

"But you did know. And you did it, even though Sandra was waiting."

"It would have been twice that, if I'd taken her back to the . . . the compound."

"So you dropped her off, and Karlo killed her. And then you realized you had a dead girl's blood all over your car."

Billy pressed the pistol to Decker's forehead and growled, "How about now?"

For the first time, I thought he might actually do it. For the first time, I thought I might actually let him.

Decker squeezed his eyes shut. Held his breath.

Billy's finger hovered near the trigger.

"Not yet," I said, grabbing Decker by the collar and hauling him to his feet. "First, he's going to get us inside."

40

We hustled him outside and dashed through the rain to the Silverado.

"They aren't going to let you in, in this," Decker said, pointing to the truck. "Or wearing that. And you think they aren't going to notice that I've pissed myself?"

"Stand out here a minute longer," Billy said, "and they won't be able to tell piss from rain."

"Okay, new plan," I said to Decker. "We're taking your Mercedes."

We stopped at Burlington clothing store, and I left Billy guarding Decker while I went inside for a suit, two expensive raincoats, both black, and a new pair of pants for our hostage. "Don't kill him while I'm gone," I said, which under other circumstances, would have been a joke.

I came back out in my new duds and tossed Decker the bag with his pants in it. Looked at Billy. "Your turn."

He came back in a gray suit and oversized raincoat, tugging at his tie. "Now I remember why I don't wear these."

Billy slid into the back seat behind Decker and said, "I know you're thinking in your little perv brain that, when we get there, you're going to give your friends some secret signal, and they'll take us out and save your sorry ass. That's a dangerous way to think."

"I'm not thinking that. Seriously."

"I'm glad to hear that, because at the first sign that your piece of shit buddies know something's up, I promise you I'll put a bullet in your head."

"That's not fair. I—"

"I don't care if it's fair. You want to talk about fair, we can start with all those women you've been helping rape for years."

"I get it, I get it. I swear to God, I'm not going to double-cross you guys."

"Maybe you better leave God out of it," Billy said. "I got a feeling He's not very happy with you right now."

⁂

THE SMARTEST thing to do would be to wait for the police to finish with the Executioner situation. The second smartest thing to do would be to wait until dark. But either choice meant a delay of hours, and Khanh might not have hours to spare. I tried not to think of the hours that had already ticked away while we tracked down the source and enlisted Decker's reluctant assistance.

Did Sun really think I would walk away? It strained credulity, but why else would he give Ashleigh back? Buying time, maybe, while he worked out whether to try and preserve his little empire or cut his losses and run? Or maybe just buying time to run.

I texted Malone and Frank the address of the compound where the women were being held. When I put the phone back in my pocket, Decker said, "They'll kill you, you know."

"You can dance on my grave later. For now, I want to know everything about that compound. Cameras, security, entrances, exits, how many guards and where they'll be. Everything."

As he laid it out, it became clear that the bulk of Sun's security was aimed more toward preventing escape from within and discovery from without than toward defending against an assault. Security cameras and a chain-link fence around the perimeter of the property kept out hunters and curious neighbors, while the smaller inner compound was hidden at the heart of a hundred and twenty wooded acres fifteen minutes from downtown.

Decker and his vetting system were their protection against infiltration. He brought them in slowly, monitoring their computers, reeling them in one small illegal digital transaction at a time. By the time a member was enrolled, he was culpable enough to be trusted. First-time entry was always through Decker. After that, each customer was given a photo membership card, which doubled as a key card for the outer gate.

The prisoners were contained by fear, despair, more security cameras, and the twenty-foot glass moat that lined the walls. Customers—"our members," Decker called them—would be at a minimum on a weekday, and the on-site staff was small. For each of the three eight-hour shifts, there was a guard for the inner gate, a "concierge," a chef, one guard manning the security cameras, and fourteen more guards whose sole purposes were to make the customers feel protected and reinforce the prisoners' belief in the ultimate power of their captors.

Add Sun to the mix, and that made nineteen.

If we were lucky, Sun's men were amateurs who would throw down their guns and surrender at the first sign of a fight. But you couldn't depend on being lucky.

Since the escape, an additional fail-safe had been added. The guards outside and the guards manning the security monitors checked in with each other via two-way radio on the half-hour, which would give us a thirty-minute window after neutralizing the guards on the monitors.

It would have to be enough.

We stopped at the home improvement store, and I ran inside for two twenty-by-twenty heavy-duty industrial tarps, twenty-five microfiber washcloths, a pack of fourteen-inch industrial zip ties, rope, two rolls of duct tape, nineteen five-inch smoke alarms with lithium batteries, and a two-story fire escape ladder with antislip rungs.

I dumped them in the back seat, shook off the rain, and said to Billy, "We're agreed on this, right? We're here to get the women out. The police can worry about the rest."

"That's the plan, but you know what they say about plans."

"Man plans, and God laughs."

"I meant the one about the mice, but that's a good one too."

41

While Billy covered Decker, I squinted through the windshield and crept along Briley to the Brick Church exit. Turned and turned again. Missed a street sign obscured by the rain and did a U-turn in the parking lot of a boarded-over filling station. A few more turns, and Billy hauled Decker out to unlock a chained security gate flanked by *No Trespassing* signs. Billy shoved Decker back into the front seat, and I pulled through the gate onto a gravel road called Timber Creek. Alongside it ran the real Timber Creek, dark and swollen, churning with whitecaps that threatened to overflow its banks. We came to a dip in the road, and I eased the Mercedes through two inches of swirling, muddy water.

Decker had said he could sell wool to a sheep, and it seemed to be true, because he sold the gate guard on Billy and me. Maybe it was fear of Billy that inspired him. Maybe it was just that a sale was a sale to him, no matter what it was. His success with the guard seemed to fortify him, and he sat up a little straighter.

The guard, a friendly looking guy in his midforties winked and waved us through. "Have a good time, boys."

We passed between a double row of small bamboo houses with thatched roofs, three on each side. Billy smacked the back of Decker's head and said, "What are those? You didn't mention those."

"Those don't matter. There're no guards there, they're just theme huts. That one's the geisha fantasy. That one's the Japanese schoolgirl or anime fantasy. That one's bondage and discipline. They each have a wet bar and big-screen TV with on-demand, in-house video, but other than that, the decor is designed to support the fantasy. Big bucks."

I said, "Do the women live in there?"

"No, a member gets a fantasy package and picks the actress he wants from the catalog."

Billy growled. "That's what we're calling them now? Actresses?"

We parked in front of the main house. Billy tossed me the home improvement bag, and we went inside. Impressive. Flagstone floors, high ceilings, chandeliers, a bronze and copper wall fountain.

Decker said, "There are rooms upstairs for members, and a community area. A wine room, a cigar room. Indoor and outdoor pools. The . . . actresses . . . live out back. Before they're allowed to service members, they're all trained in massage."

Billy's jaw clenched. "You're not selling us a membership, Decker. Best you remember that."

⸺

THE SECURITY monitors were in a back room on the ground floor. Decker pushed the door open and flashed a grin at the guy behind the monitors. It wasn't a convincing grin, for my money, but by the time the guard had time to process it, Billy had stuffed a washcloth in his mouth, and I'd bound his hands and feet with zip ties.

One down.

I ripped open his shirt and, blocking his view with my body, attached a smoke alarm to his hairless chest with two strips of duct tape. Billy said to him, "You know what this is?"

He shook his head, mumbled something around the gag.

"This here's an explosive device. There's a motion sensor attached. You try to get loose, or one of your buddies tries to get you loose . . . boom."

The guard's eyes went wide. He shook his head.

"You might not believe me," Billy said. His eyes looked feral, like a tiger's. "Maybe this is some elaborate joke. But you have to ask yourself, like Dirty Harry used to say, *'Do you feel lucky today?'*"

The guard shook his head.

"Where are the others?" I asked Decker.

"I don't know." At Billy's scowl, he hurried to add, "Honest to God! The concierge is probably in his office. The chef's in the kitchen. The other guards could be anywhere."

"Where are the women?"

"There are two big sheds out back. Sturdy. Metal. Like Quonset huts." He stepped over to the monitors and pointed. "The more experienced ones, the ones we can trust, stay in the larger one. They have a lot more perks there. Good food, nice clothes, a real bathroom. The new ones stay in the smaller hut."

"How new is new?"

"Sometimes a month, sometimes a few months. Depends how fast they learn."

Billy reached behind the monitors, ripping out wires. With the butt of his gun, he smashed the glass of each monitor. Blinding them.

Decker's presence was as good as a movie pass. Within eight minutes, the chef and the concierge were gagged and zip-tied in the security control room, each with a simulated explosive device attached to his chest. We locked them in and, three minutes later, we were heading out the back door, back into the rain, home-improvement bags in hand.

The two sheds were set back from the house, well hidden by the landscaping. Apparently, men who bought and paid for sex slaves didn't care to be reminded that their paramours were frightened women brutalized into submission.

Beside the smaller shed was an open pit, and just beyond that, a mound of freshly turned earth that could only be a grave. I walked to the pit and looked in. It was deep, maybe twelve feet. In one corner, a small pile of human bones jutted from the muddy water. I looked at Decker, and something in my face made him recoil.

The clock in my head ticked on. No time to think about the pit or what might have happened there. I found my voice and said to Billy, "Around back. I want the shed between us and the main house."

While Billy kept a watch on Decker, I laid one tarp across the glass and tossed one end of the other over the fence. Careful to place my hands only on the tarp, I climbed over and used the rope to secure one end of the ladder to a nearby tree. Then I climbed back with the other end.

I said, "There's nothing on this side to secure it to, so I'll hold this end and help the women climb over. You'll be on the other side of the wall to help them down and lead them out of here."

"What about Decker?" Billy asked.

"On top of the wall. He helps them over, and we can both keep an eye on him."

"We should have brought a bus," Billy said, reaching for his cell phone. "I'm gonna call Tommy and have him bring us one."

"Tell him to park out of sight of the cameras. We passed a Jiffy Mart not far from here. Tell him to park it there."

"Fifteen minutes," Decker said. "Then they'll find the breach, and you guys are so dead."

"You better hope not," Billy said, "'cause I guarantee you're dying three seconds before I do."

Fifteen minutes left.

I took a deep breath and kicked in the door of the shed. A dozen pairs of eyes swung toward me. This one fearful, that one defiant, this one deadened. One woman shrank back, curling her body inward to protect the baby in her arms. I recognized the mocha skin, the nap of black curls. Helix's daughter.

I opened my mouth, closed it again, suddenly unsure of what to say. Remembering Decker's words: *By the time he's through with them, they're convinced that everyone is in on it. They wouldn't go with the Pope himself.*

"We're getting out of here," I said. "But we don't have much time. Let's move."

They exchanged glances. Hopeful. Hesitant. Confused. Someone muttered something in another language. Another minute passed.

I scanned the room for Khanh. She wasn't there.

Best-laid plans.

I scanned the room again. Ten women, all young, all gaunt, all in filthy nylon slips or teddies. One face looked familiar. "Tuyet," I said.

Tuyet

*T*he man was tall, maybe six feet, and lean, his blond hair sodden, water streaming from his open raincoat, the suit beneath soaked through. She pushed herself up from the stained mattress, gave a sharp hiss of breath as her movement tugged at the thin slash along her side.

The pain brought a flash of memory—Beetle's triumphant smile as she rose from the water with the knife in her hand, the thin, sharp pain as the blade bit into Tuyet's skin, the startled "o" of Beetle's mouth when Tuyet turned the blade and slipped it between the older girl's ribs. She hadn't wanted to kill Beetle, but she hadn't wanted to die, either. Sometimes you had to choose.

"Tuyet," the man said.

Near the open door, Weasel wrapped her arms around her shins and pressed her face against her knees. She refused to look at Tuyet. None of them would meet her gaze, not since she alone had returned from the pit.

"Tuyet," he said again.

She had not seen the tattooed man in days. Since then, the Boss Man seemed angry, Mat Troi worried. Things were coming apart, but she didn't know why or how, or whether it was a good thing for her or a bad one.

She looked at the stranger, while rain pounded on the ceiling of the hut and washed through the gap Dung had crawled through. A new man. What did it mean?

He fumbled in his jacket pocket, held out a jade monkey on a silver chain.

Her heart faltered.

"Your mother left me this," he said. "You gave one to your grandmother and one to your mom before she left to find the wind tree."

Fear and hope warred within her. If he had the monkey, then he knew her mother. The Boss Man might have her, or the tattooed man. They might have made her mother tell them these things. It might be a trick or a trap, or . . .

She stared at the necklace, frozen by possibility.

He took a step forward. As his shadow passed, Weasel moaned. Gaze fixed on Tuyet's eyes, he approached her slowly, closed her fingers around the necklace. "Please, Tuyet. You know who I am. Look at my face."

She stretched out her empty hand and touched his face. Ran her fingers along his jaw and across his cheekbones. How many times had she seen that face, or one much like it, in her mother's photographs? In her own dreams?

"You are you," she said, her voice filled with wonder. "You are really you."

42

She took her hand away from my cheek.

"We have to hurry," I said. "Can you make them understand?"

She gave a small nod, then turned and tugged at the arm of a willowy girl with a broad mouth. "Hurry, we must hurry." Then she was moving, helping women to their feet, shoving them toward the door, urging them on in a mixture of broken English and her native language.

Another minute. Two.

I looked at my watch. Seven minutes left for the guard we'd captured to miss the check-in, figure two or three more while the others tested their radios, rationalized his failure to respond. They'd close the front gate. Hurry to the main house. Find the control room door locked. Another few minutes to pop the door and realize what had happened. Another few to make a plan and narrow down our location.

I stood at the open door as the women shuffled out, pointed them around to the back of the shed, then followed behind. Decker stood on the wall, helping the first of the women over, while Billy stood on the tarp, securing the ladder with one hand and covering Decker with a pistol in the other.

I turned to Tuyet. "Where's Khanh?"

"Not know. Maybe big house." Her chin quivered.

"Where in the big house?"

She closed her eyes. "Downstairs. Basement. Very bad."

I looked at Billy. "You get them out of here. I'm going for Khanh."

"What about the women in the other hut?"

I looked at Tuyet. "If I open the door, can you convince them to come?"

"Not know. They here long time. Maybe not trust."

"I'll get them on the way out." I nudged her toward Billy. "You go ahead."

She shot a longing glance toward the wall, where Decker, eyes riveted on Billy's gun, helped the next woman clamber over. Then she drew in a long breath and lifted her shoulders. "I stay. They not listen you."

Her jaw was firm, her eyes clear. Like mother, like daughter. "Okay," I said. "Billy, if I'm not back before the bad guys get here, throw her over your shoulder and carry her over."

"Aye aye, Captain." With a mock salute, Billy turned his attention to the next woman on the ladder.

Tuyet took one side of the ladder and reached for the woman's hand.

Four minutes.

I drew the Glock and headed for the main house at a run just as two men in tan security uniforms and yellow rain slickers came around the corner. They were laughing about something, and for a moment the laughter froze on their faces. They were both young, maybe midtwenties, muscled up like football players.

"Hands up," I said, pointing with the Glock.

The one on the left grabbed for his gun, and I shot him twice, center of mass, the suppressed rounds sounding like two quick sharp breaths. He gave a soft, high-pitched moan and crumpled, and the one on the right dropped to his knees and threw his hands up over his head. His eyes were squeezed shut, tears—or maybe rain—leaking from the corners.

"Don't make a sound," I said.

He nodded, his breath coming in ragged bursts. He let me stuff the rag in his mouth and bind him with the zip ties, and I rolled him into the shadow of the building to buy a little more time.

"Smart guy," I said. "Stay smart."

He nodded again, and I left him.

Two minutes.

I found the basement door and slipped through just as excited voices and the slam of the front door said time had run out.

The stairs were lit by bare incandescent bulbs. I crept down cautiously, leading with the pistol low and ready. At the bottom of the stairs was a door, and propped in front of the door was Harold Sun with a bullet hole in his forehead.

From the other side of the door came a thwack and a cry.

No time to worry about Sun. I kicked the door open and stepped inside.

My brain cataloged the details. Bare walls, an empty chair and another with a woman lashed to it. Khanh in her bra and panties, one eye swollen shut, a bloody bandage on her left hand. Her head was bent, her hair covering her face.

Andrew Talbot stood behind her in his expensive suit, one hand cupping her chin, the other clamped onto her shoulder. Suddenly, everything made sense. Sun's no-show at the park, the explosion at Helix's place. The timing of Sun's offer to make a trade. Talbot had sent out an e-mail just before that call.

Talbot had known where the investigation was going, which put him in the ideal position to deflect it. He'd been there when I'd called the police about the meeting with Sun, and as a police consultant, he even could have gotten access to the murdered girl's case files. For all I knew, Malone had shown him the file when she first asked him about Tuyet.

When he saw me, he let go of Khanh and ducked behind her, shielding himself with her body. He reached around her head, drew out a silver-plated revolver.

Khanh looked up and, in a broken voice, said, "You came."

"Brave man," I said to Talbot, stepping back past Sun's body into the partial cover of the doorframe. "Does it make you feel tough, hiding behind a wounded woman?"

Talbot laughed. "Is this the part where we share confidences until the cavalry comes? I could give you a long sad story about how my father drove my mother to suicide with a string of Asian whores, and that damaged my fragile psyche."

"That was a rhetorical question. I don't really give a shit about your life story."

"Too bad. It's an interesting story."

"I got it already. All that stuff you said about Sun was true, but it was true for both of you. Using Hands of Mercy as a shield, that was brilliant."

"Glad you appreciate it."

"To tell you the truth, it pisses me off."

"That's because you're such a white knight. You are a white knight, right? Otherwise, why would you be here? And that's why you're going to put down your gun so I don't shoot this pathetic husk of a woman in the head." He tapped the pistol barrel against Khanh's temple.

A sound came from the top of the stairs. I glanced up just as the door swung open and a startled security guard lifted his gun. I swung the Glock toward him, popped off a round. He looked down at the red stain blooming on his shirt, and with a puzzled look on his face, tumbled forward down the stairs. He lay in a heap near the bottom, wheezing a red mist.

I kicked his gun away and swung the barrel of my Glock back toward Talbot.

Talbot said, "I wish you hadn't done that. First poor Karlo—"

"I didn't kill Karlo."

"Of course not. Sun killed Karlo. But you made it necessary. And then there's Sun. I owe you for Sun. I loved him like a brother."

"He *was* your brother."

"Half. But he was weak. It was the Asian side of him. He'd have crumbled under scrutiny, and then how long before he gave me up?"

"So you killed him."

"Sometimes hard things have to be done. I learned that from my father."

"Does Claire know?"

A pained expression crossed his face. "Not yet. Perhaps she won't have to."

"You've destroyed the rescue group. Everything she worked for."

"Only if you survive to tell the tale. But even if you do, Claire will bounce back. Her type always does."

"Her type?"

"Idealists. Now, enough talk." He caressed Khanh's cheek with the barrel of the revolver. She gave a little shriek, and the Glock jumped in my hand. Talbot's mouth dropped open, and a stream of red spurted from one eye. He sank to one knee, then toppled to the concrete floor, a red pool spreading from the ruined eye.

I holstered the Glock and knelt in front of Khanh, unsheathing my survival knife. It cut through the ropes easily, and she shoved them off her lap.

I looked at the bandage on her hand, tried to think of a way to tell her I was sorry. There were no words big enough, and no time to say them, even if I could think of them. Instead, I said, "I need you to stay here. I need to go up and clear the house before the others go back out and find Billy."

"No, please." Khanh's voice broke, and she wet her lips and tried again. "Please not leave me here."

I forced a smile. "You know I work alone."

"I know." She touched two fingers to my chest, just above my heart. "You work alone. I come with you."

∽

The guard at the bottom of the stairs was still breathing, but his eyes were glazed and frightened. He wouldn't last long without a doctor. He might not last long, even with one. He scrabbled at my arm with bloody fingers, mouthed something I couldn't hear.

While Khanh put on my shirt, I found the guard's cell phone and dialed 911, then left it, line open, beside him. Then I folded one of the home-improvement cloths against his wound and pressed his hand against it while I used my new tie to secure it. He thrashed his head and moaned but I didn't let go. "Press hard. As hard as you can stand. Maybe you'll live long enough to go to prison."

A blast of static burst from the radio attached to his belt. I let go of his hand and tugged the radio free. Pressed the *Speak* button. "Listen up," I said. "Sun's dead. Talbot's dead. Savitch is dead. The police are on their way. It's all falling apart. You stay, you lose."

∽

THERE WAS no one at the top of the basement stairs. The door to the security office hung on its hinges, but our prisoners still lay trussed on the floor. The makeshift gags had been removed, and while the concierge looked at us with frightened eyes, the chef spewed a stream of invective.

Billy's spiel about the explosives must have been convincing.

I hurried out the back door, Glock in hand, Khanh at my heels. From the direction of the Quonset huts came the sound of a silenced shot. Then three more. I broke into a run.

It had taken longer in the basement than we'd planned, and the door to the larger shed hung open. A quick glance inside showed a row of beds with comforters, each with a woman in a Japanese robe sitting or lying on it, each with a wooden wardrobe beside it. One woman stood near the door, peering out. She was beautiful. Clean, graceful. Slender but well fed. Her nails were manicured. Her eyes were dead. As I passed, she jerked her head in and looked away.

Too frightened or too broken to leave.

Tuyet, sitting at the top of the ladder, squealed and started back down toward her mother.

James Decker and Mean Billy stood on top of the wall. Billy's gun was drawn, and at the edge of the glass moat lay four motionless guards.

"Jared, my man." Billy spread his arms and grinned. "Let's blow this Popsicle stand."

Decker made a half turn. He shifted his weight, stretched out his hand, and pushed. For a moment, Billy pinwheeled on one foot. His head came forward, his supporting knee bent, and he toppled straight down into the river of glass.

43

Mean Billy bellowed, and then he screamed. I shoved the Glock into its holster and ran, glass shifting beneath my shoes. I grabbed Billy by the collar, and glass bit my hands as I hauled him to his feet. Blood streamed down his face and arms. His beard and mustache glistened with red, and bits of glass fell out of the folds of his clothes and jutted from his cheeks and lips and eyelids. A large shard jutted from one eye, another from the webbing of one hand. The cuffs of his white shirt were flowered with red.

Rain bounced off the glass and I couldn't tell what was rain and what was glass. He moaned and sagged against me, and glass cut into my skin.

In the distance, sirens wailed. Another guard came around the corner. His eyes widened. He looked at the tarp and the ladder and the three dead guards. Then he turned and bolted in the opposite direction.

"Ah, God," Mean Billy said. He scrabbled at his face and moaned again as the glass in his fingers raked the skin.

"Don't touch it, Billy. God, don't touch anything."

"I can't see," he said. "Everything's red."

"It's just blood. You'll be good as new when they get you sewed up." His new suit and his new white shirt were in shreds, the cloth dark with blood and rain.

"God, my eye hurts." He moved his hand toward it, and I caught his wrist. "He blinded me, didn't he? I'm gonna be blind. That son of a bitch, that son of a bitch Decker."

The sirens came closer.

"Where is he?" Billy asked. "Tell me he didn't get away."

"Over the wall. He isn't going to get away."

"God." He moaned again. "Don't just stand here. Go get him."

"Billy, you need—"

"I need you to catch that little fucker. Can you do that for me?"

I opened my mouth to protest, but Khanh laid her hand on my forearm. "You go. I take care."

Mean Billy growled. "Go."

I gave him one last look, and as he sank to the ground, I ran for the ladder.

⟨⟩

THE WOMEN milled around on the other side of the wall. They moved aside as I dropped to the ground. "Where'd Decker go?"

The willowy girl pointed. Over the sound of the sirens, I could hear Decker crashing through the trees.

I lowered my head and ran after him. Leaves slid beneath my feet, and brambles caught at my pants legs. They slowed me down, but they slowed him more. I caught a glimpse of his white shirt through the foliage. Then another. A wave of energy surged through me, part rage and part victory. He stopped short, and I burst out of a copse almost on top of him. He cried out, stumbled, and scrambled backward on his hands and knees. Behind him, the swollen creek raged against the bank.

I said, "It's over. You got no place to go."

"I can't go to jail," he said, over the roar of the water. "I can't."

He yanked up his pants leg, came up with a thin-bladed knife, and danced forward, slashing. I thought of the fencing trophies lining the walls of his foyer, noticed how he held the knife, firm but relaxed. He knew his way around a blade.

I moved in and kicked him in the stomach. He bent double, retching and holding his belly, then slashed upward with the knife. If I'd been wearing a shirt, it might have caught the blade and deflected it. But Khanh was wearing my shirt, and there was nothing but skin between my blood and the blade.

I felt a sting, like a bee sting, and a thin line of red appeared an inch below my navel.

"It doesn't have to be this way," he said.

"Yes, it does."

"I helped you. I got you in here. Just let me go."

"I'm not a sheep," I said. "You can't sell wool to me."

His voice turned pleading. "You know what happens to guys like me in jail."

"Same thing that happened to those women you sold."

"I'd rather die." He sank into a fencer's stance, swayed lightly on the balls of his feet, choosing his moment. Fear took the edge off his finesse, but it gave him strength. The knife came down. I threw up my left arm, felt the blade bite into my cast. Set my teeth against the pain and jerked the arm upward. The knife, caught in the cast, slid out of his hand. I turned the arm and backhanded him as hard as I could with the cast.

Pain exploded from my elbow to my fingertips. My vision went gray, then white. His head snapped back and his feet went out from under him, and he staggered backward into the angry water.

He cried out, fingers scrabbling at the bank. I shook my vision clear and dove onto my stomach, grabbed his wrist with my good hand. The wet skin slipped through my grasp, and he spun away. I snatched at his coat collar, closed my fist around it.

"I've got you," I said. "Hang on."

A branch rushed by, struck his shoulder. The current roared, tugged, wrenched his feet downstream, sloshed into his nose and mouth. He coughed and sputtered, slapped at my hand.

My fingers cramped. My shoulders ached.

He turned his face up, the fear clearing from his eyes. He raised his arms and twisted in my hand, and the current carried him out of his jacket and away.

⧂

I LAY on the bank, rain washing into my eyes and hammering my scalp, my shoulder blades, the backs of my thighs. It hammered on my cast, and the pain in my arm pulsed in rhythm with my pounding heart. After a while, I pushed to my knees, rocked back on my heels, and waited for the throbbing to recede and the police to come.

The police came first.

Frank held out a hand and pulled me to my feet. "Next time you've got a shoot-out on your calendar, could you try not to book it around the biggest hostage crisis of the year?"

Malone crashed into the clearing, gun out. When she saw us, she put it away and said, "Jesus, McKean, I told you to wait."

"Nice to see you too," I said. "Is Billy—?"

"En route to Vanderbilt's trauma center, but . . . I don't know. In this weather . . ."

I closed my eyes. Billy would be fine. He had the constitution of a rhino. It would take more than a few shards of glass to take him down. Besides, he'd promised me a beer.

I tilted my face up into the rain and said, "What happened with the Executioner?"

"Torched himself," Frank said. "Sent out a whole new manifesto on the Internet, then doused himself in gasoline and lit himself up. He'd soaked the whole house. It went up like a rocket booster."

"No great loss," Malone said. "Of course, the official line is, we're so very sorry that Mr. Hogarth's illness led him to this tragic course of action, blah blah blah. Jesus, McKean, you look like you're about to heave. McKean? You okay?"

I opened my eyes, realized I still had Decker's coat collar clenched in my fist. I flexed my fingers, made myself let go. "Decker. He went into the water."

Frank reached out, plucked a sliver of glass from my shoulder. "Don't worry. We'll find him. Right now, let's get you to a doctor."

44

They found Decker's body a mile downstream, wedged beneath the roots of a half-uprooted oak. I wondered if he'd thought he had a chance, or if he'd meant it when he said he'd prefer death to prison. I wasn't sorry he was dead, but neither was I glad. Some ledger had been evened, but it was too late for the women he'd helped sell or bury.

Claire, resilient as Talbot had predicted, held a press conference. She didn't make excuses, and she didn't whitewash anything. Instead, she apologized for her naïveté, opened her books to the public, and devoted Hands of Mercy to the restoration of the women we'd rescued from Talbot's compound. Trust would be a long time coming, but looking at her sincere face, I knew it would come.

The storms passed, the air behind them hot and steaming. Khanh said it felt like home. In early June, five of us waited at the airport security gate. Khanh and Tuyet stood with their arms around each other, looking eagerly at the arriving passengers. Their wounds were healing, and Tuyet's brand was hidden by a high-collared shirt.

Paul stood up straight in his Cub Scout uniform, occasionally giving his Wolf patch a proud pat. He looked up at Jay on his other side and grinned.

A flood of people poured through the gates. They came in waves, first the Type As, heads down, taking long strides, then the regular folks, and finally the elderly and infirm and families with small children. Tuyet nudged her mother and pointed. *"Bà ngoạingoa!"*

A moment later, I spotted an airline attendant pushing a small woman in a wheelchair. She looked hunched and withered, lines of hardship webbing her face. She wore tan slacks with sandals and a white sleeveless blouse. Around her neck was a tiny jade monkey on a silver chain.

The attendant wheeled the chair through security, and Khanh and Tuyet rushed forward to take over, chattering in Vietnamese. Paul edged closer to me, pressed his back against my legs.

"It's okay, Sport," I said.

Tuyet slipped her hand into the older woman's, and Khanh pushed her over to where I stood with Paul and Jay.

"You very like him," she said, and took my hand in hers.

"This is Paulie," I said. "Paulie, this is Khanh's mom. Phen. You have something to give her."

He handed her a small velvet-covered box, then stretched up and gave her a sticky kiss. "You get well now."

She opened the box, and Dad's silver star winked up at her. She stroked it with her fingertips, and for a moment, I saw them both, a younger Phen laughing, with flowers in her hair, my father, young and uniformed, smiling in a rice paddy ten thousand miles from home. Ghosts of the living and the dead.

We stopped to pick up Billy, who hobbled out to meet us. He looked stitched together, the patch over his eye giving him a piratical look. Paul smiled and pulled up his shirt, showed the small scar where the surgeons had gone in to repair his heart.

"Look, Uncle Billy. We bofe look like Frankenstein."

Billy ruffled Paul's hair and gave Khanh a kiss on the top of the head.

Back at home, Khanh filled a bowl with spring water and flower petals. Tuyet lit a stick of incense and handed another to Paul. Together, we marched through the house, Khanh chanting a prayer and sprinkling drops of scented water, Tuyet and Paul waving sticks of incense, filling the house with sweet-smelling smoke. Jay and I walked on each side of Phen, supporting her insubstantial weight, while Billy stumped along beside us.

The house felt lighter with her blessing. But we had shed blood, and our blood had been shed. I'd added more bodies to my balance sheet. It had been justified, but no matter how justified, killing has its costs. I wasn't sure how I felt about that.

Khanh looked back at me and smiled, then walked on, chanting, not ridding us of our ghosts, for they are always with us, but maybe—at least for the moment—making peace with them.